7/17

HEIR OF
SHANDARA

Ken Lozito

Heir of Shandara

ISBN: 978-0-9899319-7-7

The author greatly appreciates you taking the time to read his work.

Please consider leaving a review wherever you bought the book, or telling your friends about it, to help us spread the word. Thank you.

Published by Acoustical Books, LLC
KenLozito.com

CONTENTS

CHAPTER 1
FAILURE

"System failure is imminent," the AI said as its monotone voice spat out critical alarms.

The old man shuffled on shaky legs across the room as if he were straining from a great weight. The aged metallic floor shuddered beneath his feet. The bronze holo display was overrun with catastrophic failure messages. The alarms he muted, not needing them to know the chaos that had swallowed all of Safanar was coming for them.

"Bring up cryo-vault ten-zero-three-nine," the old man said.

"Confirm. Cryo-vault online. Status is green."

The old man sucked in a breath of relief. "End stasis," he said, and collapsed to the floor.

A bronze panel on the far side of the room slid open, and a cryostasis tube hovered through. Tendrils of cold vapor hissed around the tube, and the red indicator light switched to green as the tube settled upon the floor. A mechanical arm rose from the platform, and a blue laser ran the length of the tube. There was a snap-hiss of the tube opening, and the occupant inside began to awake.

Bayen forced his eyes open. He sucked in quick breaths and coughed out the bitter fluid used in cryostasis. He wiped fluid from his eyes and pulled himself up.

"Stasis ended. You may now exit the pod," the AI said.

The secondary tube door that covered his legs hissed open. Bayen swung his legs to the side, placing his feet on the floor, but didn't rise. He knew better and continued to take shallow breaths until his head cleared. He flexed his feet and rubbed his hands together until the stiffness left them.

A medical bot hovered to his left, and Bayen felt the slight prick of a needle enter his arm. Within moments, his foggy brain cleared. Bayen rose to his feet, feeling more of his strength return.

"Where am I?" Bayen asked.

"Location Q34B Alpha Base," answered the AI.

Bayen frowned and looked away from the holo screen. He'd never heard of Q34B Alpha Base. His last memory was going to sleep at the palace in Shandara. His gaze darted across the screen, searching for the current date. A soft rustle drew his attention, and Bayen peered through the dimly lit room. Vibrations coming through the floor panels caused the lighting in the room to flicker.

Across the room an old man knelt, balancing himself with his outstretched hand upon the console.

Father!?

Despite himself, Bayen took a few steps toward his father and stopped. He barely recognized him. The dark hair had turned mostly gray, and his clothes draped off his frail bones. The brown eyes still had strength in them. When had his father got so old?

"Bayen, come closer," the old man said.

Bayen glanced at the readout on the console behind his father. "What have you done? How long have I been in cryostasis?"

A coughing fit stole the breath from the old man as he struggled to his feet. His once-towering frame stooped with age.

"I protected you," the old man said.

Bayen stomped over to the console; his fingers flew over the interface. "Twenty years? You kept me in cryostasis for twenty years! It was only supposed to be a few months while the cure was finished."

"The plague had already claimed your mother and sister, so with the help of the Hythariam, I had you kept in cryostasis to keep you safe."

Bayen's eyes locked with his father's. *Mother and Taryel dead?* His gut clenched. "You had no right."

"Things got worse after you were asleep. The plague spread everywhere, and armies of those creatures swarmed across the continent…" his father said with his watery eyes growing distant.

"Where are we? What is Alpha Base? What happened to our home?" Bayen asked.

His father winced as shadows of unwanted memories pushed themselves across his haunted eyes.

"It's all gone. Alpha Base was our last hope. We had to run. Shandara was lost," his father said.

Bayen gasped. *Shandara gone?* The city was a marvel of the joint efforts of the people of Safanar. One of the capitals of the Free Nations. The city had been rebuilt after High King Amorak's armies sacked the city before his father was even born.

His father coughed and continued. "Alpha Base is on a string of islands well away from the continent. We took survivors of the plague and came here to continue working on a cure."

"Do you have a cure?" Bayen asked.

His father compressed his lips in a thin line and shook his head. "No. Each time we thought we had a cure, the plague changed. It spread to the other creatures, and each iteration contained the Zekaran directive to replicate itself and hunt humans."

"What about the Hythariam, they are immune to the plague?" Bayen asked, unable to stop the growing dread creeping through him.

"There is no one else left, Son."

Bayen jerked back, his chest heaving. "I don't believe you. Stop this."

There was a loud pop, and the floor shuddered beneath his feet. The lighting in the room dimmed for a moment. Ignoring his father, Bayen returned to the console, which had the standard interface. He brought up the base's video feeds of the surrounding area. Smoke and haze billowed past, slowly giving way to a sea of glowing yellow eyes.

"Is there a way out of here? Can we get off this island?" Bayen asked, glancing back at his father. His fingers flew across the console, checking the system and defense status. Nothing was online. It was a miracle there was still power in this room. He checked the backup systems and noticed that power was being diverted to somewhere beneath them.

"What is this?" Bayen asked, bringing up the schematics of a chamber beneath them. It appeared to be a keystone accelerator, but with additional pylons configured to tap into geothermal energy deep underground.

"It can take you away from here," his father said.

"Great, let's go. We can take the research data here and go."

"I cannot leave."

Bayen faced his father, seeing the energy gathered around him. "You're keeping all those creatures at bay?"

"Even if I weren't, only one person can go through this portal."

Bayen frowned, glancing at the information on all the screens and then back at his father. "But the cure?"

His father turned away from him. "There is no cure. We stopped working toward a cure and shifted our focus."

"You just gave up! No, this can't be happening," Bayen said, his mind racing. Twenty years stolen from him and everything he knew was gone.

"We had to find another solution," his father said.

"Who is we? There isn't anyone else here," Bayen said.

A door hissed open behind them, revealing an elevator. "Please, there is little time," his father said, heading for the door. "I don't know how much longer I can keep them at bay."

Bayen headed to the door, feeling like this was futile. The elevator rapidly descended for a few moments then came to a halt. The doors opened to a blast of stifling humid air. There was a red glow at the far side of the massive cavern and the acrid smell of sulfur. A web of cables ran along the walkway that took them to a ring of metallic pylons. On either side of each pylon were glowing crystals.

"How are energy pylons going to help with the plague? That keystone accelerator is different than the others. You said the plague was everywhere on Safanar. What's all this for?" Bayen asked.

"Safanar's last hope. You, my son."

"Me?"

His father slowly nodded.

"What can I do?"

"The portal can take you back to a time before the plague."

Bayen's eyes swept the room, taking in all the equipment. The amount of energy in this cavern could destroy the entire island. "Time travel is impossible."

"The last of us devoted our remaining resources to this. Our AI helped with the calculations required for adding the fourth dimensional plane to this keystone accelerator."

"You put an awful lot of faith into an AI. How do you know if this will work?" Bayen asked.

"We don't. This is not something that could be tested. We only have enough resources for one trip. If you don't go, then we're dead anyway."

His father walked over to a console, and Bayen couldn't help but notice just how old his father had become. "You're the reason why this happened."

His father stopped what he was doing at the console, and his shoulders slumped even farther. "I know... I didn't know it then. You can stop this from happening. It has to be you. You can stop the plague from being created in the first place, and then this world will cease to exist."

"Yeah, but it could be much worse," Bayen said.

"There is no other way. We're out of time."

"Even if it means your life?"

"Better I die than let Safanar become like this," the old man said.

"But it's my life as well."

His father drew himself up. "You are a member of the Safanarion Order, Son. Who will the fate of the world fall to if not to us? There is no other way."

Bayen glared at his father. The man had stolen his life from him, and now he was being asked to sacrifice what little there was left.

"What happened to the other people here?"

"They were all killed. The forsaken surprised us. We're all that's left," his father answered.

Bayen had never seen his father look so defeated. He looked dead on his feet.

"What am I supposed to do if this works?" Bayen asked.

His father reached out toward him and Bayen stepped away. "Don't you dare. I'll do this, but you and I are finished." Bayen said scowling at his father.

"Killing me won't prevent this from happening," the old man said.

Bayen stepped back. "How do you—"

"We tried to conceive of every possible probability."

"Then what am I supposed to do?" Bayen asked.

His father's lips pressed together. "Keep Halcylon alive."

"What! He's a monster. Father, I can't do this. How will keeping Halcylon alive accomplish anything?"

The old man held up his hands. "Sam, what is the greatest probability for preventing the plague?"

The AI's monotone voice answered. "The greatest probability for preventing the plague that stemmed from the life form known as Ryakuls is tied directly to General Morag Halcylon, 55 percent."

Bayen frowned. "Sam?"

"I got tired of calling it computer."

Bayen wondered how long his father had been alone here on this island. "Fifty-five percent is hardly conclusive. What about the Eldarin?"

His father's eyes darted around as if Bayen had given word to a nameless fear.

Bayen repeated his question to Sam.

"The Eldarin represent an unknown quantity, and therefore their influence on the course of events is inconclusive."

"Do you hear that? Inconclusive. Even the AI doesn't know if this will work. Sam, what is the probability of creating a cure with all known variables in play?" Bayen asked.

"Zero."

Bayen frowned. "That can't be right. Before I went into cryo, we were close to a cure. Sam, expand upon probability of cure."

"Data input required."

"You see," his father began, "all our efforts to create a cure have failed. The plague adapts too quickly for us to stop it."

A panel opened beneath the console, and a dark metallic bracer rose upon a shelf. His father grabbed the bracer and handed it to him.

"Put this on," his father said. "It's a mobile version of Sam, and it will help keep you alive."

Bayen hesitated for a moment before taking the bracer. He placed it on his wrist and felt it conform to the contours of his arm.

His father opened a tall storage locker next to the console and withdrew a long dark staff that ended in a short sword.

"I kept it for you."

Bayen reached for the weapon. It was his favorite and by far the one he was most skilled at, but it irritated him that with Safanar crumbling all around them, his father had saved it for him. The ground rumbled beneath their feet, and steam hissed from fissures on the far side of the cavern. His father collapsed to his knees, writhing in pain. The structure around them groaned in protest.

"There's no time. They've breached the upper levels. Take the supply pack over there."

"Father," Bayen said. "I can't just leave you here."

His father's gaze drew down sadly. "I know you hate me for what I've done, and I don't blame you. I would save you from this if I could, Son."

The pylons ignited to life. Bands of electricity snapped across, and the focusing crystals flared.

A lump grew in Bayen's throat despite his anger. "How will I even know if I've succeeded?"

"Death comes for us all, Son. It's how we choose to meet it that counts. If you succeed, then this version of you will cease to exist at that precise moment."

Success means death. Failure means death. Bayen's bitter thoughts sucked away his resolve. His thoughts turned to those that were gone. Taking strength in that his actions could lead to the salvation of the only home he had ever known, he grabbed the supply pack and headed toward the pylons. The elevator doors exploded. Snarling, shadowed forms with glowing yellow eyes emerged.

Bayen watched as his father pushed out with his hands. The shadowed forms slammed against an invisible barrier. He stepped toward his father.

"Go!" his father shouted, sinking to his knees, the last of his strength giving way.

Bayen turned back to the portal. The crystals on the other side of the cavern shuddered and exploded. Flames ripped through the cavern, and Bayen leaped through the portal, leaving the doomed remnants of Safanar behind him.

CHAPTER 2
ORIGIN POINTS

Bayen had been through portals before, but this was different. The skin on his face hurt from the extreme cold. He was surrounded by a swirling mass with bolts of electricity running through it. He felt as if an invisible hand was thrusting him forward, and the swirling mass blurred away from his vision. He squeezed his eyes shut against the pain. His breath came in gasps as the crushing pressure on his entire body intensified. He squeezed through the portal and landed in a field. The portal zipped closed above him, and the air was warm and still. He sat up, and traces of frost crinkled away to the ground, quickly melting in the warm sunlight. A slight vapor rose from his things into the much warmer air. The ringing in his ears slowly faded. He shook the stiffness from his hands and brought up his wrist. He ran his fingers over the touchpad to activate the device, but it remained off. After a few more times, the device whirled to life. A basic holo interface was brought up, and the AI seemed to be running some type of automated diagnostic. Nothing he could do but wait for it to finish.

Bayen opened the supply pack and changed out of the cryo-suit he had been wearing. The AI vibrated on his wrist, and he brought up the interface.

"Sam," Bayen called.

"I am here, sir," the AI answered.

"Where are we? Can you sweep the area and report in?" Bayen asked.

"According to the local satellites, we're in the Waylands, one hundred miles north of Rexel."

"What is the current date?" Bayen asked.

The date immediately appeared on the display. It worked! According to Sam, he was back to almost a year before he was born.

"Sir, temporal matrix achieved and steady at 100 percent."

Bayen frowned. "Define temporal matrix."

"Temporal matrix is the alignment between the known time line and the anomaly."

Well, that didn't explain very much, Bayen thought. The AI wasn't all that intuitive. Bayen stood up and grabbed his halberd. It felt good to have the bladed staff in his hands.

"Please define the anomaly," Bayen asked.

"You, sir."

Bayen pursed his lips in thought. What did that even mean? *I'm the anomaly?* Try as he might, he didn't understand what the AI was trying to tell him.

"Sam, what happens to the anomaly if the temporal matrix moves out of alignment?"

"The anomaly will cease to exist, sir."

The pieces clicked into place. He was the anomaly, and if he was able to change the time line, then he would die.

"Temporal matrix alignment changed," the AI said.

"What? How? I haven't even done anything yet," Bayen said, wondering if the AI was broken.

"Updated calculations. Anomaly has approximately fourteen days until matrix moves out of alignment."

Bayen felt a sinking feeling in his gut. "Define updated calculations in context of matrix alignment."

"Time line connections with the anomaly—" the AI began.

"Sam, it's me! I'm the anomaly. I want all future references to the anomaly to be as you would refer to myself."

"Preferences updated, sir. Your connection to the time line is maintained by the energy source from your point of origin."

"Point of origin," Bayen repeated, coming to grips with what the AI was trying to tell him. "Are you saying that my connection is maintained by an energy source from the future we're trying to change?"

"Yes, sir."

"And you've calculated that the maximum amount of time that I have to do what I came here to do is fourteen days?"

"Precisely, sir."

Bayen clenched his teeth and cursed. "And after fourteen days?"

"You will be pulled back to the future, sir."

He tightened his grip on the haft of the halberd. He had fourteen days… maybe. Twenty years stolen from him. Everything he had ever known was gone. The creatures that broke into the chamber were like nothing he had ever seen. They were a mix of human and beast, coming in all shapes and sizes. Bayen called up the log on the AI, preferring to read some of the history so he could figure out a way forward. The Ryakul plague had only affected humans and had been unleashed by the Zekara. The war with the Zekara had stretched on for years. *Keep General Halcylon alive. Fifty-five percent success probability rate.* The thoughts tumbled through Bayen's mind. Was Halcylon really their best chance to prevent Safanar's destruction? He didn't like it. The Hythariam was a monster.

"Sam, can you give me the location of General Morag Halcylon at this time?"

"Unknown," the AI replied.

"Best guess then."

"Cannot estimate probability," the AI said.

Bayen shook his head and then chided himself. What would he have done if he had found Halcylon anyway? He hadn't come all this way to take up guard duty.

He needed to find another way to prevent the plague from starting to begin with. He rolled his eyes, trying to think.

"Sam, when is the first reported incidence of the plague?"

"Today, sir."

Bayen swore; if he could stop it today, would that be enough to change the time line?

"Sam, can you give me the location of Safanarion Order leader, Aaron Jace?"

Bayen's holo display above his wrist showed a flurry of activity as the AI disseminated all the bits of data flowing through the comms network.

"Sam, restrict search to encrypted security channels stemming from Hathenwood and Shandara," Bayen said, playing a hunch.

After a few moments, coordinates appeared for Aaron Jace's location, and he sent the information to his keystone accelerator. Perhaps he could stop Aaron from unleashing the plague and dooming all of Safanar in the first place. Bayen noted the matrix alignment estimate that the AI had placed in the top right corner of every screen. Fourteen days, and that was the machine's best guess. If he had more time, great, but what if he had less? Bayen suppressed a shudder, steeled his gaze forward, and stepped through the portal.

CHAPTER 3
FIRST MEETING

Aaron saw his breath rise up in the crisp air. He was up among the tallest branches of a tree, studying the Elitesman stronghold below. They had been clearing Elitesman strongholds for weeks, but this was one of the biggest they had encountered so far. The stronghold itself was composed of remnant walls of a long-abandoned castle. Trees and shrubbery grew around the walls, becoming part of them. There were easily a few hundred soldiers and Elitesmen within the stronghold, whose interior was comprised mainly of tents.

"Now comes the fun part," Verona said, coming up to a branch near him.

Aaron nodded. "Hopefully, the other teams are almost in position."

Gavril had advised them to work on coordinating their strikes as a team. The Free Nations Army, with their newest specialized recruits, needed to learn to work together. Their last encounter with a stronghold was almost a disaster. Former Elitesmen, while superb fighters, had issues with following orders and functioning as part of a larger fighting force. The younger ones were easier to retrain, as their experience within the Elitesmen Order wasn't so ingrained in them.

They still remembered what it was like before they became Elitesmen. The older Elitesmen who were not part of the Resistance gave him the most trouble, and were the riskiest to keep in the FNA. The Elitesman way was one of ruthless brutality to achieve their goals.

Dividing their number so that they were dispersed throughout the army was one way to reintegrate them back into the ever-changing world. At Sarah's request, some were assigned to help with the sick and wounded soldiers, which did help reacquaint them with their own humanity. Unfortunately, this didn't hold true for as many as they would have liked. Commanders down the chain voiced their protests at being assigned former Elitesmen among their own troops.

Isaac, a former Elitesman who was a leader among the Resistance in Khamearra, had taken it upon himself to help watch over and keep track of the former Elitesmen to ensure they were staying in line. Isaac's efforts had proven invaluable, but after many long discussions with leaders of the FNA it was decided that the most troublesome cases came to Aaron. He insisted that he get a chance to work with them before they were to be imprisoned or executed.

Gavril, who had been a colonel in the Hythariam military over a hundred years before Aaron had been born, had more than a few ideas as to how to handle those men. They were given a chance to serve within a specialized force of the FNA that was headed up by Verona and himself. Having a group of highly skilled and lethal fighting men and women earned them the riskiest of missions. Within their specialized force was a group of soldiers that were extremely loyal to Aaron, which helped with those who would get it into their head to test their mettle against the famed scion of Shandara.

"Sarik is in position," Verona said.

Aaron nodded, expecting nothing less. The young man threw himself into everything that came his way until he mastered what was taught.

"I've been meaning to talk to you about something, my friend," Verona said.

"Now?" Aaron asked with a slight grin. "Oh, is this about Iranus?"

Verona wiped his hand across his brow and frowned. "I swear he doesn't like me at all."

"That's not true," Aaron said.

"You didn't see the look on his face when he finally learned that Roselyn and I were together."

Aaron chuckled. "You probably just caught him off guard."

"That's what I thought at first, but now whenever I enter the room, he draws himself up and looks at me as though something foul has just wandered in," Verona said.

"All fathers disapprove of their daughter's significant others in the beginning. Could be worse; at least he hasn't tried to kill you."

Verona was about to answer when a voice spoke over his comms device. "Do you guys realize that Verona's comms channel is open?" Gavril asked, unable to keep the mirth from his voice.

"Thank you, Aaron," Iranus said. "I hadn't thought of trying to have Verona killed, but it's something I will seriously consider in the near future. Now, don't you have something else to be focusing on?"

Verona's face turned several shades of red before he shook his head and shut off his comms device. Aaron tried to hold his laughter in, but when he heard Verona snicker he lost it. He shrugged his shoulders and turned his attention back to the Elitesmen stronghold.

"Do you love her?" Aaron asked.

"With everything that I am," Verona answered.

"What I would do is tell him that. A little reassurance can go a long way. You may not need his blessing, but it would certainly mean a lot to Roselyn if both you and Iranus could at least see eye to eye on this."

"You make it sound so easy and straightforward. As my uncle can attest, I was reckless in my pursuits until recently," Verona said.

"Aw, hell," Aaron said.

"What is it?" Verona asked, peering into the misty afternoon cold.

"Paven's group is in the wrong place, and now he's arguing with Sarik," Aaron said, shifting his position along the branch.

"Remember what Gavril said about not swooping in. Let them sort it out," Verona said.

Aaron frowned. "Even if at the cost of lives? It's a wonder the whole stronghold doesn't know we're here." His teeth clenched down, but Gavril was right: the FNA needed to learn to function on its own.

Verona looked through his spyglass. "This just got more interesting. This is the group that has been sacking the towns north of Duncan's Port. Here, have a look," Verona said, handing Aaron the spyglass.

Aaron squinted and looked to where Verona pointed. There was a line of men leading to a tent. All of them were carrying various items of value. He scanned the stronghold and saw a group of people being led away in chains.

"They've taken prisoners," Aaron said.

Verona's eyes drew up in surprise. "Why would they do that? They haven't taken anyone before. Weren't these groups suspected to be aligned with Rordan?"

The late high king's son hadn't been seen since the High King died at the battle at Rexel. Sarah had suspected that Rordan might return to Khamearra, but so far he'd seen fit not to show himself anywhere.

"I bet a group this large is headed up by a few masters," Aaron said.

"The Elitesmen with the silver cloaks. I'm not sure our troops are prepared for something like that, and neither am I, to be honest, my friend."

Aaron nodded and handed back the spyglass. Elite Masters were among the most ruthless of the Order. They were highly skilled and could manipulate the flow of energy, depending on their own particular skill sets in working with the elements. He had faced them before at the arena in Khamearra. The silver-clad Elitesmen were as likely to kill their brethren as they were to focus upon their enemies.

"It looks like someone else took up position where Paven was supposed to be... You're not going to like it," Verona said.

Aaron frowned, drawing in the energy, and peered into the gloom. "It's Sarah."

"Wasn't she sick again this morning?" Verona asked.

Soldiers in the stronghold raised the alarm and scrambled to the walls. The FNA forces were already attacking, closing the net around the stronghold so that none escaped. Aaron drew his swords with Verona doing the same. He couldn't sit idly by while Sarah took it upon herself to join the attack. She was a match for any Elitesmen and probably the masters too, but he couldn't take the chance. Not after everything they'd been through to be together.

Soldiers poured out of the tents with Elitesmen mixed between. Some howled their rage at their former brethren who had joined the Free Nations Army. With a nod to Verona, Aaron launched into the air, using the particles in the wind to extend his jump, and landed in the middle of the stronghold. Six Elitesmen streaked in his direction with their swords drawn.

Aaron brought up the Falcons, and a few notes of the bladesong pierced the air. He charged forward, meeting the Elitesmen's attack. No longer were the Elitesmen put off by someone who could actually fight back, and they fought all the more ferociously because of it. Amid the storm of swords, the bladesong bit into the Elitesmen's blades. One after another, they threw themselves at him, bringing all their training to bear. A few unleashed attack orbs, which Aaron deflected with his blades. The crystals in the pommels of his blades glowed with the energy, casting a white glow around them. Knowledge of souls past melded themselves into his style, allowing him to quickly unravel the pattern of Elitesmen attacks. They would never surrender, preferring to fight to the death, and while Aaron would fight, it still sickened him that he had no other choice but to kill the Elitesmen. He feared the day when killing Elitesmen didn't matter to him. Then he would be like the High King, whose insatiable appetite to kill went hand in hand with his lust for power.

Verona fought by his side. His friend had grown in his abilities by leaps and bounds. Verona harbored a lifetime of fear and hatred for the Elitesmen and held no such misgivings where their deaths were concerned. Two Elitesmen sent attack orbs their way, which bounced harmlessly off an invisible shield created by Verona.

The medallion became as ice on Aaron's chest. He spun around, scanning the area, and amid the shadows two glowing red eyes bored into him. Aaron charged, closing the distance between them. The Elite Master narrowed his baleful gaze and raised his swords. Aaron swung his Falcons, and as the blades met, sparks showered down around them. The Elite Master leaped away, and Aaron followed, quickly catching up to him. The Elitesman cut to the left, heading into the courtyard. Aaron caught a glimpse of Verona following and saw that the FNA forces were pushing in on all sides.

Aaron went over the wall and was met by three Elite Masters in their silver cloaks.

A trap it is then, but not enough for this quarry.

A squad of FNA soldiers charged in, and the Elite Masters lifted their hands. The squad of men screamed in pain, their skin blistering everywhere. Before Aaron could move, the squad was already dead, their bodies steaming husks. Their blood was boiled from within. Growling, Aaron spun, sucking in a torrent of energy, and swung his swords, sending a swath of pure energy into the Elite Masters. He was on them before their bodies hit the ground. His blades cut down two of them, but the third scrambled away and came to a halt before the portcullis.

"Surrender," Aaron said.

The glowing red eyes of the Elite Master narrowed. "Never, Shandarian."

Verona crested the wall, and more FNA soldiers led by Sarah appeared outside the portcullis.

The Elite Master glanced behind him and smirked. "Your weakness presents itself, Shandarian," he said, and raised his hands.

A soldier stepped in front of Sarah and collapsed to the ground. Aaron dashed forward and was in front of the Elite Master in the span between moments. He brought down his blades, severing the Elite Master's outstretched hand.

"You will never be able to protect them all, Shandarian."

Without another word, Aaron plunged his sword into the Elite Master's heart.

Sarah helped the soldier regain his feet and closed the distance to Aaron, while the FNA soldiers fanned out through the courtyard.

"My Queen, I thought you were feeling ill," Aaron said with half a smile.

"I felt better and wanted a bit of fresh air," Sarah said.

Sarah had become the High Queen of Khamearra after they had defeated her father, the High King. Aaron had taken to calling her his queen ever since, and it had been a running joke between them.

A deep, cavernous roar echoed through the courtyard. The roar appeared to come from within the castle. In moments, more Elitesmen and renegade soldiers poured out of it. Behind them followed an immense creature easily fifteen feet tall. Dark armor covered it from head to toe, with the exception of the thick horns that protruded from its forehead. Something about the armored beast tugged at Aaron's memory.

Verona came to his side with a crystal-tipped arrow nocked in his bow. The arrow flew into the giant beast, but the exploding dust of the crystal-laden arrow barely slowed it down.

The beast's armor ended in spikes, and it carried a large twin mooned ax. FNA soldiers armed with plasma rifles fired at the beast, but the bolts were absorbed into the armor.

That's no creature of Safanar. It's one of the Zekara! Aaron thought.

The Zekara were of the Hythariam military led by General Halcylon, who had sworn to enslave the people of Safanar.

The giant ax was swung through the air, dealing crushing blows upon the FNA soldiers. The Elitesmen surrounding the beast attacked. Aaron rushed forward, heading straight for the beast. He ducked under a swing of the giant ax and hammered down upon the armored leg, but the Falcons bounced back, jarring his arms.

Elitesmen closed in behind him, and Aaron scrambled around looking for a vulnerable spot in the beast's armor. He unleashed an energy-fused kick to the beast's knee, driving it down, but the beast sprang back up and spun around, focusing on Aaron as a hound on prey.

Aaron taunted the beast, drawing it away from the others, and it roared in pursuit. As the distance between them increased, the beast came to halt and lifted the haft of the ax as if it were aiming a rifle. Aaron threw himself behind a wall. The blast of the Zekara weapon thundered against the wall.

"Aaron." Gavril's voice came through his comms device. "The beast is from the Zekara. Try to take it alive."

Another blast from the Zekaran weapon blasted a hole through the rock wall near his head.

Capture it? Yeah, right.

Aaron leaped over the wall and charged the beast. The FNA was engaged with the Elitesmen. The beast's ax swung past him, and Aaron brought the Falcons down upon the haft, cutting through it. A bolt of energy ran along the remaining haft of the ax, and the beast howled in pain, dropping its weapon. The beast's boulder-sized hands smashed at the ground, trying to get at him. Aaron backed away, looking for a way to capture the beast. A gauntleted fist sailed toward him, and he brought up his swords, funneling energy into his muscles and limbs. The gauntleted fists slammed into him, and the beast bore down upon him, using its massive weight. The corded muscles in Aaron's back groaned in protest, and they each struggled against the other. Deep within the helm were glowing yellow eyes, eerily reminiscent of the Drake. The beast roared, as did Aaron, each refusing to yield. Aaron pushed with his legs, and the ground beneath the beast's feet gave way as it slid on the ground.

Aaron heaved to the side, using the beast's forward momentum, causing it to lose its balance. The horns protruding from the helmet slammed into the wall. Aaron brought his swords down and cut one of the horns. The beast reared back in pain. Yellowish liquid dripped from the stump. The beast tore its helmet off, revealing bronze skin and white hair similar to those of the Hythariam. The beast focused its rage-filled eyes upon Aaron. The beast charged. Aaron ducked to the other side and cut through the remaining husk. With the beast's head exposed upon its armored body, Aaron waited for it to attack again. The yellowish liquid dripped to the ground and hissed as it made contact.

The beast regarded Aaron with the barest hints of a smile and charged forward. Aaron summoned the bladesong, readying to strike the final blow. At the last second, a white blur appeared out of nowhere and kicked Aaron out of the way.

Aaron spun in the air and rolled to his feet.

A figure in white armor stood, holding a staff that ended in a short sword, ready to face him.

"You'll kill us all," the man in the white armor said.

The beast narrowed its eyes at them and then tapped a button upon its wrist. A panel hissed open, and the beast's armor glowed with crimson light streaking through the cracks. In a sickening hiss, the fifteen-foot-tall body of the beast came apart, releasing a cloud of yellow particles into the air. Instead of dissipating, it continued to grow, circling around the nearby Elitesmen and FNA soldiers alike. They dropped to their knees, retching.

"Damn," the man in the white armor said. "We can't let it escape."

The cloud of yellow moved on, becoming thinner and harder to see. Anyone who came in contact was affected. Hints of the vapor headed toward Aaron.

Verona gasped at his side, and a Hythariam upon a glider swooped down.

"It's a contagion," Tanneth said.

Aaron's eyes widened, and he saw Sarah heading toward them. "Verona, shield us from the others. Don't let them be exposed," Aaron said.

Verona glanced at the fallen Elitesman and FNA soldiers then nodded. Verona's brow furrowed in concentration.

"Stay back," Aaron said and had to repeat himself several times before the others would listen. Some slammed into Verona's shield. The yellow haze had all but disappeared, but Aaron knew better. "Sarah, you need to get away from here. We've been exposed to something from the Zekara."

Sarah made as if to press forward.

"You can't help us. Get the rest of the FNA out of here!" Aaron cried. Sarah looked as if she were about to protest, and Aaron looked to the older man at her side. "Isaac, get her out of here."

The former Elitesman nodded his gray mane of hair and reached out to Sarah. In a flash, they were gone, via the travel crystal. The soldiers outside Verona's shield backed away. Someone must have given the order to set fire to the stronghold. Smoke began to rise beyond the walls of the courtyard.

Tanneth opened a small panel on the side of his rifle and then immediately closed it again. He took aim at the nearest body, and a red beam shot forth. After a second, the body was engulfed in flames.

"Burn the rest," the man in the white armor said.

"Who are you?" Aaron asked. "And how did you know about the beast?"

"We don't have time for this. Burn them before they have a chance to rise again," the man in the white armor said. He moved from corpse to corpse, severing the heads.

Aaron was about to follow, but Verona held his arm.

"Whoever he is, he helped us against the Elitesmen here," Verona said.

Beside them there were a dozen FNA soldiers that had been trapped within Verona's shield, but none appeared to be suffering from the same illness that afflicted those closest to the yellow haze.

"We must leave this place and burn it to the ground," the man in the white armor said.

Tanneth returned to them. "He's right, Aaron. We need to leave here. The contagion appears airborne but seems to have dissipated. We should do as he says and burn this place to the ground."

An FNA soldier brought out the keystone accelerator, preparing a way back to base, when Tanneth stopped him. "We can't return to Shandara or anywhere, for that matter, or we risk spreading whatever we've been exposed to."

Aaron nodded and looked at the armored stranger. "We'll leave, then you give us some answers."

The man's armored head nodded. The armor had no markings but was similar to the light armor that the Hythariam wore.

They set fire to the castle, using anything they found, and exited through the portcullis. Verona released his shield. The rest of the FNA soldiers, along with their prisoners, had long since gone through the portals back to Shandara.

"Sir, we've been exposed to something made by the Zekara," Tanneth said, speaking into the comms device. "Sending preliminary report."

"Acknowledged," Gavril said. "Recommend quarantine protocols. Since there is no one else there, you should stay in the area. We'll look at the data and be in touch shortly."

The man in the white armor removed his helmet, revealing a young face. He couldn't have been more than eighteen years old. He had dark-blond hair, and his green eyes narrowed when they came upon Aaron.

"Who are you?" Aaron asked.

"My name is Bayen. I'm of the Safanarion Order."

Aaron and Verona exchanged doubtful glances.

"I find that hard to believe," Verona said.

"Believe what you like; the truth doesn't mind," Bayen replied, and looked at Aaron. "Is all you know how to do is kill?"

"Me?" Aaron asked.

Bayen's eyes flashed. "You must have realized the beast wasn't of Safanar. Did you think of what that meant? To find a Zekaran infiltrator? You need to be prepared for a higher form of warfare."

Aaron glanced at the others, but they looked on in stunned silence. "We didn't know what that thing was. In case you didn't notice, that thing was slaughtering my men."

"That's right, you didn't know," Bayen said, stepping closer to Aaron. "It focused on you from the start."

"That's because I attacked it to keep it from harming the others," Aaron said. He couldn't believe he was explaining himself to a kid that was barely more than a boy.

Bayen glared at him, and for a moment Aaron believed he was going to take a shot at him.

"It drew you out by going after your men," Bayen said.

"Easy, guys," Verona said. "Why don't we take a minute and calm down?"

"Verona is right," Tanneth said. "Let me check us all out and send the data back to base so they can figure out what the Zekara have done." Tanneth withdrew a small scanner from his pack and began moving among the men but ignored the Hythariam.

Aaron frowned. "Wouldn't your exposure be the same as ours?"

"Yes, but the Nanites in our system are already uploading their readings, and that data is sent back to base through the comms device. For those who don't have Nanites, I will need to use the scanner," Tanneth said.

"I can tell you what it is. It's a plague the likes of which you've never seen, and it will spread," Bayen said.

"Well, you'll forgive us if we don't take your word for it," Aaron replied.

Bayen shook his head and walked off to the side.

The comms device chimed, and Aaron moved away from the others to speak with Sarah.

"I'm sorry, Sarah. I didn't want to risk you being exposed to what the Zekara released," Aaron said.

"Roselyn explained to me. Are you all right?" Sarah asked.

He could still hear the annoyance in her voice. "I feel fine, but if Verona hadn't shielded us off from the rest of you, then this could have got bad real quick. There is something else," Aaron said, and told her about Bayen.

"I don't think he's an enemy. I saw him fight the Elitesmen on his path to you," Sarah said.

Aaron nodded. "Verona said the same thing, but there's something about him that's not quite right. Remember when the barrier was in place and how Shandara felt out of balance? Well, it's similar to that, except it's focused around a person."

"If you suspect he knows more, then talk to him. We need every advantage for dealing with Halcylon."

Aaron said he would, glancing at Bayen, who had his back to him.

"Be safe, my love," Sarah said.

Aaron said goodbye and closed the channel. He thought he had been exposed to the contagion but didn't feel the effects. He went over to Tanneth.

"What do you know so far?" Aaron asked.

"I've sent the results from the scanner back to base. The preliminary results are that we're fine, but we can't be sure," Tanneth said.

"What do you mean?" Aaron asked.

"We don't know anything about this. Even a small exposure over time could eventually have the same effect as direct exposure to the cloud."

Aaron nodded. "What do you think of our new friend over there?"

Verona joined them. "Seems a bit young to be claiming to be of the Safanarion Order."

"He could have been raised by someone who was a member," Aaron said.

"Not completely unheard of, my friend," Verona said with a wink.

"We need some answers," Aaron said, and headed over to Bayen. "You said before that we needed to burn the bodies before they rise again."

Bayen's face grew ashen, and he clenched the haft of the halberd he carried. "I've seen it before."

"Where?" Aaron asked.

"Everywhere," Bayen whispered, and winced in pain.

"Are you injured?" Aaron asked, taking a step closer.

Bayen jerked his halberd between them. "Stay away from me."

Aaron was startled by the vehemence with which Bayen spoke but didn't go any closer.

"Come now, Aaron was only trying to help," Verona said.

"I've had enough of his help," Bayen said, wincing.

Tanneth brought up his scanner and looked up in surprise. "He has Nanites in his system."

"A spy," Aaron growled and stepped back, drawing his Falcons. The other men of the FNA did the same.

The FNA soldiers fanned out on either side.

"Now would be a good time to start talking," Verona said.

Bayen divided his gaze between them. "I'm no spy."

"Impossible," Tanneth said. "The only people who have Nanites in their systems are Hythariam."

"Could it be another clone?" Aaron asked.

"Maybe, but the clone only revealed itself when its life was threatened," Tanneth said.

"Fine," Aaron said, moving forward.

"I'm no clone," Bayen said, holding up his hand. "It's true, I have Nanites in my system. But the clone that infiltrated your ranks before was less than a month old, which is how it was detected. You'll find that if you use a different scan, then you'll be able to see my age is quite a bit older than that."

Tanneth regarded Bayen for a long moment and then adjusted the scanner. A thin red line appeared on Bayen's outstretched hand. Tanneth frowned at the display on the scanner.

"According to this, he's eighteen years of age," Tanneth said.

"Halcylon could have found a way to fool the scanner," Aaron said.

Bayen met his gaze. "I'm the best hope you have for saving Safanar. Right now, this world is doomed."

CHAPTER 4
WARNING

In the weeks since the battle with the High King, Shandara had become a city transformed. Many of the refugees from Khamearra and Rexel had elected to remain in Shandara and help rebuild the city. Sarah could hardly blame them. Many were either direct descendants or former residents of the fabled city. Shandara had been a tomb but was now being resurrected, and the sight of it was wondrous. People, be it human or Hythariam, worked to rebuild what had been claimed by fire all those years ago. Some had taken it upon themselves to build monuments to the fallen at various parts of the city. With the command center accessible again, they were better able to prepare the defense of the city.

Farms were springing up in the surrounding countryside. Lands that had been unable to support growth for the length of twenty-five years since Shandara had fallen were again able to do so. Some farmers had help from the Hythariam with their technological wonders to aid the fertility of the land. Others had chosen to accept the help of the Safanarion Order.

Original members of the Order had returned to Shandara. They had skills that went beyond those of martial arts. They were practitioners of gathering and sharing of knowledge. They had become adept at concealing their identities and had lived along the fringes of the lands in small towns to escape the Elite Order. Their skills in cultivating the energy to promote growth from crops were beyond Sarah. It was subtle and so slight that when she had first learned of it, she couldn't conceal her skepticism. Aaron held no such doubts, but he didn't have a lifetime of experience working against him.

The former members of the Safanarion Order brought their families and followers, with many journeying to Shandara on foot. The Safanarion Order had been originally made up of different factions, with the Wardens representing the warrior face of the Order. The Wardens were the shields and head of the De'anjard, Shandara's armies. There were factions devoted to justice and laws as well as the pursuit of knowledge. Then there were the ones who bore the mark of the leaf. That faction pursued knowledge of the living world, seeking to be in harmony.

The library within the White Rose, the palace that had been home to the Alenzar'seth for hundreds of years, had been remarkably well preserved. As different parts of the city were brought back to life, residents were also discovering much of the Hythariam underground infrastructure was left intact.

Sarah walked the palace grounds, heading to one of the new trams the Hythariam had built to make the journey across the vast city much quicker. She had divided her time between Shandara and her home city of Khamearra. She was the High Queen now, succeeding her father.

Thoughts of her father had always been a fine mixture of pain and loss. She remembered the kind and gentle man he was when she was young. The ruthless tyrant he had become ignited a cold fury that hadn't diminished, even with his death. If anything, her anger with her father had grown as she tried to hold Khamearra together. There were many opportunists that sought to take whatever they could when they learned of her father's demise.

She was lucky to have established a ruling council that could carry out her decrees. The High Council was made up of former members of the Resistance and those who had endured her father's rule but had not become pulled into its corruption.

Sarah entered the tram and was flanked by her De'anjard bodyguards that Braden, the Warden of the De'anjard, had insisted she allow to accompany her. To be honest, she suspected that Aaron had something to do with it as well. She already had to limit those who stood in line to guard her. Not only were the De'anjard with her at all times, but she was also often flanked by soldiers of the Free Nations Army who were former Elitesmen that had changed sides near the end of the war.

She had disbanded the Elite Order, giving the former members the option to serve in the Free Nations Army. Some of them, like Isaac, were too old to serve in the FNA as a fresh recruit. Isaac was among her protectors, but she hadn't said a word to him since he had whisked her away from the battle at the Elitesman stronghold. She squeezed the hilt of her sword and glared out of the window at the buildings zipping past. A faint bruise showed beneath Isaac's craggy old beard. No one would lay a hand on her without her permission. She didn't care who gave the order. She told Aaron she understood why, but understanding did nothing to quell her anger.

The fact that she had been too nauseated to leave with Aaron this morning was enough to get her hackles rising. She hated that he'd slipped away from her. *You'll pay for that, Shandarian, Alenzar'seth or not.* After a few moments plotting a revenge unworthy of her, she sighed. What was the matter with her? She could go from pleasant to furious inside a minute. She looked at Isaac and was about to apologize, but her temper flared anew. The old Elitesman's chuckle did nothing to soothe it.

The tram came to a halt, and she got out, leading her entourage. As if she needed their protection. She could best any one of them, former Elitesman or not. She set a quick pace, and in no time at all she came to a white building in the style of those at Hathenwood. Tall and circular. The doors hissed open at her approach, and she went inside. The walls had the appearance of being made of glass, but they also functioned as displays. More Hythariam technology that she had come to know in the past six weeks.

Hunched over a machine was Roselyn. Her long, lustrous raven hair was pulled around her neck and covered her shoulder. Her fingers worked the holo interface, and the images on the screens in front of her changed. She turned as Sarah entered, and her golden eyes widened for a moment before she smiled in greeting and waved her over. Sarah gave one glance over her shoulder—that was enough to tell her protectors that they weren't allowed in the lab.

"Verona said you were ill again this morning. Are you feeling better?" Roselyn asked.

"It comes and goes," Sarah said.

Roselyn nodded. "I've begun analyzing the data sent from Tanneth and the others this morning. I know you must have hated having to leave them behind, but it was really for the best. They've all been exposed. Everyone outside Verona's shield appears to be fine. Why is it that whenever Aaron and Verona are together they seem to attract all sorts of trouble?"

"They're men. Put enough of them together, and trouble has no choice but to come poking around," Sarah said, and was surprised to find herself smiling a bit. She and Roselyn had grown quite close, and Sarah felt fortunate to call her friend. Aaron and *his* ever-expanding group of friends were one thing, but they were mostly men. Sometimes, a woman just needed another woman to be around.

"That is true," Roselyn said, and her face grew serious. The screen in front of them changed, showing floating yellow spheres that were latching onto healthy white ones. After a few moments, the other spheres changed too, becoming yellow. "That's it. This is a partial re-creation based upon the data sent. It appears to be tailored for humans. Hythariam aren't affected at all."

"Are you surprised? According to Aaron, Halcylon hates all humans."

Roselyn nodded, her eyes downcast. "It shames me that something this awful is coming from one of my race."

Sarah didn't say anything for a moment. "Evil isn't restricted to a particular race. Sometimes, it just *is*," Sarah said, thinking of all the awful things her father had done during his reign and how it had become her mission to undo the damage that was done. "What does this thing that the Zekara have created do exactly? Anyone caught in the path of the cloud died. At least it appeared that way."

"That's the thing; it does more than kill. It functions like a parasite, but it still keeps going even after the host has died. Most parasites die with the host," Roselyn said.

"The beast this stuff came out of appeared to be part machine and something else."

"The Zekara are made up of the former Hythariam military. The beast was likely part of some type of research. The type that is kept secret—like what the Elitesmen have done in their Citadel," Roselyn said.

"Since the others were exposed, does that mean they're all at risk?" Sarah swayed slightly on her feet.

Roselyn grabbed a nearby chair and helped her to sit. She looked at her as if she were one of her patients. "You look a little tired; are you feeling all right?"

Sarah took a sip of water from the cup that Roselyn handed her. "I just felt as if I was going to pass out all of a sudden. Dammit, I can't be sick right now. It's been like this for almost a week."

Roselyn nodded, and Sarah thought she saw a small smile. Roselyn withdrew a small scanner from her desk drawer. "I just want to run a quick scan."

"Fine," Sarah said.

Roselyn had her lie back and ran the scanner from her head to her stomach, where she kept it for a few seconds. Sarah watched as Roselyn studied the scanner for a moment. Her eyes widened, and she looked up at her, smiling.

"You're not sick. You're pregnant," Roselyn said, beaming.

Sarah's mouth fell open. "Pregnant? Are you sure? I can't be pregnant."

"With twins actually," Roselyn said, and her fingers dashed through the holo interface. In moments, two circular images appeared with smaller ones within. "These are your children. I'd say you are five weeks along."

Sarah stared at the screen; her mouth kept opening and closing, but no words came out. "Twins," she whispered, unable to tear her eyes from the screen. She brought her hands down to her stomach.

Roselyn let out a laugh and hugged her. When she pulled back, both women had tears in their eyes.

"By the Goddess, never in my wildest dreams did I think that this is what was happening to me," Sarah said, and she looked up in alarm. "Aaron..."

"He'll be fine. We will figure out a way through this."

Sarah's eyebrows drew together. "But the war with the Zekara could begin at any moment, and Khamearra is holding together by a thread. And—"

"Sarah, everything will be fine. Trust me, we will find a way through this." Roselyn took a moment before continuing. "You do want to be a mother?"

"Of course I do. I just didn't think it would happen so soon for Aaron and me. Oh Goddess, Aaron. How do you think he will react?" Sarah's breath quickened in her chest.

Roselyn took her hand. "He loves you more than anything in the world. He will make an excellent father."

Sarah knew she was being foolish, but she could hardly keep up with her racing thoughts. "We can't tell him. At least right now."

"Why ever not?"

"He needs to focus on what he is doing. If I tell him now, it's all he will think about."

"He will find out sooner or later. You might be able to conceal it for now, but eventually you *will* start to show."

"I know, but for now I really think I should wait to tell him." *Oh Goddess, I'm pregnant.* The thought was emblazoned in her mind. *Me, a mother...* Her memories of her own mother were so distant that they were more feelings. "I will tell him, but not right now. Promise me you won't say anything."

Roselyn nodded and glanced back at the screen, her lips pursed in thought. On-screen was a depiction of the Alenzar'seth sigil, a Dragon cradling a single rose.

"What is it?" Sarah asked.

"I think I know what Halcylon has done," Roselyn said, and began navigating through the holo interface.

Sarah waited for the rapidly changing images on-screen to stop.

"This is a sample of the Ryakul poison taken from Aaron's blood when he was wounded. The poison was active in his system. We thought that the Ryakuls had poison that came out of their claws. I can't believe I didn't see this before. It's not poison but a virus seeking to spread itself. What Halcylon has done was alter the virus that changes Dragons into Ryakuls so that it affects humans," Roselyn said.

Sarah reined in her racing thoughts. "Are you saying this virus will change humans into something similar to a Ryakul?"

Roselyn tore her eyes from the screen. "Yes," she whispered.

Sarah's stomach clenched. There was no cure for this sickness. "We have to warn them."

CHAPTER 5
ZEKARA

Far to the north, deep in the forests of Safanar, thousands of Hythariam loyal to the Zekara labored. It had been two months since they had arrived upon this world, and Halcylon still caught himself gazing up at the sky. It was a beautiful world. So alive. He had almost forgotten what a living, breathing world could be like. From glorious skies overhead to the strange scents of the forests around them. The Nanites inside every Zekaran had sped up his race's acclimation to this world. The atmosphere was too rich when compared with the thin, sterilized air they had to breathe in their mountain base on Hytharia.

The home world of the Hythariam was gone. Destroyed. The singularity that had slowly been feeding off their system of planets for thousands of years had finally devoured their home. He had been born to a dying world where only the strong survived. As leader of the Zekara, he had to make tough choices. The type of choices that made those playing at being civilized uncomfortable. The harsh truth he had come to accept from a very early age was that civilization is an illusion. An illusion that allows weakness to fester and drain away from the truly visionary people. With the invention of the Nanites that kept their bodies free of sickness and prevented the decrepitude of old age, the Hythariam had conquered mortality. The ruling councils of Hytharia had been swayed to the line of thinking that immortality was against the natural order of things. *Fools.* It was the destiny of his race to spread themselves among the planets of the galaxy, but their time had been cut short. There were thousands of Hythariam with him. Easily a number that would repopulate the species that had once numbered in the billions. Now they had a lush and fertile world at their disposal. There was just the humans to deal with. He had thought to decimate their entire species, and he still planned to kill many of them. But he'd decided the rest would be enslaved.

He called a meeting for the leadership council here. It was time to move things along. Some of their number were losing the will to fight. They were being pulled into the peace of their new world, lulled into a false sense of security, but Halcylon knew better. He joined the council inside one the temporary structures they had built. A holo display of the map of Safanar highlighted the major cities. As they were wiped off the face of the planet, the fallen cities would be renamed. Khamearra lay in the heart of the west with Rexel almost in the middle, but their sights were set on Shandara. Shandara was the biggest prize and posed the most risk to them.

"Chinta, give us an overview of Shandara's defenses," Halcylon commanded.

Chinta's scarred face lifted at being called upon. The Zekaran rose to his feet and saluted Halcylon.

"Passive scans have shown that the city is heavily fortified. We know the city was all but destroyed around twenty-five cycles ago.

However, they are rebuilding it. The scans show armored shafts inside the towers along the wall and throughout the city. Our guess is that there are several different types of cannons, which would make an air assault on the city unwise at our current capability," Chinta said.

Halcylon nodded. "The outer shell of Shandara is similar to other cities on this world, but its infrastructure is much more in line with what we left behind on Hytharia. I agree with your assessment of our chances with an air assault. That's why we won't be leading off with that when we attack the city."

In the silence, Halcylon could sense the hesitation within some of the military leaders around the table. They were a silent minority but if left unchecked could fester and spread.

"Speak freely," Halcylon said.

It was Chinta who cleared his throat. "The Safanarions are stronger than we thought. They rally behind the Alenzar'seth."

Halcylon ground his teeth for a moment. "The failure of the Alenzar'seth is mine. It was my suggestion to the tribunal that he remain alive to watch us escape to Safanar."

The Hythariam around the table immediately started to protest.

"I thought that he would have surely perished upon Hytharia. How could he have escaped?" Halcylon asked, and took a moment for his hardened gaze to settle upon each of them. The question had come up before this, but there had been too much to do. Now the issue had to be addressed.

"He must have had help," Ronin, his chief science officer, said.

Halcylon's gaze settled upon the white-haired Hythariam in his gray uniform. The Hythariam was brilliant, and at times he wondered whose interests he served. Still, Halcylon needed him.

"That would mean we have a traitor in our midst," Halcylon said.

They'd had to purge their ranks in the past, but he would find other ways to use the traitors once he found out who they were.

"I will rally my forces, and we will root out anyone who is not loyal to the Zekara," Chinta said.

The others around the table gave their assertions as well, and in the silence that followed they waited for Halcylon to address them.

"I want a list of suspects brought to me as soon as possible. Unless you catch a traitor in the act, do not take any action against them. I want them watched, and I will insert them into my plans. We could always use a few infiltrators," Halcylon said.

His team recognized the value in the modifications to soldiers in the Catalyst program. They had all reaped the benefits without suffering from any of the long-term effects. Sacrifice a few to make many of them stronger.

"Do you still have need for us to capture more humans?" Chinta asked.

Halcylon glanced at Ronin, for whose experimentation the humans had been required.

"I have enough for now. I'm ready to give my report if you're ready, sir," Ronin asked.

Halcylon nodded.

"I've been successful in adapting the Ryakul virus to human physiology, using additional protocols that I think you will find interesting," Ronin said, and a list of attributes appeared on the holo display.

Halcylon scanned the list, as did the others.

Ronin continued. "We're all familiar with the tenacity with which the original strain seeks to spread itself. What I've been able to do is to encode a prime directive into it, similar to what we normally do with the Nanites. The virus seizes control of the central nervous system, in particular the brain. We've added a mechanism for delivery in each of the infiltrators we've sent out," Ronin said, and the holo display changed to show the small canisters equipped by the infiltrators. "Humans caught in the direct cloud will change almost immediately. Those with less exposure will change, but it can take some time."

Chinta frowned. "What happens when your toxic cloud dissipates?"

"Think of it as adding a spark to some tinder. Those coming in direct contact with a human already infected will become infected themselves," Ronin answered.

Brutal images of the various ways the virus could spread through humans played for them. Halcylon killed the display and drew the attention from the others. "Our path will take us through the most heavily populated areas. They will soften our enemies before we arrive. We cannot cloak our main force for much longer. The power requirements are draining our reserves faster than we originally thought. Any more than that will affect our ability to fight."

The Ryakul virus was something new he'd added to his plans after seeing how effective it was against the Dragons of Safanar. Ronin was the scientist, and he was the general, but what he'd kept secret for the length of their isolation was that he had built quite an understanding of applied science. It was a weakness the traitors had exploited before the barrier cut off their access to Safanar eighty cycles ago. He trusted Ronin as much as any other scientist, which wasn't all that much. Within Ronin's modification to the Ryakul virus were his own protocols that would automatically trigger under certain circumstances.

Halcylon changed the holo display to show a map of the land.

"Militarily, there is no army that can stand against us. Our reckoning with the human race begins now. We will use every means at our disposal to make them suffer for what they have done to us. They are weak, scattered, and without strong leadership. And they will all fall before the might of the Zekara."

Chinta and his other commanders studied the map that showed a simulation of the troop movements in his attack plan.

"I hate to lose the element of surprise. Won't they realize where we are heading in the end?" Chinta asked.

"I'm counting on it," Halcylon replied.

CHAPTER 6
WOUNDED

The Eldarin were of a higher order of Dragons known as Dragon lords. Their domain went beyond the realm of Safanar. They were both spiritual and physical beings, and their fate was tied to Aaron.

The Eldarin honored a sacred trust with the Ferasdiam marked. In saving his life, an Eldarin had become infected with the Ryakul virus. The effect on a normal Dragon was to become a Ryakul. A beast devoid of a lifebeat. The Dragon ceased to be, but for the lifeless husk of what once was. Aaron remembered the Eldarin changing before his eyes and attack one of its own. The mournful howl of the other Eldarin still plagued his dreams. His stomach clenched at the thought, and Aaron suspected more and more that his fate and that of his people was tied to the Eldarin.

The Dragons and Ryakuls were enemies that had been fighting a war for survival for the past sixty years. The FNA hunted the Ryakul, but Aaron was afraid it wasn't enough. There was no cure for the Ryakul virus. Roselyn, a Hythariam scientist and healer, had explained that the virus permanently changed those infected at their fundamental level. If Halcylon was truly able to modify the Ryakul virus so that it affected humans, then all the people of Safanar were in danger.

Night had fallen over their camp. There were more than a few suspicious glances toward Bayen and at each other. The few Hythariam with them kept a careful watch on them all, looking for signs of being infected. No one wanted to talk about what they would do if one of them was.

"Not sleeping?" Verona asked.

"I doubt anyone is going to sleep tonight," Aaron said, and glanced at Bayen, who had positioned himself away from the others.

"The watch has been set, and I've sent four to scout the area a bit," Verona said, and watched Bayen for a few seconds. "Not your biggest fan, I'd say, my friend."

Aaron frowned. "He's hiding something. I just can't guess what it is. His answers raise more questions."

"He does seem rather familiar," Verona said.

"He's supposed to be our best hope against this plague. Not sure if I believe that, but he believes it. I don't know whether to have him bound or reach out to him." Aaron returned his gaze toward Verona.

"How long are you going to avoid carrying it?" Verona asked.

"What do you mean?"

"The staff. The rune-carved staff to be exact. You've barely touched it since the battle with the High King."

Aaron shifted his gaze away. "So many Dragons fell at the battle, and the Eldarin... I can hear their call, Verona. When I sleep. When I'm awake. It's like they're reaching out to me, but I don't know how to help them. I'm afraid."

"I have an idea about that—" Verona began but was cut off by a scream.

The clouds shifted past, distorting the moonlight, and beyond the campfire they heard another scream echoing. Aaron drew his swords and moved to the edge of the firelight. Tanneth engaged his helmet, which covered his head instantly, and trained his plasma rifle into the gloom. A foggy mist rolled in around them. The night erupted into a series of growls coming from directly ahead of them. The FNA formed a circle around the fire and kept their weapons at the ready.

Four of their number who had been patrolling the area were missing. An FNA soldier stumbled from the fog, calling for help. His uniform was shredded across his chest, and blood covered his hands. The soldier hunched over, gasping.

"What happened to you?" Aaron asked but didn't move any closer.

The soldiers raised their weapons, and the terrified man kept glancing over his shoulders.

"He's infected," Bayen shouted.

"We don't know that," Aaron said.

The man collapsed to the ground, his body going into convulsions. Behind him, three large figures emerged from the gloom. Tattered remnants of their FNA uniforms were the only way to tell they had once been men. Their eyes glowed yellow, and their elongated features stretched upon blackened skin that still held a pasty whiteness. In the split second that it took for Aaron and the others to realize what they faced, the infected bounded forth, using their arms to propel them forward with inhuman speed.

Aaron charged, bringing his swords to bear, and was joined by Bayen moving just as fast as he. Aaron dodged the black claws and hacked away at the vicious attacks of the infected. Grisly body parts still twitched on the ground, and Aaron was careful not to get any of the black liquid on him. Aaron heard Bayen's halberd whirl through the air as he dispatched the infected nearest him. Flashes of golden plasma bolts lit up the area as Tanneth tried to shoot the third infected. The infected man bolted to the side in a twisted leap, his claws raking across several men in his path. Attack orbs from a former Elitesman tore through the infected man, engulfing him in flames.

Aaron saw Verona standing over the infected man who'd come just before the attack.

"Verona, please, help me," the infected man cried, and curled into a ball.

Verona froze with his sword hanging loosely by his side. The man lashed out and clawed Verona's leg. Several plasma bolts struck the man, and he fell back. Verona looked down at his leg, seeing the blood mix with the black liquid in the wound. Verona rubbed at the wound with his sleeve. His eyes darted up and met Aaron's as he stumbled to the ground.

"He's infected," Bayen said, coming to his side.

"We don't know that," Aaron replied.

Bayen leaned in so only Aaron heard. "Killing him now would be a mercy," Bayen whispered.

"I'm not killing him!"

"He'll kill us all. If you won't, then I will," Bayen said, and moved forward.

Aaron grabbed him by the arm and yanked him back. "No you won't."

Bayen glared at him and then glanced down at Verona. "You can't save him," Bayen said, and backed away, muttering under his breath.

Aaron came to Verona's side. There was a shallow gash on his outer thigh. Tanneth handed him some water, which he used to clean the wound. *It's a shallow wound. He can't be infected, can he?* Aaron called for strips of cloth and tied it above the wound.

"This may slow the virus," Aaron said, and stared at Verona, looking for some sign.

Verona met his gaze. "I don't feel anything, but Aaron, if I start to turn into… one of *those* things… you need to do it."

Cries of the wounded men drew their attention. They'd collapsed to the ground. Their pleas to save them became harsh growls as the minutes dripped by and their skin became pasty gray. The FNA soldiers around them looked on helplessly and glanced back at Aaron. Aaron reached out with his senses, seeking the lifebeat of the fallen soldiers, but there was nothing but darkness. In minutes, they went from normal human beings to lifeless shells, their bodies still convulsing while their limbs extended, changing into something inhuman.

Bayen watched him expectantly. Aaron nodded to the soldiers that held the plasma rifles ready. The soldiers made quick work of it and burned the remains.

"They're the Forsaken," Bayen said. "If you take any wounds from their claws or teeth, then you're as good as dead."

Aaron's hands balled into fists. "Do you know the location of Halcylon and the Zekara?"

"Killing him won't stop this," Bayen said.

"It's a start," Aaron said.

Tanneth called him back to Verona, who was sitting up.

"His wound is changing," Tanneth said.

The skin around the wound was turning black but hadn't spread.

"I'm afraid I have something to tell you, my friend," Verona began. "Roselyn has put the Nanites into me. She has been adapting them for us. I think they are fighting the infection."

The Nanites. One of the Hythariam's greatest scientific achievements that allowed them to extend their lifetime, cure diseases, and augment themselves in a number of ways. By the same token, the inception of the Nanites had led to vicious civil wars that, in turn, had led to the collapse of their world. In the hands of a monster like Halcylon, Aaron had experienced firsthand what the Nanites were capable of. The Eldarin had healed him, and he wondered if he could do the same for Verona.

Aaron drew in the energy and saw Verona's lifebeat pulsing in rhythm with his beating heart. The lifebeat encompassed his whole body, springing from Verona's head. At the location of the wound there was a small mass of swirling darkness. Aaron reached toward the wound with a tendril of energy, urging the body to repair itself.

Nothing happened.

The wound itself was a shallow gash and nothing else, but the flesh just beneath wouldn't react to anything that Aaron could do. He could try using the Falcons and keying the bladesong. Aaron shook his head; it wasn't the amount of energy that was failing but his lack of knowledge.

Tanneth brought out his scanner and ran it over Verona's wound. "The Nanites appear to be stopping the spread of the infection, but they can't rid his body of it."

"Cut it out of me then," Verona said.

Aaron glanced at the others. "There is no guarantee that it will work."

"There's no guarantee that it won't work either, my friend," Verona replied.

Aaron nodded. "We'll need to seal the wound after," he said.

An FNA soldier handed him a sharp knife. Aaron washed it as best he could. Tanneth withdrew a small tube from his pack and adjusted the dial on top. He motioned for the knife, and a beam of light came from the tube. Tanneth moved the light up and down both sides of the blade.

"It's clean now," Tanneth said, handing the knife back to Aaron.

"Hold him down. This is going to hurt."

FNA soldiers surrounded them, taking positions so that they could keep Verona from moving. One handed Verona a piece of leather that he could bite down on. The wound was on the outer thigh. Aaron brought the knife just outside the blackened area of skin and looked up at his friend. Verona nodded for him to begin.

Aaron swallowed some of his angst away and steeled himself to the task. He drew in the energy, enhancing his strength so he could make a clean cut. With one final nod to Verona, Aaron cut deeply into his flesh. Verona screamed, his body went rigid, and the FNA soldiers clamped down to hold him in place. The darkened flesh fell to the ground, and blood rushed the area. Tanneth used the laser to cauterize the wound. Verona's muffled groans gave way to silence. They burned the remains.

Tanneth scanned the wound. "I don't detect any traces of the infection."

Aaron released the breath he was holding and gave Verona a pat on his shoulder. "You said before that the Nanites send a signal so they can report in. How come you weren't able to detect them before?"

"Roselyn must have changed the protocol to hide the test. Which means she did this without the approval of the council," Tanneth said. "It's not as bad as it sounds. It was always the intent to share all of our technology with the people of Safanar."

"I don't know if they're ready for this, and honestly the decision is beyond just the council," Aaron said.

Tanneth nodded. "We'll need to keep an eye on Verona. The Nanites only slowed it down, and he was lucky the wound was so small."

"We need answers, and we're not going to find them by staying here," Aaron said, and glanced at Bayen, who stood off to the side. He was hunched over with his back to him. "I think I'll start with him. Let's break camp."

Aaron headed toward the mysterious member of the Safanarion Order. He approached silently.

"...The probability is still estimated at 55 percent. Thirteen days, twelve hours, and thirty-seven minutes until matrix moves out of alignment," a low voice said.

Aaron cleared his throat, and Bayen cursed and spun around.

"I think it's time you and I had a talk," Aaron said.

"You got lucky. I'm not sure he's out of the woods just yet," Bayen said, nodding toward where Verona lay.

Aaron studied the young man. The way Bayen glared at him as if Aaron had wronged him somehow. "If there is a chance that we can save him or anyone else exposed to one of those things, then we should take it," Aaron said.

"You haven't seen what I've seen."

"You can't expect anyone to fight at your side if they believe that you'll just strike them down the moment they get wounded by one of those things," Aaron said.

"They're called the Forsaken because once you're infected, there is no cure. Striking down a Forsaken is a mercy both to the infected and the rest of us," Bayen said.

"How can you be so sure? Tell us what you know, and maybe we can find a way to beat this."

Bayen didn't say anything but kept watching Verona. *What happened to him?* Aaron wondered.

"When you fought before, you protected the men around you, so I think we're on the same side, but if you don't work with me, then I'm not sure there is much point in you staying with us," Aaron said.

Bayen tore his eyes away from Verona. "I don't know where Halcylon is, but I can tell you where he is going to be."

"How do you know where he's going to be?" Aaron asked.

"You wouldn't believe me if I told you. Halcylon is heading through the Waylands."

Aaron frowned. "You said you're the best hope for saving Safanar. What does that even mean?"

"You've seen the Forsaken. Now imagine this happening in a city or multiple cities," Bayen said.

That haunted look in Bayen's eyes gave Aaron pause. Verona rose to his feet and waved over at them.

"You were lucky this time," Bayen said. "Next time, you may not have a choice."

Tanneth ran over. "We've just got a report from Hathenwood. There is a large force heading toward Rexel."

"From where?" Aaron asked.

"They are coming in from the north. This is no remnant fighting force of the former High King's army. Gavril just sent this over," Tanneth said.

The comms device on his wrist lit up, and a small holo display appeared. The picture was from one of the many reconnaissance drones they had flying overhead. The picture showed the tracks of vehicles traveling over land, and the only place they could be heading was Rexel. Bayen was right. Halcylon was heading to the Waylands.

"We need to warn them," Aaron said. "I know we're supposed to stay in quarantine, but if the rest of us haven't been infected yet, then it's a risk we're going to have to take. We leave now."

CHAPTER 7
OLD FOES

Night would soon fall on Shandara, and Sarah glanced at the city skyline. The gleaming spires of White Rose Palace stood proudly in the distance. Neither she nor Aaron had so much as set foot inside the home of his ancestors. There hadn't been time. She suspected the palace and what it represented made Aaron a bit uncomfortable. The man wouldn't think twice at leaping through a sky filled with Ryakuls, but put one of the grandest palaces of all Safanar and the mantle that goes with it in front of him, and he hesitated.

Aaron didn't crave power, which was one of the things that drew her to him. That and his broad shoulders and those dark, piercing eyes. Sarah brought her straying thoughts to a halt and slipped her hand down to caress her stomach. If the Goddess Ferasdiam smiled upon them, then their children would grow up here. She pictured it in her mind. A time of peace. A time when their world wasn't in danger from powerful tyrants. Aaron feared becoming like her father, the High King. Both were Ferasdiam marked, making them the most powerful among them. Where her father had been consumed by his gift, using it to gather power and control everything around him,

Aaron used his gift to give hope where there was none. He fought against overwhelming odds to a victory that hadn't cost him his soul.

He asserted that he was the possibility of what any of them could achieve. The belief was bound to his very core, but after the battle with the High King, he feared walking in her father's footsteps. She wasn't naive enough to believe that it could never happen, but her faith in Aaron was secure. He would give his life so they could all live, and that was what frightened her the most. Their children deserved to have their father in their lives. Sarah would challenge the Goddess herself if it came to it. People who were Ferasdiam marked throughout history had one commonality that was universal to almost all: They died young. Her father had been an exception, and he became a monster.

Sarah returned to Roselyn's lab, but just outside the doors she heard voices from within.

"...It doesn't work the same as on the Dragons?" Iranus asked.

"No, Father. They've made it more aggressive, and they've tailored it for humans. It's also highly unstable."

"Unstable? What do you mean?"

"The base virus that appears in the Ryakul venom spreads itself through a host at an alarming rate. Since Halcylon had it modified for humans, there is a chance it will spread to other species, including Hythariam," Roselyn said.

"I see, but viruses usually only cross similar species."

"That's not all of it. The Safanarions have a connection to their world and other life forms the likes of which we've never seen. This gift manifests itself in small ways in many of them, but for others, like the former Elitesmen and Safanarion Order, their gifts are an order of magnitude above everyone else," Roselyn said.

"Are you saying that the likeliness of the infection spreading to the other species is dependent upon whom they've infected?"

"That's my theory. Halcylon's scientist should have known better than to create this," Roselyn said.

"The general is considered a hero to his followers. He can be quite persuasive. Have you been able to make an antiviral that can also prevent it from spreading?"

"Father, they weren't able to do that back on Hytharia before the civil wars happened."

"They weren't you, my dear. I'll bring this to the FNA, but there is another reason why I'm here."

There was a long moment of silence, and Sarah leaned in to hear better.

"Verona is a good man. You would see that if you gave him a chance," Roselyn said.

"He is reckless. The lifespan of a human is barely a hundred years. He will be an old man, and you will still have the measure of your life to live."

"Did you say something similar to Aunt Cassandra before she married Reymius?" Roselyn asked.

Sarah stifled a gasp. She hadn't known that one of Aaron's grandparents had been a Hythariam. Aaron was the child of three worlds. Earth, where he was raised and the home to his father. Safanar, where his mother had been raised before fleeing to Earth at the fall of Shandara. His grandmother, Cassandra, was of the Hythariam and had fallen victim to the Drake.

"We could extend their lifespan and help them in a number of different ways," Roselyn said.

"The Nanites have been both a curse and a blessing upon the

Hythariam. Do you think that humans would fare any better, given such a burden?"

"They might not make the same mistakes we have," Roselyn said.

"You always see the best in people. It's part of what makes you a brilliant healer, but in this I'm not sure I can agree. Some of them have proven to be very wise and good, but by the same token many have not. It's not because of pride or arrogance that I've always argued against sharing the Nanites with the people of Safanar. It's fear of the repercussions of what will happen to them if we were to do such a thing."

"What if the Nanites help prevent the Ryakul virus from spreading?" Roselyn asked.

"Does it?" Iranus countered.

"I'm not sure—" Roselyn began, but something chimed in the background.

Sarah heard the shifting of feet.

"What is this?" Iranus demanded. "These are Nanite update logs. The protocols have been changed to come directly to you rather than through our main systems in Hathenwood."

"Verona has the Nanites in him. I've been adapting them for humans," Roselyn said.

Iranus gasped. "You had no right to do this. You've broken the decrees set from the council."

"Then have me arrested," Roselyn said.

"You don't understand the gravity of what you've done. The people of Safanar aren't ready for this, and they might not even want it," Iranus said, and Roselyn gasped.

"What is it?"

"Verona's been hurt."

Hearing the shakiness in her friend's voice, Sarah went through the doors, abandoning the pretext that she had not been listening in on their conversation. "Are they all right?"

They turned toward her, surprised by her sudden appearance.

"I'm not sure," Roselyn said.

Sarah joined them. Roselyn read through the report on her holo display, and the frown on her face deepened the further she read. "The Nanites report a foreign entity with virus classification and then skin trauma." Roselyn repeated the last words to herself.

Iranus scanned the report. "It says he was wounded before he became infected, but it doesn't look like they were able to beat the infection."

"They slowed it down," Roselyn said, and then looked at Sarah. "The Nanites don't just beat infections. They enhance our own immune systems so that it can better withstand an infection."

"I don't understand where the skin trauma comes into play," Iranus said.

Sarah thought about it for a moment and divided her gaze between the two of them. The Hythariam for all their brilliance had forgotten a form of disease prevention that they probably considered to be too primitive.

"They cut out the infection," Sarah said.

Roselyn gasped and then nodded. "That makes sense. Tanneth is with them. He could tell whether the infection had spread. But if they didn't get all of it, the virus could spread again."

"I understand your hesitation regarding the Nanites, but are there any alternatives? If the FNA were to face an army of these things, then it would be disastrous for them," Sarah said.

"The Nanites might help in some cases. Looking at the report,

Verona was very lucky. The wound was shallow, but if it had been worse, then cutting out the infection wouldn't have worked because it would have killed the person we're trying to save," Iranus said.

"Were any of the Hythariam exposed to this virus?" Sarah asked.

"Yes, but it appears the Hythariam are not affected by it. The virus shuts down for now at least," Roselyn said.

Sarah frowned. "You think that will change?"

"Exactly," Iranus said. "Viruses can change and even jump between similar species. For all our differences, we are also quite similar. In time, our race could be affected by the virus."

"Father, I'm going to put my proposal before the council to formally begin human trials with the Nanites," Roselyn said.

"One case hardly proves anything. Have you considered that it was Verona's abilities that slowed the virus and not the Nanites?"

Roselyn frowned. "No, I hadn't considered that. Then I will need samples of the actual virus to test against. Without samples, we can't learn anything more. Working with the data from the Nanites isn't enough."

"Why?" Sarah asked.

"Because we need to be able to test against the virus as it attacks living tissue. This way, we can study how it works and figure out a way to prevent it," Roselyn said.

Iranus turned away from them and scanned the room, focusing on nothing in particular. "Finding samples shouldn't be much of a problem before long," Iranus said quietly.

"How?" Sarah asked. "They've been burning the bodies to prevent the sickness from spreading."

"There will be more instances of these events. Aaron and the others may have stumbled upon this when they faced that creature, but

Halcylon has a plan. He will move toward more populated areas, and the sickness will spread," Iranus said.

"Goddess be merciful," Sarah whispered.

"Merciful indeed," Iranus said. "We will begin sending out warnings and information about the virus. Containment measures may need to be taken. There are going to be a lot of tough choices ahead."

The door to the lab opened, and Isaac came through. The former Elitesman, who had aided the Resistance in Khamearra, still wore his dark leather duster, though it now had the gold bars of an officer in the Free Nations Army.

"Your Grace, I'm sorry to disturb you, but we've had word from Khamearra," Isaac said.

"What is it?" Sarah asked.

"There have been unexplained deaths in the city. They seem to be primarily targeting former Elitesmen," Isaac said.

Sarah frowned in thought for a moment. "Who else are they targeting?"

"Some were healers, and then there was the head chef for the soup kitchens that feed the poor in the city. We had assigned former Elitesmen to protect and help with those duties as part of your request to reintegrate them into a more civilized world. The deaths seemed random at first, but the method was consistent among them. Some simply fell to the ground and were dead before they hit. Others would begin screaming at something only they saw. Then they would commit suicide. I witnessed the death of one, and just before he died he whispered, "The Prince of Khamearra has returned," Isaac said.

"Rordan," Sarah hissed.

"That's what I was thinking," Isaac said.

"How is he able to kill people?" Roselyn asked.

"He's using some type of amulet crafted by Mactar," Sarah said. "We had thought it was an apprentice amulet that the Elitesmen used to speed up an initiate's ability to work with the energy."

"We?" Roselyn asked.

"When Braden and I were in Khamearra," Sarah said.

"How is the Warden?" Isaac asked.

"Committed to rebuilding the De'anjard," Sarah answered. "I need to return to Khamearra to deal with this."

"But Sarah—" Roselyn began.

"I know Rordan best," Sarah said.

"This is what he wants. To draw you out," Iranus said.

"I can't sit idly by while he murders my people," Sarah said.

"I'm not suggesting that you do, but you do have resources at your disposal," Iranus said.

"And I intend to use them," Sarah said, and turned as if to leave.

"But Sarah, you can't just throw yourself in danger, what about the —"

"Roselyn," Sarah said, and shook her head.

Isaac and Iranus traded glances, and then Sarah felt the slightest touch across her senses.

Isaac gasped. "By the Goddess, you're pregnant. I can sense the lifebeat of another in you."

There was a long moment of silence as they all waited for Sarah to speak.

"Yes," Sarah said, and felt the edges of her lips curving upward, but she clamped down on her emotions at once.

Isaac's eyebrows drew up. "Aaron doesn't know?"

"No, he doesn't. I only found out a little while ago with Roselyn's help. I will tell him, but now isn't the right time."

"My Lady, I shouldn't have come. I cannot put you in danger. I had thought you would be able to help with what you knew about Rordan, but now..."

"No, Isaac, coming to me is exactly what you should have done. Life won't stop because I'm pregnant. I am going to Khamearra. I will find my brother, and he'll answer for the crimes he is committing," Sarah said.

"We can send additional protection with you," Iranus said. Isaac all but glared at the old Hythariam, but he continued anyway. "There are some rules that apply to all species, and this one holds true, as I've fallen into its folly before: One doesn't simply argue with a pregnant woman once she sets her mind to something," Iranus said with a rare broad smile. "Let me be among the first to congratulate you, my dear."

Of all the things that Sarah had thought to hear from Iranus, this was not among them. Despite herself, she felt a surge in her heart that would have her floating to the stars. "Thank you," she said. Her eyes brimmed with tears, and for once she didn't care. Under the shadows of danger all around them, their babies shone like a beacon of hope within her. But first she needed to deal with her brother, Rordan. She needed Khamearra's leaders focused upon the Zekara, who could easily turn their attention to her homeland as well as Shandara.

"I would join you, but I need to keep working on countering this Ryakul virus," Roselyn said.

"I understand, and thank you," Sarah said.

Sarah left the room to find the hallway lined with heavily armed FNA soldiers. Most were from Khamearra. She sensed the lifebeat blazing within them, marking them as former members of the Order of the Elite. They were all battle hardened, and any semblance of softness had left them long ago. But something else lingered in the eyes of the former Elitesmen, a light that she hadn't seen in any of them when they'd served her father. The soldiers came to attention and brought their fists across their hearts. Sarah saluted them back in turn and made the mark of the Goddess upon her forehead. She offered a silent prayer that they would make it safely through this.

Isaac cleared his throat. "Your Grace, Khamearra awaits."

Sarah nodded, and the former Elitesman brought out his travel crystal. In a flash of purple oblivion, the hallway disappeared around them.

CHAPTER 8
ALLIES

A small holding sat nestled along the eastern borders of Khamearra. Prince Rordan had journeyed here with his father and two brothers a few years ago. This was before he found out he had a sister. The day she returned to the High King's court, startlingly beautiful and perfect in such a way that he despised her almost instantly. The fact that she thwarted all his attempts at removing her from this life infuriated him. Now, Sarah had been proclaimed High Queen of Khamearra, when the title should have come to him as High King Amorak's rightful heir. He was the eldest son after all.

Weeks ago, he had returned to the palace, expecting to be welcomed as the next High King. Instead, the guards attempted to arrest him. Proclamations had been posted throughout the city of the disbandment of the Elite Order. The authority of the Elitesmen had been revoked. Soldiers of the Free Nations Army working with the Khamearrian Army had joined forces to remove the Elitesmen from power. They were to be arrested and faced with a choice of exile or enlistment in the Free Nations Army. More than half of the surviving members of the Elite Order had elected to throw their lot in with their former enemies. The whole thing stank of the Heir of Shandara's influence. As Aaron was Ferasdiam marked, it would be suicidal for Rordan to face him in open combat, but he had other ways to strike out at the Alenzar'seth.

"Your Grace, there have been more inquiries into your whereabouts," Darven said.

Rordan eyed the former Elitesman. The man had been paired with Mactar for a number of years and was an apprentice of sorts. Mactar hadn't been seen or heard from since their army had been defeated. Many believed the old Dark Master had perished in the battle. Rordan didn't believe the rumors until Darven had sought him out and confirmed it for him.

"Well, I have been drawing attention to myself," Rordan said. The power was in him now, loitering beneath the surface. The amulet that Mactar had left him had opened the door and taken his abilities to another level. He could reach out with the energy and stop a person's heart almost instantly. The one caveat was that he needed to be close to his intended target. He didn't know why, and Mactar wasn't around to ask. Another ability had manifested itself within the past week.

"Have you practiced the meditation exercises that I taught you?" Darven asked.

"Of course. How else do you think my father's former staff at the palace met with unfortunate ends?" Rordan said. In deep stages of meditation, he was able to focus upon a single person and use the energy to nudge their thoughts. As he learned to focus more, and with the help of the amulet to focus his power, he was able to do more than just nudge a person's thoughts. Some he could bend to his will, while with others he turned their dreams into nightmares.

His skin had become a pasty white, a side effect of the amulet, but he didn't care. Even the Elitesmen within their midst gave him a wide berth now. He supposed he couldn't blame them because they had become his practice targets while he honed his abilities. It was good that they feared him now. Fear was something these Elitesmen understood, and it was that fear that would make them useful for what he had in mind.

"Do you think she will come?" Rordan asked.

"Sarah will come. Your sister will never let the deaths you've caused go unanswered," Darven said.

Rordan nodded and resumed his pacing. His thoughts were clearer if he kept moving. "Do you think *he* will come as well?" Rordan asked.

"Probably; I bet he hardly leaves her side."

His gut clenched at the thought, and Rordan kicked over a chair. "I need to get them separate."

"You should remember that Aaron Jace is, in fact, human. He can be beaten. He can be outwitted. One just needs to find the right leverage to keep him at bay or a distraction to keep him looking in the direction that you want," Darven said.

Rordan stopped his pacing. "Why does he hate you so much? I remember his reaction to you when we first saw him in Shandara. He knew who you were, but how could that be?"

Darven stopped sharpening his blade. "I was with your brother, Tye, when he tried to capture Aaron. He killed your brother but not before my dagger found its home in his mother's chest. That's why he wants to kill me."

Rordan's eyes widened. "You killed his mother... So that's how the rest of you escaped."

Darven nodded. "There wasn't much time for a better plan. Aaron wasn't nearly as battle tested as he is now. Taking him on alone now would be a path to a quick death."

"I don't need to take him on. At least not directly. It's my sister that I will kill first. Then the throne of Khamearra will be mine as it should have been," Rordan said, wiping his hands upon his pants. People always gave him strange looks when he did this, but Darven was too smart for that. The skin on the back of his hands always felt as if there were tiny things crawling on them. The release he had was when he took a life, but the feeling always came back. Slow at first, but steadily building over time until he gave in and went on the hunt for his next victim.

"Have you given further thought to my proposal?" Darven asked.

"The one where we reach out to the army of Hythariam that we're not sure exist? No, I haven't," Rordan said, and resumed his pacing.

"They exist. Mactar was aligned with them. At least he told me himself before he died. Regardless, I've seen a report come in from one of our remote encampments. They've been contacted, and there was talk of aligning against a common enemy," Darven said.

"They approached us? How did they even know that they were one of ours? And what do they want in return?" Rordan asked.

"All good questions, my Lord," Darven answered. "They've given us a means to contact them," Darven said and set down a small black oval object on the table in front of him.

"What is that?"

"It's a means to communicate with them. All you need to do is touch the top."

Rordan frowned in thought for a moment and crossed his arms tightly in front of him. "Why me?"

Darven glanced at him with a slightly amused expression. "Because they said they wanted to speak to you."

Rordan tilted his head for a moment, considering. "Me specifically?"

"You are the prince and heir apparent to Khamearra's throne. That is, of course, unless you want to submit to the rule of your sister?" Darven asked.

Rordan glared at the former Elitesman. "You know I don't."

"I wasn't advising one way or the other. I was merely pointing out the options. Now, are you going to contact our potential allies or not?" Darven asked.

Rordan unclenched his jaw, and his gaze returned to the small black oval object on the table. He slowly reached out and pressed his thumb onto the center. The metallic surface beneath his thumb glowed. Small legs unfolded themselves and pushed the device up. After a few moments, a face with tan skin and golden eyes appeared above the glowing object. Rordan glanced at Darven, who nodded for him to speak.

"I was told you wanted to speak with me. I am Prince Rordan of Khamearra."

Chapter 9
COUNSEL

Bayen sat hunched over, glaring at the small holographic display above the bracer on his wrist. Matrix alignment estimate read 86 percent. He had been here less than a day. How had the matrix alignment decreased so much since then? He'd looked at the estimate, expecting it to be near 93 percent. He had fourteen days until the temporal matrix was pulled out of alignment and he was forced to go back to the future. That meant that there should have been a steady decline of 7 percent each day. It was more than double that.

"Sam," Bayen whispered. "Why has the alignment decreased so much?"

"Calculations are adjusted based upon new input," Sam replied.

Bayen cursed inwardly at the designer of this simple-minded artificial intelligence that he was forced to contend with.

"What has changed?"

"The plague has been released," Sam said.

"But we were able to contain it," Bayen said.

"As instructed, I've been monitoring communications."

"Right, communications between Hathenwood and Shandara."

"I've expanded my parameters to include communications from the group known as the Zekara," Sam said.

"You were able to crack the encryption on their communications channels?" Bayen asked.

"No, sir. I already have the keys that unlock their comms channels," Sam said.

"Do you have system access?" Bayen asked, fighting to keep his voice down. If his little AI could get system access to the Zekara, then they could cripple their forces and perhaps turn the tide of this war before it had a chance to really begin.

"Negative, sir."

Bayen swore and drew a few glances his way. Aaron was speaking into his own comms device and didn't hear him.

"Is keeping Halcylon alive still our only hope of curing the plague?"

"Keep General Halcylon alive. Fifty-five percent success probability rate."

Bayen pursed his lips in thought. The answer hadn't changed. Still, he had less time to stop the plague from getting out of control.

"Sam, what happened? Why do I have even less time than we thought?"

"Infiltrators are moving into position around the continent. Should they be destroyed, then their self-destruct mechanism will release the plague," the AI said.

"Is there any way to stop them from self-destructing?" Bayen asked, and after a moment added, "And disable them at the same time?"

Never trust an AI to not state the obvious, and allowing the infiltrators to roam free wasn't really an option.

"The self-destruct is engaged automatically upon catastrophic failure of the host or if the host chooses to engage it," Sam said.

"There must be a way to prevent the sequence from starting. A design flaw of some kind," Bayen said.

"Accessing known infiltrator design. One moment please," Sam said. "There is a sequence that can be followed that will both disable the infiltrator and stop the self-destruct protocol. It requires close proximity to the infiltrator," Sam said.

The holo display showed a few images of the actions required to disable the infiltrator. It wasn't your typical hack-and-slash until it stopped moving, but precise and targeted hits carried out in just the right order.

"Can you get this information into the hands of Free Nations Army? Particularly"—Bayen paused for a second, trying to recall the name of the Hythariam general that served in the beginning—"Gavril Sorindal?"

"It would require leveraging the nearest comms device to send the information. This communication could later be discovered, and our presence would be detected," Sam warned.

"It's a risk we need to take. If we can get the FNA to neutralize the infiltrators, that would buy us some time to prevent the plague from spreading so rapidly."

"Confirmed, sir. Data packet sent."

Bayen frowned for a moment. "Whose comms device did you use?"

"T-thirty-one-H," Sam replied.

Bayen rolled his eyes and shook his head. "A name, Sam. I'm looking for the user of the device."

"Apologies, sir. I gave you the device's unique identifier. The current user of the device is known as Tanneth."

Bayen glanced over at the Hythariam and cursed inwardly. Tanneth was clever enough to know if his comms device had been tampered with. It was only a matter of time. Bayen glanced back over at Aaron. He was so different from the man he knew, but some things were the same.

"Planning your next argument?" Verona asked, approaching from behind him.

Bayen quickly covered up his bracer with the sleeve of his cloak. "With who?"

Verona's lips curved in a half smile. "I understand why you wanted to kill me."

"You were very lucky. Anyone else would have been dead."

"Still, you seem hell-bent on challenging Aaron at every turn"

Bayen clutched the haft of his bladed staff. "Someone should. If you don't, then what he does could doom us all."

"Aaron wouldn't let that happen. You know, when I first met Aaron, he had secrets that were weighing him down. They constantly ate away at him and almost became his downfall."

"Really, and what did he do?" Bayen asked.

Verona met his gaze. "Well, he trusted me, for one. Eventually, he shared his burdens with the rest of us. Friends help each other, and right now you look like you could use a friend."

Bayen looked across the way at Aaron but didn't say anything. *Success means death. Failure means the end of the world,* he thought.

"Another time perhaps," Verona said, and took a few steps away. "Just remember: Bearing a burden alone is the surest path to defeat. Aaron taught me that."

Bayen's breath caught in his chest. "What if my burden is meant to be carried alone?"

"Carried, perhaps, but you don't have to stand apart from the rest of us to do so. Just think about what I said."

***

"They don't think we're infected," Aaron said. The holo display above his comms device showed a miniature depiction of Sarah from the shoulders up.

"That's good. Roselyn pieced together what happened to Verona. The fact that he has the Nanites in him didn't sit well with Iranus," Sarah said.

"They saved his life," Aaron said, and suppressed a shiver at just how close he had come to losing his friend forever.

"What is it?"

Aaron frowned. He should have known better. If he denied anything, she would see right through him. "I keep thinking what if it had been you."

Sarah's gaze bored into his. "Then you would have done what had to be done."

"I won't do it," Aaron said.

"I trust that when the time comes for action to be taken, you will do what you believe is best in your heart," Sarah replied.

They didn't say anything for a few moments, and Aaron silently cursed the distance between them. He wanted to be with Sarah and not speaking through a damned comms device.

"I keep hearing the Eldarin. At first, it was only in my dreams, but it's coming more frequently. It's like they are close but just out of reach. I don't know how to help them, and I need to. Not only because of what they've done for me, but they are tied to this."

"How?" Sarah asked.

"All life is connected. The Eldarin are able to traverse different planes of existence. But with one of them infected with the Ryakul virus, I feel like things are spiraling out of balance. They're not ordinary Dragons. They are something else entirely. Something… more."

"You could seek out Tolvar's help. He might be able to guide you in this," Sarah said.

"That's a really good idea. I hadn't thought of him," Aaron said, remembering the mysterious group of people that roamed the lands. He and Sarah had spent barely a day and night among them, but they had been able to shield themselves from the Drake somehow. Tolvar had known his grandfather, Reymius, before he went to Earth. Aaron hadn't seen or heard from Tolvar since before they first traveled to Shandara. It was Tolvar who'd revealed his presence to the Hythariam, and they had come just in time to save his life.

"Tolvar will be disappointed if you're not with me," Aaron said.

Sarah shook her head. "I'm sorry, my love. I must return to Khamearra. Rordan has turned up there."

Aaron frowned. "Can't Isaac handle this?"

"They don't know Rordan like I do," Sarah said.

He couldn't tell much from Sarah based upon the holo display alone, but something was tugging at him. "Are you sure you're okay? I can meet you in Khamearra. We can do this together."

"No. I will deal with Rordan. You need to focus on the Zekara and the Eldarin. Do you have the staff with you?"

"It's here," Aaron said.

"You must carry it. Do not fear the Eldarin."

"I fear that I might not be able to help them," Aaron said, but he didn't give voice to his other fear that had been gnawing away at him.

The High King's words echoed in his mind. *You've felt it, haven't you? The thirst. That feeling of holding people's lives in your hands. They are so easy to manipulate and control.* Aaron had used his abilities to open his companions up to the energy, but there was more he could do. The High King had used everyone around him. He had corrupted what it meant to be Ferasdiam marked: those chosen by the Goddess. The ones marked by fate. Aaron clamped down on his racing thoughts. He wouldn't be like the High King. *Even if it's the difference between victory and defeat for all of Safanar?* Aaron brushed aside the dark thoughts and drew in the energy around him. He reached through his connection to Sarah, seeing the golden brilliance of her lifebeat, but there was something different. A brighter flare that hadn't been present before.

Sarah gasped. "Stay safe, my love. I shall contact you tomorrow," she said quickly, and the holo display went dark.

The moment passed, and Aaron shrugged his shoulders. Another time he would ask her about what he saw.

CHAPTER 10
ATTACK

North of the kingdom of Rexel was an ancient watchtower called Elden Hold. It had been hundreds of years since the people who inhabited the lands beyond Rexel's immediate borders had pledged their loyalty. The troops of the watchtower mostly dealt with bandits who preyed upon trade caravans that moved through the area. Aaron and the others had set up camp within view of the ancient tower. An airship formerly from the Rexellian Air Corp, and now of the Free Nations Army, had been dispatched to scout the area. Scouting efforts with the airship had ceased the moment they learned that the Zekara's path led them straight to the watchtower on their way to Rexel.

"How is it that now we can see them coming but not before?" Verona asked.

"It was the airship captain," Aaron said. "Then it was later confirmed by the flyer-class SPT."

"Wait, I know this one," Verona said, pressing his lips in thought. "Stealth Personnel Transport. For all the Hythariam's technological wonders, they aren't very imaginative with their names."

"We're a practical race," Tanneth said. "I supposed that if *you* were to name the vessel, it would be something flashy like Shadow Stalker."

Verona laughed, as did the others. "Don't be silly. Shadow Stalker is a terrible name. Were I of a mind to put a name to the flyer-class SPT, it would be with more style than the simple names you give to such wondrous things."

"This should be good," Aaron said, and the others waited for Verona.

"Nighthawk," Verona said after a moment, and nodded to himself. "That's what I would call it."

"Truly, your ability to name our machines is awe inspiring," Tanneth said dryly.

The others around them laughed, and Verona joined in.

"Fine, we'll stick with your non-imaginative name, but I will come up with something better," Verona promised. "Aaron, on Earth what do they call ships like what the Hythariam have?"

"Oh, um," Aaron stammered. "I wasn't in the military."

"Surely they named their airships and the like," Verona said.

"Of course. I think they were named with the job they were designed for. Off the top of my head one was called a Strike Eagle."

"Strike Eagle! Now that's a name. Much more imaginative than what the Hythariam call their ships," Verona said.

Tanneth shrugged his shoulders and laughed. Aaron caught Bayen watching them and waved him over. Much to his surprise, the young man came to join them. At the same moment, Verona's comms device chimed, and he moved off to the side. Reinforcements had been arriving, steadily swelling their ranks. Upon learning that General Halcylon had the Zekara on the move, Aaron proposed to take a fighting force north to strike at them. Gavril, the most seasoned soldier among the Hythariam, seconded the idea. Hopefully, this would buy time for the people of Rexel to build up fortifications. He would also look for an opportunity to take Halcylon out. That was the riskiest and the least-known part of his plan with their small army.

"Who is he talking to?" Marek asked. The man was in his mid-forties and was of the Safanarion Order. Not all of the Order had been at Shandara when the kingdom fell. Some had been able to escape, though while still being hunted by the Elitesmen. Marek and more of the Safanarion Order had returned during the battle with the High King's army.

"He's talking to Roselyn," Aaron said, glancing at Verona, who wore a puzzled expression.

Verona closed his comms link and rejoined them. "Our job gets a bit more interesting, it seems. Roselyn and the other Hythariam scientists need for us to collect samples of the Forsaken, should we encounter them. They can't make a cure for the virus without them."

The soldiers who had seen and fought the Forsaken glanced at the others. All had the grim set lines to their face that no amount of additional armor could protect against. Word had quickly spread about what had befallen those who became infected with the Ryakul virus.

"A sample? We're heading into battle, not some stroll through the forest," one soldier said.

Aaron held up his hands, drawing their attention to him. "This is important. Without a cure, everyone else could become infected. It doesn't matter who you are. A virus can strike indiscriminately."

"Except the Hythariam," another soldier said.

Aaron glanced at the FNA soldiers around him. They each came from different parts of Safanar. Some from Khamearra, others from Rexel. Former members of the Elitesmen Order were peppered through their ranks, along with the Hythariam. Guilt can weigh heavier than a mountain, and Aaron saw it reflected in the gaze of every Hythariam he saw.

"You're correct," Aaron said. "The Hythariam as of right now are not affected by this plague, but look around you. This divide that would force a wedge between us is exactly what the Zekara want. General Halcylon wants us to fight among ourselves. It will make his job of extermination easier. Do not be fooled that what the Zekara throw at us will have no effect on the Hythariam. What affects one of us affects all of us. The Hythariam among you stand at your side as comrades at arms. We created the Free Nations Army to stand against the threat to this world, side by side. That doesn't mean we stand without fear. It means we stand together to meet this threat and defeat it together. It's our commitment to remain united even in the face of our death. Especially in the face of our death. That's what Halcylon and his Zekara cannot take from us. That's what is going to see us through the eve of these dark times. There is no them or us. Not in the FNA. We are Safanarions, and we will stand together."

There was no great cheer that erupted from the soldiers' lips, and Aaron didn't expect any. What he saw was the blaze of grim determination reflected in all those around him, and it filled his heart. His gaze swept the crowd and lingered for a moment upon Bayen, whose scowl had vanished from his face, replaced by hard determination.

"Well said, my friend," Verona said.

"They needed it," Aaron said. "Now, how are we supposed to collect samples? What exactly does Roselyn need?"

Verona swallowed grimly. "This is where it gets messy. These are her terms. Ideally, living tissue, but parts from any victim will help."

Aaron frowned. "Living tissue. She wants us to capture someone who has been infected," Aaron said, bringing his fingers up to rub the bridge of his nose in thought. "I'm open to ideas."

"I doubt we can knock one out, and judging by the way they moved, a pit wouldn't work either, as they would just scale the walls," Verona said.

"Your Grace, I have a suggestion," Marek said. "The Elitesmen were quite skilled with hunting people down and capturing them. Perhaps they have a few tricks up their sleeves that could help us."

Aaron nodded. "Put to good use for a change. Would you mind checking into it and letting us know?"

Marek saluted with a fist across his heart and left them.

"Do you have any ideas, Tanneth?" Aaron asked.

"Capturing is not among my skills," Tanneth said, frowning. "I think we'll need to try a few different things."

"Agreed; if we see an opportunity, then we should take it," Aaron said.

Tanneth left them to go make some preparations.

"Things were much simpler when we were just facing the High King," Verona mused.

"I don't think they were simpler, but..." Aaron caught Verona's telling gaze. "No, I won't do it."

"My friend, whether you like it or not, it *is* an option."

Aaron clenched his teeth. "I won't become *him*, Verona."

"No one is saying you have to be the High King. The man was evil, malicious, and cruel. None of those describe who you are," Verona

said.

"I won't seize control of anyone in a battle or any other time."

"Even if the difference is between victory and defeat?"

"What would we have won then? You would trade one tyrant for another."

"My friend, I believe in you. I trust you. You are the brother that I never had. There is no way that you could ever walk the same path as the High King."

"He was Ferasdiam marked."

"So what? Ferasdiam marked may be *what* you are, but that doesn't define *who* you are," Verona said.

Aaron knew in his heart that Verona spoke the truth, yet still the fear remained. Desperation has a way of dooming the souls of all.

"You could try using your power to capture one of the Forsaken," Verona suggested mildly.

Aaron frowned. "I don't think so. If they're anything like the Ryakuls, then I'm not sure that will work. I have the same reaction to them as the Dragons, remember."

Verona shrugged his shoulders. "How could I forget the day we met? Still, we've both come a long way since then."

"You know you could try what you're suggesting as well," Aaron said.

"Me?" Verona gasped. "I'm afraid my connection to the energy isn't quite as strong as yours, my friend."

"How many times have I told you it's not about strength? It's about focus. I may be Ferasdiam marked, but what I really am is the possibility of what anyone can achieve," Aaron said.

They noticed Bayen standing near them, clearly listening to what they were saying, but it was the look in his eyes that piqued Aaron's curiosity. The young man had been so guarded with them, it was rare to see him look almost untroubled.

Aaron nodded to Bayen. "Do you think the new armor will help against the Forsaken?"

Bayen thought about it for a moment, glancing at the soldiers around them. Most were wearing the thin, dark armor of Hythariam design. Some elected to stick with their chainmail and gauntlets, not trusting something so flimsy. "Protection can only help these men. As you've seen, it doesn't take much for the Ryakul virus to turn people into the Forsaken."

"Indeed that is the case," Verona said.

"We can try to fight them at a distance, but eventually we'll find ourselves in close-quarters combat. I hate to think of the Forsaken running loose in a city," Aaron said.

Bayen clenched the haft of his bladed staff, and the tightening of his eyes was the only indication of the fear Aaron sensed in him.

What does he know? Why won't he tell us?

Bayen had the look of a seasoned soldier, which wasn't much of a surprise given the world of Safanar. It was his familiarity with Hythariam technology that made him stand apart. Technology was still new to most Safanarions, but with Bayen it was as if he had seen it before. Familiar with it as if it had always been around him. Aaron would need to keep an eye on him. He didn't know if he trusted him or not. What if Bayen was some type of spy put in their midst by Halcylon? He had fought well before. One might say he was ruthless, but what made him so?

Aaron turned his attention northward and signaled to the others. It was time to move out. They carried little with them. They needed to move swiftly and with minimal noise. The army of the Zekara was coming. Even if the Zekara had managed to somehow evade detection so far, his instincts told him that Halcylon had prepared enough. Now the war would begin in earnest. Verona handed him the rune-carved staff, and Aaron reluctantly took it.

They left the Watchtower of Elden Hold, moving swiftly on foot. A portion of them used the Hythariam gliders strapped to their feet but stayed low to the ground. Others were former Elitesmen who had no issue with setting a pace that no ordinary fighting force could match. This was an elite fighting force armed with plasma rifles and crystal-tipped arrows. A fair number carried Shandarian shields found in the weapons caches. For a moment, Aaron wished Braden was with them, but the Warden of the De'anjard had his task with defending Shandara.

The former Elitesmen still carried their blades, and many were highly trained in using attack orbs. It was a skill that Aaron hadn't learned yet. He had spent enough time dodging those types of attacks that he didn't want to learn it.

The rune-carved staff felt light in his hands, but he sensed the energy gathered within it. Along the fringes of his senses, he almost heard the rumbling of the Eldarin. Death was the only release for a Dragon infected with the Ryakul virus, but did the same apply to the Dragon lords?

Tanneth scouted ahead of them with two Hythariam trailing behind him. Aaron wanted to join him, but as Gavril and Verona would constantly tell him, he needed to learn to let others share in the task of protecting their world. It was probably for the best because Tanneth was more adept at sneaking around than Aaron was.

His fist clenched around the haft of the rune-carved staff. Would the Zekara sink into disarray if he took out Halcylon? If he could cut the head off the proverbial snake, as it were? Would Halcylon's thirst for vengeance die with him, or would some other take up the reins? Aaron pulled in the energy around him and ran ahead of the others. Verona and Bayen were nearest him, with the rest of the FNA following closely behind.

The landscape passed them in a blur, giving way to forest. Their plan had them circling around, using the forest as cover so they could sneak up on where they suspected the Zekara to be. Aaron glanced behind him as their elite force moved through the forest. The speed and efficiency with which they moved was impressive. Now that they *were* on the move, Aaron wondered what they would encounter from the Zekara. Gavril had briefed them on the known capabilities of the Hythariam military before the barrier had separated Safanar from Hytharia. They didn't know what General Halcylon was able to bring with him though the portal. Even though Aaron had been held captive at the time, he'd been in no position to actually see what they brought with them.

The miles flew by, and the sun shone overhead. Aaron's comms device vibrated upon his wrist, and he answered.

"We've taken up position on the far side of the valley. We set detonators that should evade detection by anything the Zekara would use," Tanneth said.

"Good," Aaron said. "Hold position. Maintain comms blackout. After the first detonation, we'll move in and begin the attack."

Aaron called for a halt. They were several miles east of the valley and more than thirty miles north of the Watchtower of Elden Hold. They settled down and waited. Verona and Marek joined him.

"I need someone to keep an eye on Bayen," Aaron said quietly.

Marek frowned. "Do you suspect foul play?"

Aaron shared a glance with Verona. "I don't know. That's the problem."

"We could remove him?" Marek asked.

"No," Aaron said. "I don't believe Bayen means us harm. I'm just not sure about his motives. I want two eyes on him at all times. Especially during the attack."

Marek saluted with a fist across his heart and left them.

Aaron caught Verona watching him from the corner of his eye. "You don't approve?"

"About keeping an eye on Bayen? No, I think that's a good idea. However, I don't think he will stray far from your side, my friend," Verona said, and strung his bow.

They were quiet after that, waiting in silence. Most of the soldiers kept their attention to the west, the direction they had to go. The former Elitesmen were easy to spot among them as they radiated a calmness. To them, battle was a way of life. A way to establish dominance. The few weeks with the Free Nations Army couldn't rid them of that. The others with them were made up of the best soldiers from the various nations. All were battle hardened, with some having faced each other upon the field in the not too distant past. Aaron hoped he wasn't leading them to their deaths. No amount of preparation could rid Aaron of the angst he felt in his gut. What if he was wrong? To allow the Zekara to march upon Rexel unopposed was most certainly not the right thing to do. They all agreed, but there was still a gnawing doubt that there was something he was missing.

"Verona," Aaron said.

"I'm with you, my friend," Verona answered.

The barest hint of a smile tugged at the corners of Aaron's mouth. "Til the end?"

"Yes, but Goddess willing, it will be many years from now. When we're old, fat, and have no hair left," Verona said.

Aaron extended his senses away from him. Subtle vibrations from the ground sent tiny alarm bells that the Zekara were approaching. Almost at the same instant, Bayen caught his gaze and nodded to the west. Aaron held up his hand and signaled to the others. Weapons were checked and held ready. The rune-carved staff was held loosely in one of his hands and a small curved throwing ax in the other. Aaron glanced above them. There was a small whirl of air as something passed his field of vision, momentarily distorting it.

Drone!

Aaron motioned for the nearest soldier armed with a plasma rifle and pointed overhead. The soldier nodded and peered through the scope, scanning above them. A Hythariam near him checked his comms device and shook his head. It wasn't one of theirs. They hadn't deployed their own drones due to the risk of alerting the Zekara of their presence.

The Zekara, however, *were* using drones to scout the area. Aaron couldn't be sure if they had been detected or not. Several FNA soldiers had their rifles trained upon the drone targets above them, waiting for the order to shoot them down. Aaron waited, his throat thickening as the moments passed by.

An explosion from the valley caused them all to spring into action at once. The FNA soldiers fired their rifles, taking out the drones above them. Aaron leaped up, going from tree branch to tree branch. The ones that could follow him up into the dizzying heights of the trees did, while the others raced along the ground. As they closed in, they passed through a translucent shroud. On the other side, shifting through the shadows, were dark shapes. The soldiers fired their weapons. An ear-piercing alarm was raised, and the dark shapes lifted themselves from the forest floor.

The thinning forest in front of them became a sea of glowing yellow eyes. Blackened, deformed heads cocked to the side like a hunter catching the scent of its prey. Then the Forsaken charged.

How could the Zekara have hidden so many of them?

A volley of crystal-tipped arrows was unleashed into the charging Forsaken. The explosions stalled the charge for mere moments before the Forsaken began to attack again in earnest. FNA soldiers fired their rifles, and former Elitesmen sent attack orbs, but the Forsaken kept coming even as they were being mowed down. The Hythariam among them charged forward, attempting to shield their human counterparts. The Forsaken all but ignored the Hythariam, with a singular focus on the humans.

Emerging from the smoke came towering, black-armored Zekara soldiers. A maelstrom of bolts belched from their weapons, and it was all the FNA soldiers could do to scramble for cover. Several pockets of FNA soldiers were left exposed, and heavy fire from the Zekara kept them pinned down. Aaron heard the guttural roars of the Forsaken, followed by the rapid clicking of snapping teeth closing in on them. Aaron leaped down. The runes along his staff flared to life as it whirled through the air. Aaron released a jolt of energy with each blow to the Forsaken. His appearance upon the battlefield drew the attention of all the nearby Forsaken. Glowing yellow eyes shifted toward him. He was surrounded by hundreds of Ryakul-human hybrids devoid of anything they were before, except for a faint whisper of what they'd once been.

FNA soldiers charged toward him, and the Forsaken renewed their frenzied attacks, bringing down soldiers as they tried to reach him.

The soldiers that went down began writhing. Their eyes bulged in fear as they looked to Aaron to save them.

Bayen landed near him. "Shield!" he shouted, slamming his bladed staff to the ground. A barrier shimmered into existence, rapidly extending to either side.

Aaron drew in the energy and pushed outward from the rune-carved staff, forming a second barrier that quickly overtook the one Bayen had formed. The Forsaken hurled themselves at the shimmering barrier, but it held them at bay. In a frenzy, they immediately fanned out to the side, trying to find the barrier's end. Bright flashes of light slammed into the barrier, but Aaron felt none of it. He tethered the barrier deep beneath the ground in the same manner as the barrier that had stood at Shandara, holding the Zekara at bay for over eighty years.

"Fall back!" he shouted.

The soldiers began retreating, but for the ones writhing on the ground. Bayen moved away with the others but kept watching him, waiting to see what he would do with the doomed FNA soldiers caught on their side of the barrier. Clenching his teeth, Aaron grabbed a plasma rifle from a nearby soldier, took aim at the dying men, and fired. Others joined in and kept firing their weapons until their fallen were nothing more than charred husks.

Finding the end of the barrier, the Forsaken threw themselves around the edge. Verona fired crystal-tipped arrows at them. The towering Zekara charged toward the barrier and in the last second leaped into the air, clearing its height. The powered armor housing the Zekara barely showed any signs of weakening as they dropped down to the ground. Aaron tossed the rifle back to the soldier and ordered him to retreat. He turned back to face the charging Zekara, creating a smaller barrier in front to deflect the bolts fired at him. He only needed to buy the FNA some time to retreat, and then he could catch up with them.

As the Zekara passed by a rocky outcropping, one of them went down as if his legs had been cut out from under him. A figure half their size pounced on the fallen soldier. Gleaming claws tore through the armor with blinding speed. The Zekaran soldier cried out in pain before being cut off. The translucent figure atop the dead soldier charged forward, closing the distance on the two others.

The surrounding forest blended in around the creature, and a dim memory tugged at the edges of Aaron's thoughts, taking him back to being held captive on Hytharia. A similar creature had helped him escape the dying world.

Thraw!

Aaron grabbed the small curved ax that hung on his belt. Summoning the energy, he sent the ax streaking across the way. The ax slammed into the charging Zekara with such force that he was blown back several feet.

Thraw closed in on the remaining Zekaran soldier and dispatched him as quickly as he had the first.

Thraw skidded to a halt in front of Aaron.

"You must flee, human. It's not safe for your kind here."

The Forsaken were circling around the barrier.

"Fight with us," Aaron said.

Thraw's green eyes flashed, and the skin along his body rippled.

"Come with us, Thraw. You saved my life. Allow me to repay the debt I owe you."

Thraw narrowed his gaze at him. "Hythariam fight at your side."

"Yes. They fight the Zekara just as you do."

Verona called after him from the trees.

"I will come with you, human," Thraw said.

Aaron severed the tethers that kept the barrier in place and darted away from the advancing Forsaken. Thraw matched his speed, running on all fours. Aaron took in more energy and went faster. Sounds of pursuit eventually faded into the distance. He needed answers. How had the Zekara known they were coming? Where had they got so many Forsaken from? They must have been rounding up people from the smaller northern towns, but how had they missed it? They needed to evacuate the towns and farms between here and Rexel. Otherwise, those people would be doomed.

Then Aaron recalled that the Forsaken had been drawn to him upon the battlefield. It was almost as if they had known to look for him. What was it about him that drew the Forsaken to him like moths to a flame? Could General Halcylon have that kind of control where he could have the Forsaken focus on a specific person?

Aaron slowed, joining Verona and the few remaining FNA soldiers waiting to go through the portal opened with the keystone accelerator. None noticed Thraw, whose skin easily adapted to his surroundings. He could sense Thraw through his connection to the energy. Bayen glanced at him before going through the portal. Perhaps Aaron wasn't the only one to know of Thraw's presence. Aaron nodded to Verona and went through the portal, with Thraw going through at the last moment.

Chapter 11
THREAT

The mobile command center was essentially a hovering fortress. Halcylon remembered when they had hundreds of these vehicles. Equipped with multilayer attack and defense capabilities. His engineers had migrated the cyber warfare suite to the vehicle's main systems. He could have used several more command centers, but most had been destroyed on Hytharia.

There was nothing left of the Hythariam home planet. After they dealt with the human menace, they would set their efforts at rebuilding Safanar to Hytharia's former glory. Those were the reasons he gave to the Zekara he had left behind, much to their disappointment. They would have followed him even with their families in tow, but in truth he didn't need them. The few hundred nonessential Hythariam would only slow them down.

"An effective test, sir," Chinta said.

"Indeed it was," Halcylon answered. "Has there been any sign of the Safanarions since their attack?"

"None. They've retreated into the woods. The Forsaken have performed better than I expected," Chinta said.

Chinta, like his other commanders, had expressed serious doubts about infecting the humans with the Ryakul virus, even with Ronin's modification of the original strain. Ronin was a miracle worker. The commanders had cited risks, such as a lack of control, as their numbers grew. They had several hundred from the crop of humans they had taken from the smaller towns, and that number would continue to grow.

"They performed their task well. They fulfilled their purpose better than expected. It was embedded into the strain to spread itself. Once the humans are infected, they are easily controlled. This is a powerful weapon we have, and all we have to do is point it in the right direction," Halcylon said.

Ronin joined them, leaving his lab for the first time in days. His gray science officer's uniform was impeccable as ever. His calculating golden-eyed gaze swept each of them in turn.

"I've reviewed the feeds from our drones. The infected humans reacted to one particular human with more focus than all the others. I think you can guess who that is," Ronin said.

"*Him?*" Halcylon asked, and Ronin nodded.

Halcylon still didn't know how Aaron Jace had escaped Hytharia before the planet was destroyed. He'd sentenced the human to death by leaving him on their dying planet, thinking it a fitting end, but now he regretted not killing the human when he had the chance.

"Is this some type of glitch, or is this a problem?" Halcylon asked.

"The behavior is indicative of when two natural enemies meet. We've seen the pattern before with the Dragons. Once they become a Ryakul, the virus is ever working to spread itself. Dragons, hating what is happening to their species, work to eradicate the Ryakuls. The oddity here is that the virus reacts with even more intensity with this particular human," Ronin said.

Chinta rapped his armored fist upon the table. "What difference does this make? He's a human and therefore susceptible to the virus."

"The difference is— " Ronin began, barely hiding his irritation with the commander, and brought up the holo display showing the events the drone captured before it was destroyed. "The difference is that this isn't just a few Forsaken reacting to a nearby human. This affected all the Forsaken in the immediate area. They focused in on him like a beacon. We need to understand why that is."

Halcylon watched the video feed and nodded. "I see your point, Ronin. It's hard to tell if the Forsaken were out of control during this time."

"It is hard to tell. As soon as the humans retreated and there was some distance between the Forsaken and Aaron, their behavior returned to normal," Ronin said.

"I have no doubts we will see Aaron and this Free Nations Army of his before long. We can't halt our efforts because of some peculiarities with the Ryakul virus. Would I like to understand this better? Of course, but we have a tight time line. If the Forsaken want to concentrate on this one human, then that's fine with me. It will mean more of their side will get caught in the crosshairs as they try to protect Aaron. This could actually serve our cause well. Remember, the Forsaken just need to do some of the heavy lifting so we can conserve our troops for the real fight," Halcylon said.

Chinta agreed almost immediately, but Ronin was still concerned about this new development, which gave Halcylon some pause.

"I don't think they will try another surprise attack again and will more than likely consolidate their defense for the city of Rexel. We should be ready for another attack regardless," Halcylon said.

"We've found the bodies of three of our soldiers that I think you need to see," Ronin said.

Halcylon nodded, and they left their mobile command center. Their march was halted for now, but they would resume within the hour. Ronin led them toward the edge of the forest.

"I had the bodies cordoned off after I reviewed the feeds from the drones," Ronin said.

A pair of soldiers remained focused on the forest away from their temporary camp. No doubt the feeds in their helmets had already alerted them to their approach. Upon the ground were three shock troops with their powered armor gashed open.

Halcylon frowned. "Claw marks?" he asked.

Chinta squatted down, running his fingers along the gashes on the back of one of the soldiers' legs. "This is something new. Could this be a beast the Free Nations Army brought with them?"

Halcylon studied the wounds, his mind rebuilding the demise of his soldiers with forensic detail. "No, I've seen this before. This is the work of a hunter from Hytharia."

"Project Thorn?" Ronin asked.

"I'm not familiar with Project Thorn," Chinta said, looking up from the dead soldiers.

"Genetic modification to our soldiers," Halcylon said. "Cross-species modification to be exact. At least that was the start of it. Once the project yielded results, we stepped up the enhancements. One of things the project achieved was merging our species with that of a maul-cat."

Chinta's eyebrows raised in alarm. "I thought the maul-cats were too vicious to be controlled."

"Not when you add certain genes from the Hythariam, particularly those for intelligence," Halcylon said.

"The only reason it worked is because we have a common ancestor," Ronin said.

"We used them for covert operations. The maul-cat's ability for blending in with its environment is unparalleled. I haven't seen claw marks like this in a very long time," Halcylon said.

"No ordinary claws, even from a maul-cat, could cut through our armor, especially the armor of the shock troops," Chinta said.

Ronin gave a single nod. "Their skeletal structure was reinforced to make up for their inferior size."

"Inferior size?" Chinta asked.

"They're only four or five feet in length, but don't let their size fool you. Their strength rivals that of any Hythariam, even in powered armor or with Nanite enhancement. Maul-cats were picked because of their durability, but the project was abandoned," Ronin answered.

"All true," Halcylon said. "However, we kept a few in cryostasis."

"Why was the project abandoned? By the sound of it, they made lethal killing machines," Chinta said.

"Intelligence," Ronin said. "The maul-cat's intelligence grew by leaps and bounds when crossed with our species."

Chinta smirked. "I bet they wondered why they had to take orders."

"It's worse than that. We're their natural enemies, and no amount of genetic modification could change that," Ronin said.

"We tried," Halcylon said. "But it made them much less effective in combat. What we were able to do is focus them on particular targets. Once the targets were taken out, we lured them to a place so they could be recaptured. The real question is how a maul-cat is here on Safanar in the first place."

"You said before that a few were kept in cryostasis. Were they brought here along with everything else we were able to scavenge?" Chinta asked.

Halcylon shook his head. "No. They were deemed nonessential."

"Could this be the work of the traitors? Perhaps something they had kept here on Safanar to be used if the barrier between worlds went down?" Ronin asked.

Halcylon glanced at the bodies again. "They wouldn't have the stomach to create one. It was a black ops project. None would have had access, which can only mean one thing."

"What's that?" Chinta asked.

"That we have some traitors within our midst. How else would a maul-cat suddenly appear?" Halcylon said.

Chinta frowned. "Are you sure? It's possible, but highly unlikely. What good would one maul-cat be? How much damage could it actually do?"

Halcylon signaled to the other soldiers to fall in and led the others back to camp, his mind racing with the implications of the appearance of the maul-cat. *Who would be the target? Me?*

"I want guard details put on all commanders around the clock. They don't get a moment alone. I want all our equipment checked and rechecked with a sporadic schedule," Halcylon said to the soldiers, who nodded and spoke into their comms devices. "These creatures were designed to strike from the shadows. Any of us could be the target. They were designed to be able to overcome hardened military assets. They're equipped to evade our means to detect them."

Chinta's deadpan expression became grim as his military-trained mind worked the details and came to grips with what he was being told.

"There are protocols to be followed so that we can detect them,"

Ronin said. "Sir, with your permission I would like clearance to review the specifics of Project Thorn. Perhaps there is something there that I can use to help protect our leadership."

"Granted," Halcylon said, and he watched Ronin's back as he headed off to do his work. He started a mental list of who would have had access to release a maul-cat. It wouldn't be that simple. The traitor would have needed to know how to bring the creature out of cryostasis and imprint a target. The list grew shorter, and his head science officer was at the top.

There *were* other means he could employ through the use of the Nanites to ensure compliance among his more questionable subordinates, which he had avoided so far. Using the Nanites for widespread control came at a price, with initiative being primary among them. It was a subtle thing to retrain someone's mind, and there was always the risk of a breakdown. He knew Ronin had been among the traitors living on Safanar who had come back to Hytharia. The scientist had changed sides, and it was with his talents that they had been able to modify the Ryakul virus to affect humans.

"Sir, I have a question if you don't mind?" Chinta asked.

"By all means," Halcylon invited.

"This place we're heading. Rexel. It's not a high-priority target. I'm not certain why we're going to attack it. I'm not questioning the order. You say wipe that city from the face of the planet, then I will do as you command. But still, some of us are wondering why we didn't head straight for Shandara."

"We're going to the place the humans call Rexel to teach them something," Halcylon said.

"What's that, sir?"

"We're going to teach them about defeat. We're going to teach them about fear and hopelessness. Right now, our enemy thinks they have a chance to defeat us. Our passive scans of Shandara show that the city has heavy defenses in place. Defenses I think we can overcome, but I want them put off balance. I want their world crumbling down around them. They don't have the capacity to defend the other cities, and they know it. The way we defeat Rexel and unleash the Forsaken upon the land will scatter them like bugs. In the days ahead, they will learn to fear their betters. I may even entertain offers of surrender after a time—but not until after many of them are dead and gone. We will have our vengeance for the fate these humans cursed us to. They thought to lock us away on our dying planet. We will soak the ground in human blood before this is over, and they will answer for all the Hythariam not with us today," Halcylon said.

Chinta saluted him with fire in his eyes. Halcylon knew the word would be spread. He was the heart of the Zekara, and all of Safanar would feel the fires of his rage before he was done.

Chapter 12
FAMILY MATTERS

Sarah had thought she could simply return to Khamearra and hunt for her brother Rordan, but she was mistaken. No longer could she simply go about her own business. As High Queen, she had responsibilities and duties to attend to.

The day-to-day business of running the city had been placed upon the shoulders of her administrators—at least the ones she'd kept in service after she ascended the throne. And in no uncertain terms had she put it to those administrators that the practices afforded under her father's rule would not be tolerated under her own. That wasn't to say that corruption all but disappeared because it hadn't. Despite the monster her father had been, he had instilled a follow my command or else mentality among the city's administrators. Once they were put to work, the administrators who ran the city executed their tasks with rigid efficiency. They had no choice under her father's rule, or their lives and the lives of their family were forfeit. Fear inspired results in the short term at least, but it wasn't the loyalty that Sarah wanted to inspire as Khamearra's High Queen.

But Sarah's chief responsibility was leadership, and she'd engaged with the highest leaders first, as soon as she'd returned. Sarah was no stranger to the city and had plenty of ideas on how to improve how it was run, but to get the best from her people she needed for them to trust her enough to suggest improvements as well.

That was one of the cornerstones of Shandara's greatness: the value of contribution and coordinated effort. One of the best appointments to a post had been Nolan, the district captain who'd aided the Resistance at great risk to himself and his family. She had promoted him to captain commander in charge of all Khamearra's districts. She would be meeting with him soon, but at the district headquarters of the captain commander and not at her office in the palace. If word spread that the High Queen was in court this day, then she would never get anything done.

And Isaac's report of Rordan's activity had her worried. There had been a time when she had thought that Rordan might be swayed from their father's influence, but he had descended onto a dark path. Rordan had been the most levelheaded of her brothers. He had none of Primus's insecurities or Tye's need to garner their father's attention. Rordan had proved to be the cleverest of her brothers, but her presence had always threatened them.

Now Tye and Primus were both dead. Tye, with Mactar's prodding, had thrown himself at Aaron and had died in the process. Primus had been killed when he tried to kill her at Shandara. Rordan was hers alone to pursue. She would not burden Aaron with this. He had enough to deal with, and truth be told, Rordan was her mess to clean up.

Now that she was here, she yearned to be at Aaron's side. But she couldn't let Rordan move around her kingdom, killing indiscriminately. Like it or not, she was best suited for tracking

Rordan down and stopping him once and for all.

A soft knock came at the door to her office.

Isaac stuck his head in. "Your Grace, General Khoiron is here as requested."

"Send him in, and please come in as well, Isaac."

After a few moments, Isaac returned with the craggy-faced general. His weathered hands looked as if they could squeeze blood from a stone.

General Khoiron raised his fist to his heart and bowed his head respectfully. "Your Grace, when I offered my services I had thought you would have taken me up sooner rather than later."

"We've had a bit of house cleaning to attend to, my Lord," Sarah answered mildly.

"I hope the information I've supplied from my agents proved useful," Khoiron said.

Sarah studied the old general for a moment, considering. "Indeed it has. Make no mistake, General, I know what you've done in my father's service. What I would like to know from you is why you offered your services to me."

The old general eyed her with steel-gray eyes that matched his hair. "Yours is the stronger claim to the throne, your Grace. I've seen what your brother can do, and he never would have made a good king. The people want you, and a majority of our armies are loyal to you. I've spoken at length with the Free Nations Army general who calls himself Gavril. A Hythariam. He knows his business, your Grace. He makes a compelling argument of the threats that face us all."

"Where do you stand then?" Sarah asked.

"Wherever you command me, your Grace," Khoiron said. After a few moments, he continued. "Your brother brought up the warning given to him by the Heir of Shandara. He urged your father to seriously consider it, but Amorak would hear none of it. At the time, I agreed with him. Better to face an enemy you can see than concern yourselves with something that may never come to pass."

"You know that I stood with the Resistance and fought with the Free Nations Army against the armies of Khamearra," Sarah said.

"I won't stand here and say I lived a lifetime of regret serving under your father because I didn't. I served my king proudly. I brought glory to this kingdom. The king didn't need to exert his influence to get me to do what he required. I stood apart from his other generals because I delivered results, and I wasn't foolish enough to incur his wrath. I would serve you, my queen. You have problems to face, and quite honestly, you need me. You need my agents to help you hold this kingdom together—especially with the Zekara," Khoiron said.

Sarah knew the old general wasn't being boastful. She did need him. Men like Khoiron lived for the challenges she faced. He was a brilliant tactician. "You accept that the Zekara are a threat to us all then?" Sarah asked.

"Yes, your Grace. As I've said before, speaking with the Hythariam general was enlightening, and we can now trace some of the strange reports from my agents to Zekaran activity. At least that is my hunch," Khoiron said.

"What strange reports?"

"Disappearances, your Grace. Not just a few people, but entire towns full of people gone. My agents reported evidence of them being rounded up by tall black-armored warriors. The description of the warriors matched the attacks on this city. I knew immediately that this was not the work of the Free Nations Army, but the descriptions were clearly of the Hythariam. After speaking with Gavril, it didn't take much to convince me of the threat we are now facing."

"This is the first I've heard of people gone missing."

"When I got the report, I wanted to see the area for myself. I came to Isaac here and asked if one of the former Elitesmen could take me up there with the use of the travel crystal," Khoiron said.

"I took him myself, your Grace," Isaac said. "It was just as he said. The people were rounded up and taken from their homes."

Sarah knew from Aaron that the leader of the Zekara, General Halcylon, blamed humans for his race's suffering.

Khoiron cleared his throat. "Any idea why they would be capturing our people?"

"The leader of the Zekara is called General Halcylon. He is taking the people to build up an army," Sarah answered.

"A peasant doesn't a soldier make," Khoiron quoted.

"That is correct, but they don't need to train them. The Zekara have the power to change people into creatures like the Ryakuls," Sarah said, and proceeded to explain the origins of the Ryakuls and how they were once Dragons. Halcylon, she told them, had managed to modify the virus so it would affect humans.

"This could throw everything into chaos," Khoiron said.

"The Free Nations Army believes that the Zekara will be focused on taking Shandara," Sarah said.

"Why?"

"Because Shandara represents their biggest threat. The Hythariam worked with the Shandarians for years getting the city ready in the event that the Zekara invaded."

"Please forgive me, your Grace. The Zekara, are they not Hythariam?" Khoiron asked.

"They are indeed the same race, but the Zekara were mostly made up of Hytharia's most ruthless military faction. They hold humans responsible for their suffering for the past eighty years. It was Aaron's great-grandfather, Daverim Alenzar'seth, who perceived that some of the Hythariam were a threat not only to Shandara but to all of Safanar. He created the barrier that kept the Zekara from invading. The barrier was linked to a living member of the Alenzar'seth line."

General Khoiron's eyes widened. "We never knew. The High King ordered us to invade Shandara, and the reason for that campaign's success was because we had agents on the inside of the city. A man called Tarimus was instrumental in our armies gaining access to the city. We took them by surprise, but we had no idea what was at stake even after Shandara was all but destroyed. Our armies journeyed back across the lands with kingdoms swearing fealty to your father."

"The Zekara are the real threat now. They will not offer us any quarter," Sarah said, trying to avoid the shame she felt at the historical events that occurred before she was born. She remembered yearly celebrations of her father's victory over Shandara, which had been left a wasteland. That is until Aaron returned. The barrier that had protected their world from the Zekara had been slowly siphoning away at Shandara and the surrounding lands, making them unlivable. In addition, the Ryakuls, under control of the Drake, had made the ruins of Shandara their home.

"The Zekara won't ignore us forever," Khoiron said. "If I had a weapon such as this Ryakul virus to use against my enemies, I wouldn't just limit its application to where I was at the time. If they can control them? Then it's a safe bet to assume that more of these Forsaken could start to show up. Do we know how the sickness spreads?" Khoiron brought his hands together as he paced.

"The Zekara have a means to spread it from a canister when they are killed. It is the opinion of the Hythariam that this is a limited application. Based on what we've seen, if you're bitten or wounded from a Forsaken's claw, then you will be turned into one of them. Once someone is infected, their body begins to change, but they are able to infect others within minutes before the transformation completes," Sarah said.

"How long does the transformation take?" Isaac asked. The former Elitesman had been quiet until now, letting the old general ask his questions.

"It depends on how bad the wound is. The greater the wound, the quicker the infection acts," Sarah answered.

Khoiron stopped pacing. "What do they look like after the transformation?"

Sarah sighed, thinking of the soldiers that had died at the camp. She felt her muscles tightening in readiness and glanced at Isaac. Aaron had ordered him to take her to safety. Knowing it was the right decision didn't make leaving any easier. "I've only seen those newly infected. Their skin blackens, and their eyes fade. They become— crazed and will attack as if in a frenzy."

Khoiron nodded. "They can still be killed."

"Yes," Isaac said. "They must have the bodies burned. According to the Hythariam, it's the best way to contain the virus."

Khoiron ran his hand along his craggy cheek in thought and shook his head. "We need to warn people, but at the same time this could spread chaos and discord among them. Opportunists could use this as an excuse to take out their enemy."

Sarah nodded. "That is the reason why I wanted you involved. I want you to work with Isaac and Nolan to help secure not only this city, but the smaller surrounding kingdoms as well."

Khoiron frowned in thought for a moment. "The new captain commander of the city. Wise choice in putting him there."

"Part of me wants to spread the word about the Forsaken to everyone and trust that people will use good sense. At the same time, I know that doing so may cause more harm than good," Sarah said.

"What would you have us do?" Khoiron asked.

"To start with, I want you to leverage your network of agents. Tell them the truth and how best to deal with the virus," Sarah said.

"That's a good start, but they will need support. It sounds like this virus could get out of control quickly," Khoiron said.

"Agreed," Sarah said. "We'll send support. Soldiers where we can. Soldiers dressed as civilians where we can't, and I will engage the leaders of the smaller kingdoms. They can cascade the knowledge about the virus as they see fit. At the same time, I want your agents to report any sightings of the Forsaken."

"This will take time—" Khoiron started.

"This begins now," Sarah said. "We can't afford to delay. Use the former Elitesmen here under Isaac's command. We have some comms devices that can be used. Train your agents in their basic use."

"You'll need to have someone show me their basic use, my Lady," Khoiron said, his craggy face lifted in a smile.

"I will have one of my men show you," Isaac said. "I can assign some of my people to help, but I will need more than half for our task, your Grace."

General Khoiron glanced between the two of them. "I had assumed that the Forsaken is what brought you back to Khamearra. Am I wrong?"

"It's part of the reason. I'm here to help hunt down my brother," Sarah said.

Khoiron's eyebrows drew up. "He's returned to the city?"

Isaac frowned. "We're not sure."

"What do you mean, you're not sure? Amorak had Rordan training with the Elitesmen. Surely you can track him down with them," Khoiron said.

"It's not that simple," Sarah said. "Rordan was given some type of amulet that augments his powers."

"Who gave him the amulet?" Khoiron asked.

"We believe the amulet was left for him by Mactar," Sarah answered.

"Curses," Khoiron swore. "I always told your father he was too indulgent with that man. Was this amulet similar to the apprentice amulets that Gerric used to force on the Elitesmen?"

Isaac frowned. "For a general, you seem to know an awful lot about Elitesmen practices, but to answer your question. Yes, it's similar."

"It's my business to know the inner workings of sects like the Elite Order," Khoiron said.

"Why did you ask if it was similar to apprentice amulets?" Sarah asked.

"Something I heard Mactar say—hint at really. Something about young men who sought power were the easiest to bend to your will," Khoiron said.

Something tugged at the edges of Sarah's thoughts, but she couldn't quite pin it down. "Mactar was full of secrets, and since Rordan may have gotten his amulet from Mactar, then it's safe to assume that it came with strings attached. Mactar didn't share power unless he could use it as a way to control you. He tried a number of ways to ensnare me into his schemes, so it's not too far a leap to believe that he did the same with my half brothers as well."

"So the amulet augments Rordan's powers, and with Mactar dead and gone, there is no one left to control him," Khoiron said.

"It's more complicated than that. Rordan is not simply more powerful, more adept at using the energy. To tap into the energy around us requires a strong mind. That's why the Safanarion Order forbade the use of apprentice amulets," Isaac said.

"A strong mind?" Khoiron asked.

Isaac smiled. "Something you don't know? Yes, being open to manipulate the energy around us taps into the very foundations of the soul. The soul can be old. Without a strong sense of self, one could fall under the influences of souls past."

"So you see, General, we're facing more than my brother. The users of such amulets become drunk on power and addicted to its use," Sarah said.

"Can't you just take the amulet from him?" Khoiron asked.

"We need to find him first. I last saw Rordan here at the palace. This was before the battle at Rexel. Rordan was slipping then. Changing into something else almost entirely," Sarah said, her thoughts beginning to race. "Tarimus!"

Isaac and Khoiron exchanged glances.

"Colind's son. What about him?" Isaac asked.

Sarah felt the pang of Colind's loss. The Lord Guardian of the Safanarion Order had traded his life to rid the world of Mactar. She missed the old man and hoped he was finally at peace. "Tarimus was under Mactar's control since before the fall of Shandara. What if Mactar started the same process with Rordan, only he wasn't able to finish it because he is dead?"

Khoiron nodded. "A means to control. The idea has merit, your Grace."

Isaac frowned. "It is a good idea. We searched Mactar's chambers here at the palace but didn't find anything."

Sarah shook her head. "No, he wouldn't keep it here. Mactar would have kept it at his castle."

"But Garret reported that Colind destroyed the castle," Isaac said.

"That's true, but it couldn't hurt to look around. We can still keep looking for Rordan here, but I want to take a look around at the ruins of Mactar's castle," Sarah said, her mind made up. She needed to finish this business of stopping her brother quickly so she could focus on the Zekara with the others.

"Your Grace, I will take my leave of you and set about the task that you've given me," Khoiron said, and left the offices of the High Queen.

"Shall we, my Lady?" Isaac asked.

"No contingent of soldiers to bring with us?" Sarah asked.

Isaac chuckled. "Oh, they're just outside your office. You see, I figured you'd want to head off as soon as possible. So I keep a ready force charged with protecting you while you're here that can leave at a moment's notice."

Sarah nodded, resigned to the fact that her days of charging off alone may very well have been behind her. The price of becoming the High Queen.

CHAPTER 13

SHARED BURDENS

After coming through the portal, Aaron and the others checked themselves for injuries. Luckily, none of them had any bites from the Forsaken. *It was something at least*, Aaron thought. Despite their careful planning, it appeared that the Zekara were ready for them. Aaron shook his head, clenching his teeth. They might have surprised the Zekara, but the surprise was twofold with the FNA being blindsided once again.

Aaron glanced north and could almost make out the Watchtower of Elden Hold. He had sent word to evacuate the old watchtower. Tanneth had made the report to Gavril, who was in Rexel.

"Prince Cyrus has been informed, but he wants to speak with you," Tanneth said, and activated the portable holo display. After a few moments, the head and shoulders of Prince Cyrus, ruler of the Waylands, looked up at them. Rexel was the capital city of the Waylands and had allied with Shandara against the High King. Cyrus had been his grandfather's friend before he had fled to Earth with Aaron's mother.

Gavril joined them. Although Gavril was Hythariam, he didn't have the golden eyes that dominated their race. Instead, he had green eyes that clearly showed their distinction on the holo display. Gavril was formerly of the Hythariam military before they fled to Safanar.

"I didn't think the Zekara would have so many of the Forsaken with them," Aaron said.

"How is it that we couldn't see them?" Verona asked.

Bayen, who was off to the side, appeared as if he were about to speak but at the last second decided not to.

Strange, Aaron thought.

"It's called a cloaking net," Tanneth said.

"You've seen them before?" Aaron asked.

Tanneth shook his head. "No, like you, this is the first time. Gavril informed me what it was. We don't have anything like that at Hathenwood or Shandara. The power requirements are extremely high. Essentially, they are projecting the known image of the area in front of them through the use of the drones."

"They must have known we were coming," Verona said.

"I think they guessed we would attack at some point along the way," Aaron said. "We knew this would be a fight going in, but the Forsaken are something else entirely. It looked like they had hundreds of them. We need to clear the people out between here and Rexel."

"All the people?" Verona asked.

"Yes," Aaron answered.

"That's a tall order, my friend."

"We don't have a choice, and neither do they. If they stay, then they will fall victim to the Zekara and be turned into one of the Forsaken," Aaron said.

"Is there no other way?" Prince Cyrus asked.

Aaron shook his head. "I don't think anyone could hide from the Zekara for very long. They would need to get more than a few miles away. Having them on the open road or fleeing through the surrounding forests would leave them exposed."

"You may not have noticed, my friend," Verona began. "Rexellians are a stubborn lot. Many will be reluctant to leave their homes undefended."

Aaron was silent for a moment, his face growing grim as his gaze took in those around him. A part of him couldn't believe what he was about to say, but what choice did they have? "If they won't leave their homes, then we should consider forcing them to. We don't have a choice. If they stay, the Zekara will turn them into the Forsaken, and we will be facing them at Rexel."

An uneasy silence sank in on them, but Aaron saw a flicker of understanding among the Hythariam in their ranks.

"You can't be serious. I won't have my people rounded up like a herd of cattle," Prince Cyrus said.

"I'm not saying that we show up and take people out of their homes," Aaron said. "Tell them of the danger. They will listen to reason."

"If there is one thing I've learned from being a ruler of my own kingdom for over thirty years it's that a mob will never listen to reason. If I were to do as you suggest and force people from their homes, then there will be blood in the streets," Cyrus said.

Aaron's eyes darted around. He certainly didn't want that type of blood on his hands, but how could he protect the people if they didn't listen to reason? "We can warn them then and let them decide for themselves."

"That I agree with wholeheartedly," Cyrus said.

"Uncle," Verona said, "Aaron is right. I've seen the Forsaken firsthand. If the people don't quit their homes and seek refuge in the city, then they will most certainly die, along with their families."

"You speak the truth," Gavril said. "Like Aaron, you have the purest of intentions, but this is a slippery slope. I agree with the prince. We warn them of the danger and tell the people where we think they will be safest, but the decision of whether they yield to such advice is entirely up to them."

Aaron felt his stomach clench, remembering the sight of the Forsaken throwing themselves against the barrier. They were mindless and singular of purpose. It was a fate he wouldn't wish upon anyone. After a moment, he recognized the wisdom in the words being spoken. Forcing them from their homes, that was the way of the High King. They were on a slippery slope indeed.

"You're right. I apologize for making the suggestion," Aaron said.

"It's all right. You've seen firsthand the danger we will be facing. It's enough to affect all of us," Gavril said.

Bayen mumbled something under his breath. Aaron couldn't hear what he said, but he could have sworn it was something about half measures.

"Who came to our aid during the battle?" Verona asked.

Aaron glanced to his side and gave a single nod to Thraw, who had stayed silent, cloaked in plain sight at his side. The short hair along his body changed color from matching the ground to a sleek black figure. The others gasped at Thraw's sudden appearance.

"A maul-cat," Tanneth hissed.

"Only partially so, Hythariam," Thraw said.

Thraw's dark features were more feline in shape, with rows of pointed teeth framed within a powerful head. The corded muscles rippled as if the maul-cat was about to spring. The Hythariam around them took a step back, aiming their weapons at the maul-cat.

Aaron held up his hands. "Lower your weapons. His name is Thraw. He helped us against the Zekara."

Gavril's gaze bored in Thraw's direction. "Aaron, you don't know what this is. This is a creature from Hytharia."

Thraw's green eyes narrowed as they swept those around him. "If any of you were my target, then you would already be dead."

"Thraw helped me escape Hytharia when Halcylon left me for dead," Aaron said.

"More likely you were a means to its own ends," Gavril said.

Thraw blew out a loud breath through his snout, making more than one Hythariam twitch. "It was mutually beneficial."

"I invited Thraw to come. He took out three heavily armed Zekara," Aaron said.

Gavril shifted his gaze from Thraw to Aaron. "This creature is not your friend."

"Why don't you tell them about me then, Hythariam? Tell them what you've done to my kind," Thraw said.

"I've done nothing to your kind," Gavril said, and shifted his gaze to address the rest of them. "The creature before you was created in a lab with traits of a Hythariam and a maul-cat. The maul-cats were an apex predator on Hytharia. They can easily blend in with their surroundings and can kill with lethal efficiency. That was before some of my race began experimenting on them. They sought to use the maul-cats' capabilities to their own ends. However, they couldn't be trained even if the cubs were taken at birth. It was then that our scientist sought to enhance them. Merging with the Hythariam added to their intelligence. They were able to imprint targets upon their minds, and the maul-cats would be sent out."

Aaron looked at Thraw, and the maul-cat met his gaze evenly. There was intelligence and cunning behind the creature's eyes, but Thraw had helped him. It was one of the clearest memories he had of being held captive upon Hytharia.

"They were used as assassins?" Aaron asked.

"Yes," Gavril said. "I've never seen one alive. I've only seen the aftermath of the destruction they cause. They were used to infiltrate enemy installations to take our key targets. The facilities where the maul-cats were created had been destroyed before we ever found the portal to Safanar."

"You keep saying created," Verona said. "Do they not, you know, get together and have a few cubs?"

Aaron felt his lips curve into a small smile and shook his head. "It sounds like they were created in a lab."

Thraw stretched out his front legs, extending sizable dark metallic claws that protruded from his paws. As he pulled his legs back, the claws retracted.

"It sounds like the scientist did more than combine the traits of one species with that of another," Aaron said.

"They were enhanced," Gavril said.

Aaron sensed the unease from the Hythariam soldiers that were part of the group, and Thraw's challenging stare didn't make them any more at ease.

"You said they were used as assassins. Do you know anything more about them?" Aaron asked.

"Yes, they were. This is the part I'm least familiar with," Gavril admitted. "Somehow, the maul-cat hybrids were imprinted with a target, and once imprinted they would stop at nothing to achieve their goals."

Aaron glanced at Thraw. "Who is your target?"

Thraw regarded him for a moment. "General Morag Halcylon."

"Halcylon is your target?" Aaron asked, and the maul-cat nodded.

"That's just it, Aaron. You can't trust anything the maul-cat is telling you. It was created to deceive. Lying isn't beyond its capacity," Gavril said.

Thraw let out a low growl.

"Everyone here has the capacity to deceive," Aaron said, and turned back to Thraw. "Why did you save me on Hytharia?"

"Mutually beneficial," Thraw said.

Aaron's gaze hardened. "I mean before that. You were watching me."

"You resisted Halcylon. You could have killed him yourself but didn't. I was newly released from my tank and didn't seize the opportunity," Thraw said.

"Released? You mean someone let you out?" Aaron asked.

Thraw nodded his large head.

"Maul-cats were too dangerous to keep conscious without an imprint. There was a risk of having them turn against their captors," Gavril said.

"Still," Aaron said, "someone set him free, and if they imprinted Thraw to target Halcylon, that means there are those among the Zekara that could be allies."

"The enemy of my enemy is my friend," Verona said.

"Do you know who set you free?" Aaron asked.

Thraw shook his head.

Aaron cocked his head to the side. "Why come to my aid?"

"As I said, human, it was mutually beneficial."

"You will call me by my name, or I will revert to calling you maul-cat, is that understood?"

Thraw studied Aaron for a moment and nodded.

"I don't mean on Hytharia. I meant here on this day," Aaron said.

Thraw's gaze softened slightly as he glanced away from Aaron for a moment. "Halcylon is too well protected."

"You think that I could get you close enough to Halcylon to kill him?" Aaron asked.

Thraw didn't say anything in reply, but the answer was clearly stated in his eyes.

Aaron glanced at the others and lingered for a moment on Bayen, who appeared slightly alarmed.

Gavril cleared his throat. "They are usually forbidden from trading their lives for their targets, but it's not unheard of if the target has a high enough priority. That's one thing I know about the imprint process. After they successfully meet their objective, they return to whoever set them free."

Aaron glanced back at Thraw. "Is that right? What will you do if Halcylon is killed?"

"I don't know. That part of the imprint is not revealed until the objective is met," Thraw said.

"Well, since Thraw was released upon Hytharia, there is little chance of his returning there. Do you think anyone back at Hathenwood would know about this?" Aaron asked.

Gavril shook his head. "This was purely a military program. I'm sure we could learn a great deal from—Thraw, but that would require cooperation."

Thraw bared his teeth at the hologram.

"Thank you, but I don't think that will happen," Aaron said.

"We'll start sending out evacuation groups to the surrounding areas. I urge you to move quickly. Halcylon will press his advantage now that part of his capabilities has been revealed," Gavril said.

Aaron nodded. "We'll see you at Rexel," he said.

The holo display winked out, and Aaron told the others to be ready to move out soon. Verona and Tanneth joined him. A few moments later, Marek joined them as well. Thraw hadn't moved and had remained so still that you could barely see him breathe.

Aaron turned back to the maul-cat and rubbed his chin, gathering his thoughts. "I need to know if I can trust you."

"We have the same goals, hu—Aaron. We both wish to kill Halcylon," Thraw said.

"Thraw, I give you my word that no one here will try to harm you while you're with us, but I expect the same from you. Can you agree to that?" Aaron asked.

"Agreed," Thraw said, and then his snout crinkled as he sniffed the air.

Aaron noticed Bayen standing close by and watched him with a raised brow. Bayen then walked over of his own accord.

"This one smells... off," Thraw said.

Aaron narrowed his gaze, wanting to ask the maul-cat what he meant. A hazy memory pushed its way into his mind from his time as the Zekara's prisoner and Thraw saying the same thing about him. His instincts told him that they needed the mysterious youth. "What can I do for you, Bayen?"

"The prince doesn't understand what he will face when the Zekaran attack. If the people won't listen, then they should be forced to leave," Bayen said.

"We've already been through this," Aaron said.

"Nothing is gained by half measures. Each person we save is one less we have to fight," Bayen said.

"My uncle has the better way, my young friend," Verona said. "We cannot force people into our protection."

"You just don't get it. If they're not with us, then they're against us whether they realize it or not. The Zekara are not honor bound. Their rules of engagement are quite clear," Bayen said.

Aaron stared at Bayen for a moment. The young man's cold blue eyes seemed so familiar. Bayen's mouth was drawn down as if he was constantly clenching his teeth. *What happened to you that made you so... ruthless?* Aaron wondered.

"We're not going to do this," Aaron said.

"Do what?" Bayen asked. "Speak the truth? Anyone who gets left behind will die," Bayen said, his raised voice drawing attention from the nearby soldiers.

Aaron kept his temper in check and took a breath. "I fear for those who will get left behind, but Prince Cyrus's orders stand. We will help people retreat to the safety of the city. Unless you have a better suggestion or something you wish to share with the rest of us?" Aaron asked.

Bayen stood there for a moment, glaring at Aaron, then turned and stomped away. A moment later, Aaron noticed that Thraw was missing. Aaron glanced in the direction that Bayen headed and saw the faint outline of the maul-cat creeping along the edges of the forest. Thraw turned his head, and his green eyes calmly returned Aaron's gaze. Aaron realized that the maul-cat had let him see him so that he knew where he was going.

"We know the Zekara are heading for Rexel. Let's make their road more interesting for them," Aaron said.

"How?" Tanneth asked.

"That's what I would like for you to work on, but I'm worried that our comms devices are being monitored. I want us to limit their use for a time," Aaron said.

Tanneth shook his head. "They cannot decode our messages."

"Are you absolutely sure about that? Let's consider for a moment that they could. We could use that knowledge as we coordinate. Know what I mean?" Aaron asked.

Tanneth spared a glance at Verona, who nodded.

"I thought you said you weren't part of the military where you come from?" Tanneth asked.

"I'm not," Aaron said.

"My friend, you have an absolutely devious mind," Verona said.

Aaron looked in the direction that Bayen stormed off to.

"What is it, my friend?"

Aaron shook his head and turned back to Verona. "What if Bayen is right? We're trying to fight this war with our integrity intact. Halcylon has no such issues."

Verona pursed his lips together. "It's because of our honor that people follow us. It's why the Alenzar'seth were so revered throughout the lands."

"I understand that, but still, Verona. What if Bayen is right? An army of Forsaken could fracture the alliance we've built with the Free Nations Army. Just when we're coming together. According to Sarah, nations that haven't been anything but enemies are actually on speaking terms in an attempt to work together. If this turns into a war for survival, I'm afraid it will drive us apart," Aaron said.

"And we'll be playing right into Halcylon's hands," Verona added.

"Exactly," Aaron said.

A shadow raced across the grass toward the opposite side of the clearing, snatching their attention. Across from them, the sun reflected off the emerald hide of a Dragon. The Dragon was nowhere near the size of the Eldarin, but the raw power of its gaze was enough to steal the breath from the most stalwart of warriors.

A soft gasp escaped Aaron's lips, and he felt a probing along his senses. His last encounter with Dragons had been during the battle with the High King. The Dragons had been drawn to the battle because of the Ryakul presence.

Aaron drew in the energy and leaped across the field toward the Dragon. He landed softly, using the particles in the air to slow his descent. A blast of air blew from the creature's nose. Verona landed a few paces behind him, and the Dragon growled deep within its throat. Aaron held up his hands and bowed his head. Verona stayed where he was.

I would speak with the one marked by fate. We of the old world honor the sacred pact with Ferasdiam's blessing.

Aaron heard the Dragon's deep voice inside his head. *You honor me,* Aaron replied.

Battle is imminent; why have you not called upon the oaths sworn as part of the pact? the Dragon asked.

I'm afraid that further battle will see the end of your kind, Aaron said. Holding the energy, he felt the powerful emotions pouring off the Dragon. The very same reflected in the majestic creature's wild eyes, which bored into him. Aaron dropped his chin to his chest, breaking eye contact.

If that is our fate, then it is our sacrifice to make. Do you know nothing of our kind, Ferasdiam marked? There is imbalance in this world, and it grows with each passing moment.

Aaron felt his throat tighten. How could he summon the Dragons to a battle that could see the end of their kind?

The imbalance spreads. We feel it among the higher planes. You must sense this as well.

Aaron drew in a shaky breath. *The Eldarin don't wish for you to fall.*

The fallen ones cannot be allowed to roam free. They are a blight upon this realm, and they must be stopped!

Aaron staggered back, yielding to the crushing rage exuding from the Dragon and felt his own rise to the surface.

An ancient one has fallen, and the imbalance spreads. Sacrifice is demanded, the Dragon pressed.

Aaron lifted his head and met the Dragon's gaze. *Then I sacrifice myself.*

No!

The Dragon stomped forward, its claws digging into the ground.

The marked must unite us. The tide must be turned, or all will perish. We will always honor the sacred pact.

Aaron knew what the Dragon was saying. The power had been growing within him. The very same power that corrupted High King Amorak into the monster he had become. The High King had believed himself to be a god and had used his power to subvert the people of Safanar. He wouldn't walk the same path.

What is the sacred pact? Aaron asked.

The Dragon drew his head up, bathing in the radiance of the sun.

Safe guardianship of this realm. We've seen you battle. Yours is of the old blood who have not been among us since the time of the pact. You are Safanar's champion, and we will heed the call of the Ferasdiam marked.

The Dragon launched into the air with a great swath of its wings and flew away.

Aaron released the breath he had been holding, and the energy left him. Darkness pressed in on his vision, and he sank to his knees. Verona rushed to his side and steadied him.

"I didn't think it was my place to approach, my friend," Verona said.

Aaron nodded, still gaining his bearings. He sucked in a few breaths and steadied himself before rising to his feet.

"Not a gentle meeting?" Verona asked.

Aaron shook his head. "They're angry."

Verona snorted. "Don't tell me you've earned the ire of a Dragon now, my friend."

"They want me to summon them to the battle," Aaron said.

Verona nodded. "My friend, you have the noblest of intentions. You think to protect the Dragons from annihilation by not calling them into battle. But you forget that whether they battle or not is entirely up to them."

"They will come. Even if it means their end," Aaron said.

"I've seen you throw yourself into the thickest part of any battle more times than I can count. What makes your sacrifice any less than theirs—or mine, for that matter?" Verona asked.

Aaron's shoulders slumped, and he felt a heavy weariness spread through him. "It doesn't. I've just lost so many people along the way…"

"We can't win against Halcylon unless we work together, and in order to work together the burden must be shared. Even if it means we lose some of our friends along the way," Verona said.

Aaron unclenched his jaw to speak. "I would bear it all if I could."

"But you don't have to, and honestly you can't. The Dragons understand this. You just need to accept it."

Aaron brushed his weariness aside and pulled in a small amount of energy from the earth. "Thanks, I needed that."

Verona grinned. "As the good Admiral Morgan is fond of saying, we all need a good kick in the pants once in a while. Yours just happened to come from a Dragon and, well, me. I've said it before, my friend. I will see this journey through to its end."

Verona was his first real friend when Aaron arrived on Safanar from Earth. Whether it was the Goddess's blessing, fate, or just plain old-fashioned good luck, he counted himself truly fortunate to have such a friend.

CHAPTER 14
CASTLE RUINS

The sun cast its warmth upon a small northern town in Khamearra. The townsfolk went about their business with more of a spring in their strides since Sarah had been there last. No doubt the absence of the castle that had served as Mactar's home fueled such happiness. Both the castle and its master were gone. Thinking of Colind's sacrifice to end the life of Mactar was bittersweet. She had grown very fond of Colind, who had helped nurse her back to health after Aaron had rid her body of the Nanites. She knew that Colind would rest easier knowing that he'd traded his life for Mactar's, but she missed the old Lord Guardian of the Safanarion Order. Despite his own grief, his counsel had always been wise.

"*This* was where Mactar made his home?" Isaac asked. They were outside the town, just beyond the boundaries of the castle.

"Not what you expected?" Sarah asked.

Isaac scratched the back of his head and shook it. "Not at all. I expected something grander."

Sarah shrugged and led them up the path to the charred castle ruins. A few remnant walls looked as if a good wind could blow them over.

The men Isaac brought with them were all former Elitesmen. When she disbanded the Elite Order, the members who chose to serve had the option to join the Free Nations Army. They were to serve at the lowest possible rank where only merit would gain them authority. After a year of service, they could apply to the Safanarion Order. Shortly after the battle with her father, Aaron had input the year of service in the FNA as the bare minimum prior to an application into the Order, and Sarah had agreed. The former Elitesmen with them had all served the Resistance in Khamearra during her father's reign, so there was an element of trust that had already been established. They all wore plain blue uniforms of the Free Nations Army with the exception of Isaac, who still donned his black leather duster over his clothing. As Isaac put it, his loyalty was to her, and at his age he wasn't about to don a uniform.

"The place is a wreck. I'm not sure what we hope to find here," Isaac said.

"I'm going to look around. Have the men form a perimeter just in case. I would prefer it if they stay out of the castle grounds," Sarah said.

It had been many months since she had been to Mactar's castle, with the last time being upon her father's business. This was shortly after Aaron had arrived at Safanar from a place he called Earth. She had practically jumped at the opportunity to deliver her father's summons to Mactar and see him squirm. Unlike her brothers, she had kept from being pulled in by Mactar's manipulative designs. He was attracted to her, and she learned early on how to deal with the attentions of powerful men. She had become ruthless on occasion because there were those in power that only respected strength. She knew her father kept sending her to deal with Mactar as a way of dangling a much sought after prize. Those days were now gone, and how different her life was now. She was the High Queen of Khamearra. Her little girl's dreams of love had faded along with her childhood long ago. That is until fate had thrown one Aaron Jace in her path. Her eyes softened as they drifted to the east, where she knew Aaron was preparing for battle with the Zekara. A small flutter caused her stomach to tighten. She wondered if that was their babies growing inside her.

She needed to deal with Rordan quickly so she could return to Aaron. Once she told him of the pregnancy, he would likely try to keep her from the fighting. Many that followed them would agree with him, and he might even be right, when her belly started to swell. That time was not yet, and her place was fighting at Aaron's side.

Sarah turned back to the twisted, charred remains of the castle. Melted glass had pooled around broken frames with parts glistening in the sunlight. It was a fitting end to all the evil that had been hatched inside. The effects of Mactar would be felt upon the nations of Safanar for many years to come.

She felt something pushing on the edges of her thoughts about her last visit here. She had just sent Mactar to the palace in Khamearra through the travel crystal. Perhaps she needed a different perspective. She drew in the energy and leaped atop one of the few remaining walls. The blackened ruins had long since cooled, and Sarah leaped again to the far side of the castle where Mactar had kept his prized possessions. Some of those possessions had value, but most wouldn't give them a passing thought until they learned that they were trophies taken from Mactar's conquests. She remembered one of Shandara's standards had hung on the wall. One of his most prized possessions from the fall of Shandara. She could only imagine the blow to his pride when he learned that he had not rid Safanar of the Alenzar'seth line, of which Aaron was the last. Not the last anymore—she corrected herself as her hand caressed her stomach.

A partial frame stuck out amid a loose pile of rubble. The bronze laurel work tugged at her memory. Her eyes swept the ground and then came back to the bronze frame. She grasped the edges of the large frame and pulled it out of the pile. The frame was twisted and bent on one side, but there was one corner completely intact. A mirror shard was firmly attached to the corner. This was the mirror that hung on the wall where she had last encountered Mactar. He had been calling out to someone...

"Tarimus," Sarah whispered. Mactar had used the mirror to control Colind's son, Tarimus. Tarimus had effectively allowed her father's armies into Shandara before she had been born. The reward he had been given was to be trapped within the netherworld.

"Your Grace, are you well?" Isaac asked, crossing the castle ruins in short energy-enhanced leaps.

"I'm fine," Sarah answered. "This was Mactar's; he used it to control Tarimus."

Isaac frowned, staring at the mirror shard. "You think this is tied to the amulet that Rordan is wearing?"

"Mactar didn't give it to him out of the goodness of his twisted heart. No, he had an angle. There was something in it for him. While the amulet may augment Rordan's powers, there is always a cost for such gains," Sarah said, and focused on the shard with a tendril of energy. Tiny crystallized dust was infused into the mirror shard and frame. She could sense the power within the shard respond to her.

"Do you know how it works?" Isaac asked.

"I think this shard is connected to the amulet that Rordan now wears," Sarah said.

Isaac nodded. "I can sense that the shard is infused with energy."

Sarah twisted the frame corner with the shard, breaking it off. She wiped the dirt from the shard, and she felt a small tendril of energy cluster to where her fingers made contact. She immediately heard her brother's voice.

"This is what they've sent me?" Rordan asked, sounding unimpressed.

"It's a magnificent specimen, your Grace. And they promised more," a voice answered.

"It is rather large, Darven," Rordan said. "We would be hard pressed smuggling it into the city, but I do like the black armor. If these Zekara can deliver on their promise and provide an army of these, then that could tip the balance in our favor for retaking the city."

"I think a test is in order. We should really see what this thing can do, your Grace," Darven said.

"Agreed. What do you have in mind?" Rordan asked.

"Perhaps a visit to the palace—" Darven began. "Your amulet," Darven whispered.

"What about—it's glowing!"

With a gasp, Sarah released the mirror shard.

"What is it?" Isaac asked.

"I heard Rordan's voice. The shard is connected to the amulet somehow," Sarah said.

Isaac's gaze darted to the shard. "What did you hear?"

"They're planning something at the palace. The Zekara have reached out to him somehow."

"How would the Zekara even know about Rordan?"

Sarah shook her head, her mind going back over what she had heard. "There was someone else with him. Darven was his name."

Isaac's lip curled. "He was Mactar's apprentice. A former member of the Elite Order who managed to break away."

"I know who he is now," Sarah said. She would have loved to get her hands on both men, but Aaron most especially would want to get his hands on his mother's murderer. Darven had managed to elude them for some time, and Aaron had put aside his reckoning with the former Elitesman for now.

"We should return to the palace and put the guards on alert," Isaac said.

Sarah shook her head. "No. If we did that, then we would alert Rordan that we know something. When I used the mirror shard, his amulet started glowing, and they noticed. I'll need to be more careful."

Isaac nodded. "Ah, I see. Perhaps a smaller number of us could keep our eyes open. Did you hear anything else useful?"

Sarah repeated what she had heard, but it didn't make any more sense to Isaac than it did to her.

"Let's spring the trap," Sarah said.

Isaac's eyebrows wrinkled in surprise before he narrowed his gaze. "You're worse than Aaron with throwing yourself into danger. I almost hate to ask, but what do you have in mind?"

Sarah's lips lifted in a half smile, and with a hungry glint to her eyes, she said, "My brother wants to take the throne. Fine, let him try. We'll let it be known that the High Queen will be in court tomorrow. He can spring whatever trap he has in mind. We'll have the court filled with soldiers. Some will be in uniform with others appearing as nobility."

"A bold plan, my Lady. There is just one thing that we're not taking into account," Isaac said.

"What's that?"

"Rordan is able to stop a person's beating heart. The murders seem to occur without the victim knowing what is happening," Isaac said.

"It won't be like that with me. When my brother comes after me, he will want to look me in the eyes. My instincts tell me that Rordan needs to be within a certain distance to kill a person, otherwise I would already be dead."

Isaac nodded. "I would agree with that assumption."

"Good. If Rordan comes within sight of me, he won't get a chance to use his powers," Sarah said.

She and Isaac left the ruins of Mactar's castle. The others rejoined them, and together they returned to Khamearra.

CHAPTER 15
SOMEONE TO LEAD

Bayen and the others arrived outside the walls of Rexel, the capital city of the Waylands. Before Bayen's time, the Waylands central location had been the mutual meeting place for the nations of Safanar. During Bayen's lifetime, it had become a land ravaged by constant war, the battle line being steadily pushed back to the doorsteps of Shandara. He didn't remember much more after that because that was when he went into cryostasis. His father had told him they were weeks away from a cure. Cryostasis was supposed to be a precautionary measure. He had told his father he would go into cryostasis while the cure was being finalized. Instead, he had woken up almost twenty years later to a world a heartbeat away from being consumed by the Ryakul virus. He hated his father for stealing that time away from him. How could he have done that to him? The fury that had been so prevalent before came and went in waves. Seeing a younger version of his father almost made him more human. Bayen pinched his lips together in frustration. He needed to focus. His father had died so that he could travel back in time to save their world. That's what he thought happened, but sometimes he felt his father's presence.

They approached the northern city walls. FNA soldiers along with Rexellian regulars rushed about, making preparations. He had to close his slack-jawed mouth more than once. The city was so clean, and the palace was intact. It was everything he had been told it would be. Even at this distance, just outside the city, the palace gleamed like a beacon of hope. Rexellian pride showed upon the well-kept buildings and streets. The people that traversed them moved with purpose, but he could sense the fear as well. *Not enough fear,* Bayen thought. *These people don't know what's coming for them.*

They had spent the remainder of yesterday and part of today convincing townsfolk of the impending danger. Some left their homes, choosing to take refuge in the city. Others believed they could hide while the Zekara passed them by. Those were the ones that were already dead. They just didn't know it yet. Bayen glared at Aaron. *You should have listened to me. Now we will only face those people in battle,* Bayen thought bitterly.

The bracer upon his wrist vibrated lightly.

"What is it, Sam?" Bayen asked quietly.

"Temporal matrix alignment is at 70 percent."

Bayen barely suppressed the shudder that went through him. He had been sent back here to prevent the plague from occurring. That was his primary goal, and it was ultimately the one he was failing to accomplish. He wasn't a scientist. He didn't know all that was involved with the portal that brought him back in time, but he knew he was still connected to the future. He felt the pull of the future as his time in the past was running out. It was like his mind was trying to be in two places at once. Halcylon was crucial to Safanar's survival. Yet it was that same Hythariam who wanted to wipe humanity off the face of Safanar. Bayen clenched his teeth. His task sickened him. How could keeping Halcylon alive be Safanar's only hope? The AI was adamant that this was their only option.

Bayen knew he could get past the Zekaran defenses and take out Halcylon. The temptation of doing so was almost overwhelming at times. He suspected he wasn't the only one thinking the same thing. He took some time to review the information stored in the AI's database. At some point, the Ryakul virus would try to spread itself to subvert all life on the planet. The Zekara believed they would be safe. They would be wrong. Bayen spent a fair amount of time pursuing what-ifs and going back over what he had learned, hoping to gain insight into something all the ghosts of futures past had missed, but he couldn't make any connections.

Bayen glanced at the people he traveled with. A much younger version of his father and uncle. They were men he idolized as a child. Most of the people he'd recently met were already dead, and the very thought chilled him. At the rate the temporal matrix was falling out of alignment, he had about a week before he was snatched back to the future and his own demise. Had his presence here already changed things, and was that why he had less time than he had originally thought? He wasn't sure. He didn't feel like anything he had done so far had had much of a chance to prevent what was to come. Perhaps if they could stop the Zekara here then the divergence of the Ryakul virus would never happen. This begged the question of how could they defeat the Zekara and not kill Halcylon.

He had planned to stick close to Aaron. Earlier that day, he had sensed Tanneth watching him and confirmed that at some point a passive scan of his AI band hidden in his bracer had occurred. Bayen didn't let on that he knew Tanneth suspected him for the liberty of his comms device. He hoped that the information on how to disable the Zekaran infiltrator would help prevent the spread of the Ryakul virus.

"Hello, Bayen," Tanneth said, walking up to him.

Bayen nodded in greeting.

"A group of us are going to check the defenses along the perimeter and in the city. I thought maybe you'd like to join us since you're so familiar with Hythariam technology," Tanneth said.

Yup, he suspects.

"I would be delighted to," Bayen said, and followed Tanneth and the others.

***

Aaron watched the airships hovering in the sky. Even the ones augmented would be hard pressed to stand against what the Zekara brought with them. Still, some kind of air support was better than none at all. The airships would prove useful if the Ryakuls showed up, but against combat drones or flyer-class SPTs, there would hardly be any contest at all.

"Where to, my friend?" Verona asked.

"Your uncle wanted to see me when we got to the city," Aaron said.

They rode in one of the smaller airships that could safely carry about ten people. They were the prototypes of the current airship model that gave the FNA a decisive advantage over the High King's army.

Aaron's gaze swept over the city as they drew steadily closer to the palace.

"I have Tanneth keeping an eye on Bayen," Aaron said.

Verona nodded and pursed his lips as if deciding whether he should say anything. "Have you spoken to Sarah?" Verona asked.

"Not since yesterday," Aaron answered. When Verona didn't say anything further, Aaron turned to face his friend. "What is it?"

"Nothing."

Aaron could tell that whatever was on Verona's mind clearly wasn't nothing. "Is there something I should know?"

Verona let out a nervous chuckle and shook his head. "Given what we're about to face, I'd say there is a lot we all could benefit from knowing."

The rest of the trip to the palace was made in silence, each man quiet in his own thoughts. The small airship docked at one of the lower spires, and Verona led Aaron through the palace. The lower levels of the palace were a rush of activity. Many of the servants were packing things up and carrying off valuables. Messengers were speeding through the hallways.

"This doesn't bode well," Verona said.

"Perhaps it's just a precaution."

Verona shook his head, frowning. "When valuables and such are being packed away, then my uncle is already considering that the city could fall in the coming days ahead."

Aaron didn't know what to say. It was a hard thing knowing that one's home could be lost. He'd had no warning when his own home had been burned to the ground. The same night his parents died. Their loss was always with him, and there were still times he wished he could talk to them.

Verona's eyebrows drew up, and his normal worry-free expression returned. "Perhaps you're right, and it's just a precaution. Besides, we're better prepared than we were for the High King. At least we know there is an army heading here and not about to appear out of thin air."

Aaron put on a brave face for his friend, but deep down he knew there was no comparison between the threat of the High King and the Zekara. They were about to face their gravest threat, and Aaron truly didn't know how this was going to end. This fight was meant to be fought at Shandara. Rexel just wasn't equipped to repel an advanced Hythariam army like the Zekara. They would fight—of that he had no doubt, but he couldn't help thinking that so many of them were going to die. A flash of the darkened limbs and the fanatical attacks of the Forsaken appeared in his mind. Perhaps death wasn't the worst thing that could happen.

They arrived at Prince Cyrus's office. The main hall had become more of a planning area than a place for the prince to hold court. The guards posted outside the office opened the door, and they entered. Aaron remembered the first time he had been brought here. Colind had advised him to seek out Prince Cyrus to help him get to Shandara. The prince had been reluctant to believe who Aaron really was. It was his grandfather's letter that provided enough evidence for the prince to help him.

The office was well lit with natural light coming through the tall windows off to the side. In the middle of the room sat the prince behind his ornately carved desk. The gray-haired prince nodded in greeting and dismissed the others from the room.

"Uncle, we've come as you've asked," Verona said.

Cyrus's lips lifted in a smile that crossed between grudging respect and the apparent fondness that the prince clearly felt for his nephew.

"I believe that I asked to see Aaron here," Cyrus said, leveling his gaze at Verona for a moment. "You can stay. In fact, I'm glad you're here, as what I'm going to say affects you as well."

The prince invited them to sit on the wooden high-backed chairs in front of his desk. Aaron and Verona waited for the prince to sit down first before they sat in their seats.

Prince Cyrus regarded the pair for a few seconds. "It's things like that that make me feel as old as I must look to you."

"I was always taught that showing respect is never a bad thing," Aaron said.

There was a small knock on the door, and Gavril entered. The Hythariam wore his dark armor with lines of cyan running along the edges. He was formerly of the Hythariam military and had helped Aaron on his quest to save Sarah from the Drake.

"Have you told them yet?" Gavril asked.

"They've only just arrived," Cyrus said.

Gavril nodded, and his green eyes drew down for a moment.

"Uncle, what's going on? As we made our way here, we saw things being packed up and taken away," Verona said.

Aaron didn't say anything but waited for the prince to say what he had to say.

"I've ruled this city for almost forty years, and in that time I've learned that you prepare for things as best you can. At the same time, you should also prepare for the worst. The worst being the very real possibility that this city falls tomorrow," Cyrus said.

Verona swore and shot to his feet. "You can't be serious. You're giving up?"

Aaron turned to his friend. "That's not what he's saying."

The seconds slowly dripped by and Cyrus rose to his feet. "Let me be clear. No one is giving up. Least of all me."

"But you're packing things up. We convinced people to come here because it was their best hope for safety," Verona said.

"And it is. That hasn't changed," Cyrus said.

"We have evacuation plans in place should the city fall tomorrow," Gavril said.

Aaron divided his gaze between the two of them. "Shandara?" he asked.

After a moment, the prince nodded and looked at Verona. "A ruler needs to consider all the possibilities, Verona. Not just the ones he prefers. You are my heir, and although we haven't always seen eye to eye, I've always considered you a son."

Verona sucked in a breath and ran his fingers through his hair. "Rexel will not fall," Verona said. "Excuse me, I need to get some air," he said, and left the room.

No one said anything after the door shut, but Aaron saw the signs of strain around the prince's eyes.

The prince returned to his desk and took a large swallow from the tankard on it. "He was always idealistic. It's an admirable quality, but sometimes it can prevent one from seeing all sides."

Aaron nodded but didn't say anything. He had a feeling that the prince and Gavril weren't finished.

Cyrus's slate gray eyes peered at him as he set his tankard down upon the desk. "What I'm about to say, you will like even less than what my nephew has heard."

Aaron met Cyrus's gaze and waited.

"We need a leader. If you don't take up the mantle of leadership of this alliance, then someone else will," the prince said.

Aaron sucked in a breath. "Leadership is required, but you and everyone else want something more from me."

The prince snorted. "You're already walking the path of ruler whether you want to admit it or not. Some may call you king.

Proclaim you the ruler of Shandara, and with Sarah at your side, you become the most powerful couple Safanar has ever seen. People already defer to you, even on the Hythariam side."

Aaron glanced at Gavril, who gave him a single nod.

"We owe a great deal to the Alenzar'seth, Aaron. That much is true. Beyond that debt, you've inspired my race to once again reach for something better. Iranus has said it many times. Even when you went off on your own to combat the Drake and save Sarah. The solution you found worked out for the best for everyone. A leader must be able to forge his own path," Gavril said.

"I won't be the High King. I won't become Amorak," Aaron said.

"No one believes you would become like him," Cyrus said. "Ferasdiam marked you may be, but you've inspired the trust and loyalty that spans the many kingdoms of this world. Tales of your deeds have spread far and wide."

Aaron stood up and crossed the room to gaze out of the window. "I'm surprised to hear this from both of you. I would have thought that living under a tyrant was enough to dissuade these types of actions. Especially you, Gavril. You've seen the collapse of your whole society. Desperation has a way of sapping the souls of even the best of us."

Hythariam and human regarded him in silence.

Aaron sighed. "If I do this. Become this leader. It's temporary. Once the danger passes, we all sit down and figure out a more democratic way to establish leadership. This alliance was put together from a mutual need to stand together. Once the danger passes, I would expect that people would return to the way things were before."

Cyrus pressed his lips together. "That's just it. Things will be different. Some may want to go back to the way things were, but many others won't. Do you honestly believe that when Jopher, for instance, succeeds his father as king of Zsensibar that things won't change once that happens?"

Gavril came to his side. "Things change in time, Aaron."

"The ruling council of the Hythariam agrees to this?" Aaron asked.

Gavril nodded. "Some proposed the idea. You are the link that binds the Free Nations Army together. Those of us that know you know that you do not lust for power. You fear its use, and at the same time, you can take action when the situation calls for it. These are the qualities of a wise leader. One I'm proud to say I follow."

Aaron should have seen this coming. He had avoided it thus far. There were so many others more qualified than he to lead the FNA. But none that the different nations of this world would follow.

"I can't do this alone," Aaron said.

The two came to stand next to him at the window overlooking the palace grounds.

"You won't be alone in this," Cyrus said.

"What we're proposing is a ruling council made up of the various kingdoms, but we need a leader. Someone with authority to point us in a direction," Gavril said.

"It's too much power for one man," Aaron said.

"Who would recommend in your place then?" Prince Cyrus asked.

"Well, you actually. You put this alliance together. The Free Nations Army was formed because of you," Aaron said.

The prince shook his head. "I'm unfit to lead us. The Free Nations Army is here because of you. Shandara inspired many people of Safanar and has become a legend since it fell. With the return of the Alenzar'seth and you curing the land by removing the barrier between worlds, you've performed miracles in the eyes of many. The people needed a place to flock to, and Rexel was that place until Shandara could be rebuilt. The people who came to join the Free Nations Army didn't come for me. They came for you."

"It's not just humans, Aaron," Gavril said. "Many of my own race made their intentions known that they would stand with you."

Aaron didn't know what to say. What could one say to this? He was honored and overwhelmed at the same time. What did he know about leading people? So many lives would be in his hands. What if he failed?

"You see, Aaron," Cyrus said, "you are the bridge between the Hythariam and the Safanarions. I'm ill equipped to take this on, and the people of Safanar will never follow the Hythariam."

Aaron glanced at Gavril.

"It's true," Gavril said.

"I'm not even a true Safanarion. My father is of Earth," Aaron said.

"Yes, but your mother is from Safanar," Cyrus said.

A bridge between two races. Sarah had hinted to him on occasion that something like this would come to pass. He had ignored it. There was too much work to be done. He was a fool, and Cyrus was right to question him. Who else could lead them?

"You've made your point, but I want to stress that this appointment is temporary. We can sit down after the war and come up with a better way. I get the feeling that there is something else that needs to be discussed regarding the defense of Rexel?" Aaron asked.

"Indeed there is," Cyrus said, and gestured for them to come back around the desk.

"Should we send someone for Verona?" Aaron asked.

"Probably best that what we're about to discuss be kept from my nephew for the time being," Cyrus said.

Aaron nodded, and from the back of his mind, he saw High King Amorak grin. *I won't become like you.*

CHAPTER 16
COMMANDER

After meeting with Gavril and Cyrus, Aaron entered the main hall. People and Hythariam clustered around various tables established for different purposes. There was a line of people waiting to gain entrance to the main hall, and by the looks of it they had been waiting for a long time. The guards saluted Aaron with fists across their hearts, and Aaron did the same in response. Ten city officials sat behind the first table and routed the requests one at a time. It appeared to be a frustratingly slow process. As Aaron walked past, there were more than a few people whispering in hushed tones. Behind that first table were runners who carried the messages from the city officials. The use of comms devices hadn't been fully introduced outside the FNA, and the lack of it was showing up here.

He had left Gavril and Prince Cyrus a short while ago, intending to find Verona. His friend had been upset at the thought of the city falling to the Zekara. Aaron liked the contingency plans even less should the city fall. Both Gavril and Cyrus had lived through the fall of Shandara, and should Rexel share that fate, they would strike a blow to their enemy that would stop them in their tracks.

Gavril sent word through the comms device that the leaders of the
Free Nations Army would be meeting and voting to make Aaron the
commander of the FNA. Aaron had no problems fighting, but it was
the weight of this war being thrust upon his shoulders that gave him
pause. Acceptance would come in time. They had to stop General
Halcylon and the Zekara, or the people of Safanar would be wiped
out. If only Halcylon could be made to listen to reason. Safanar was a
big world. Surely they could find a way to coexist. The Zekara
longing for vengeance went deeper than mere blame for the
Alenzar'seth and the barrier that kept them from Safanar. Having
spent some time among the Zekara as their prisoner gave him some
insights into them. On a very deep level, they longed for a reckoning
for the destruction of their home world. Perhaps the death of the
human race upon Safanar would grant them that reckoning, but
Aaron doubted it. The destruction of their home world that took
many years to happen brought forth a cunning ruthlessness that still
caught the Safanarions by surprise. How did one defeat such an
enemy without being just as ruthless? Desperation was a sickness that
sapped the souls of nations. The scars were endured by generations
long after the war was over.

On the far side of the main hall, where Cyrus's throne had been,
was a holo projector showing a high-level view of the city. Aaron
spotted Verona studying the map and conversing with the military
leaders gathered around the display. The range of the holo display was
easily ten feet, with the ability to zoom in or out as they desired.

Those gathered around the display stopped what they were doing to
acknowledge Aaron. Prince Cyrus and Gavril entered the main hall
from a smaller door from the prince's office and joined them.

Gavril went over to where a Hythariam soldier stood before his personal display.

"We're patched in," Gavril said to the prince.

Prince Cyrus nodded and asked for their attention. "We're being joined by various factions of the Free Nations Army throughout the land for this portion of the meeting. Myself and Iranus, who sits on the ruling council for the Hythariam at Hathenwood, originally conceived the FNA as a way for our people to stand united. To many, the word *nation* is foreign to our ways. Kingdoms have been around much longer. While the FNA is made up with the participation from kingdoms throughout Safanar, we will not refer to ourselves as such. Our world is changing, and if we're to adapt, then we must be able to change with it. Like many of you, I'm not about to give up my sovereignty to join in the FNA, but we must recognize that with an alliance of this size, a clear leader must be selected. Many of you are either rulers in your own right or generals serving your kingdoms. One of the things that hindered our fight against the High King was a lack of a clear commander of the Free Nations Army. We rallied behind Shandara and the Alenzar'seth against the High King, but what I'm asking for this day is a commitment not only to stand with your fellow nations that comprise the FNA but to accept the fact that for the good of the whole we need some type of authority for which to act."

Many people spoke out at once, voicing their questions and objections alike. Did the prince believe he should command the FNA? The Hythariam? What about Khamearra? Cyrus waited patiently for them to quiet down.

"If I may continue," Cyrus said, "I would call to a vote that Aaron Jace of the house Alenzar'seth be our commander."

There was a wide range of responses and a large showing of support.

Aaron found that many more people were looking in his direction than before.

"Prince Cyrus, I wish to speak," a voice said, and the holo display showed the broad-shouldered king of Zsensibar.

"Of course, King Nasim, we welcome your counsel," Cyrus said.

"My questions are for Aaron," King Nasim said.

"I will answer any question that you have," Aaron replied.

"My son, Jopher, speaks very highly of you. Your influence upon him has had a profound impact on the man he has become. For that, you have my thanks. However, I have serious reservations about making you the commander of the FNA."

"I would be surprised if you didn't have reservations," Aaron said.

"You are Ferasdiam marked. This has given you great power. High King Amorak was also Ferasdiam marked. Is this true?" King Nasim asked.

"He was," Aaron said, and several people gasped.

The holo image of King Nasim regarded Aaron for a moment. "There were reports of the battle where the High King could seize control of the people on the battlefield. Even against their will. Do you have the same power as the High King?"

Aaron met the king's gaze. "I do," Aaron said.

"What assurances can you give us that you will not be as Amorak was?"

"His actions already speak to this, your Grace," Verona said. "I was there when Aaron fought the High King. Even in the face of defeat, Aaron would not control someone against their will or even if they wanted it, for that matter. I know this because I asked—no, I begged him to do so."

There were several murmurs throughout the main hall. Aaron

remembered all too well his battle with the High King.

"The fact of the matter is that beyond my word, there is nothing else I can do to prove that I will not use my power as the High King did," Aaron said.

"Even in the face of defeat, you wouldn't?" King Nasim pressed.

Aaron glanced around at all the expectant gazes as they waited for him to answer. "If the fate of Safanar hung in the balance, then I would consider it," Aaron said.

King Nasim turned to face Cyrus. "This is too much power for one man. If we make him the commander of the Free Nations Army, we put ourselves at risk of another High King Amorak."

Aaron was about to answer, but Cyrus cut him off.

"It should be known that Aaron himself brought these objections up to myself and Gavril when we spoke of his nomination," Cyrus said.

King Nasim turned back to Aaron. "You agree this is too much power for one man?"

Aaron nodded. "In peace time, I agree. However, this is a time of war. If we're divided, then the Zekara will defeat all of us. The FNA needs to be able to act quickly. My condition for being the commander of the FNA is that the powers bestowed upon me be revoked when the war is over. New leadership is to be established and certainly not limited to one person regardless of what race they are from."

Approving nods came from many in the main hall—from men and Hythariam alike.

"We can't win this war without the Alenzar'seth," someone said.

Aaron held up his hands, and an uneasy silence settled in. "I'm a believer in the rule of law. This is no secret. I will fight the Zekara with all that I am regardless if you make me the commander of the Free Nations Army. That is my pledge to all of you here today and is part of the oath of the Safanarion Order."

Quiet murmuring spread through the main hall and over the open comms channels. Many in the main hall gave approving nods.

Verona leaned in and spoke so only Aaron heard him. "I think you've won them over."

"I was being honest," Aaron said.

"I know, my friend. All they have to do is dare to believe."

Prince Cyrus cleared his throat. "We will now put it to a vote for the commander of the Free Nations Army."

It took several minutes for everyone to cast their votes, which was a somewhat new concept to many of the smaller kingdoms. A majority agreed that Aaron was the best choice. Cyrus looked at Aaron expectantly.

"I'm honored by your faith in me. My first order, and I hope this will allay the fears of those who voted against this appointment, is to establish a guideline whereby the powers of the commander of the FNA can be revoked, even during wartime. My hope is that this post will outlive me, and I want to reduce the risk of any entity entering this office if it were tyrannical in nature," Aaron said.

If there had been any doubts as to Aaron's intentions, they all but vanished. He meant what he said, but he also knew they had a long, difficult road ahead. Having too much power was only one of the objections that Aaron had made. He was being called upon to command the armies of the FNA and had relatively little experience when compared with someone like Gavril. The Hythariam colonel had assured him that he would learn and that Aaron had all the right instincts. Regardless, he made Gavril his second in command.

"The Zekara are within a day's march from the city by now. In addition to our own state of readiness, we need to go over the Zekara's capabilities," Aaron said.

Gavril brought up his comms device and began tapping in commands. The holo display cycled through images of the Zekara. "We've learned a great deal from your last encounter with them. During the short battle, their cloaking abilities diminished, allowing our satellites to get a clearer image than we had before. Until then, we'd only seen the evidence of a large attack force making its way toward Rexel."

"Do we know where they came from? Were any left behind?" Aaron asked.

"They emerged from the mountains in the north. We can trace their route but haven't seen where their encampment was. Anyone left behind would be noncombatants," Gavril said.

"Once the Zekara went on the move, they must have known that they couldn't mask their presence for long. Also, if they had keystone accelerators, then they would have pounced on us already," Verona said.

Aaron frowned. "Not necessarily. There are three reasons why that may not be the case. First, keystone accelerators require a lot of power to work. With all the equipment that the Zekara brought with them from Hytharia, their tech base must be strained. Second, they needed to gather people up to turn them into the Forsaken. Halcylon is ruthlessly practical. He won't waste his resources if he doesn't have to."

"And the third reason?" Verona asked.

Aaron looked around at the others grimly. "Intimidation. He wants us to know they're coming."

"That was our estimation as well," Gavril said. "We've sent out information about the infiltrator you encountered, along with a way to disable them without the release of the virus. It's not proven, but we believe it will work."

"You gleaned that much from the little bit of information we sent back to you? We destroyed the original because of the contamination risk," Aaron said.

Gavril nodded. "That and Tanneth's analysis."

Aaron frowned. Tanneth hadn't said anything about this before. He made a mental note to ask him about it later.

"The troops outside the walls will need to be agile. We need to be able to dig in and move quickly," Gavril continued, taking them through the defenses they had built outside the city walls.

Thinking of the coming battle, they needed to look for opportunities to take out General Halcylon. Gavril believed that the Zekara would never surrender. The Zekara had been an elite fighting force for the Hythariam military. Should their leadership fall, there was a clear chain of command. Gavril took them through Rexel's defenses and where they would stage their attacks. They had eight flyer-class SPTs outfitted with phase cannons. They had crystal tipped arrows in abundance. Specialized quivers had been designed to prevent the arrows from clashing together and triggering an explosion. The crystallized dust was embedded into the tips of the steel arrows, which were designed to break apart when they hit something solid.

"I have a suggestion. More of a hunch," Aaron said, drawing everyone's gaze toward him. He held up his comms device. "We've been working under the assumption that the Zekara are not able to listen in on our conversations through comms. I don't know if I believe it. I think we should speak in codes for a while. We took the Zekara by surprise, but they were better prepared than I would have thought."

"What makes you believe they can listen in?" Verona asked.

"Let's assume, for the sake of argument, that all the advantages awarded to us with the use of Hythariam technology have been compromised by the Zekara. They might not know everything we have, but we should consider the possibility and build it into our plans," Aaron said.

Gavril nodded. "We've been training the officers on communication protocols."

King Melchoir Nasim's image appeared on the holo display. "My forces will be ready to strike at your command. Where will you be during the battle?"

Aaron had anticipated the question. "I will be leading strategic strikes into ranks of our enemy. Our strike force is made up of the best of the FNA and is composed from your fellow nations."

King Nasim frowned. "As commander, I urge you to remain back and coordinate the battle on a more tactical basis."

"As Ferasdiam marked, my place is in the fight," Aaron said.

Gavril's green Hythariam eyes drew up in concern. "I think the king is suggesting that when the enemy does strike that you look before you leap. Halcylon will not put his entire plan into motion at the beginning of the battle."

This drew a chuckle from Verona. "They certainly know you, my friend."

"Halcylon is aware of what you are capable of and will include that into his own plans," Gavril advised.

The discussion weighed on until Aaron felt his head was likely to burst. He studied the map of the city and its outlying areas, looking for anything they could use to hold back the attack. Prince Cyrus had been preparing to defend his city from attack for months. The most insecure places were the areas that expanded beyond the city walls, including the FNA training grounds. Aaron tried to push off the gnawing feeling that the Zekara were simply going to overwhelm their forces. He knew it was fear of the coming battle. Although the Zekara had superior technology, the FNA had the combined strength from drawing upon all the people of Safanar. Prior to this meeting, Prince Cyrus had urged Aaron not to bring the De'anjard into this fight. The De'anjard, or the shields of Shandara as they were known, were attracting new recruits. They now numbered in the thousands. Since finding the weapons caches, they were well armed. Braden was doing a phenomenal job of whipping them into shape.

The meeting came to a close, and Aaron dismissed everyone but Cyrus, Gavril, and Nasim. They were the core of his advisory council. Verona left to speak to Roselyn over comms.

"There is something we haven't considered yet. The Dragons," Aaron said.

"What about them?" Prince Cyrus asked.

"They will be drawn to this battle because of me. I want the word spread that we are to give the Dragons support wherever they happen to be," Aaron said.

Gavril chewed on his bottom lip. "Makes sense. You're worried about more of them being turned into Ryakuls."

Aaron nodded. "That and the extinction of their race."

"What about the Eldarin?" King Nasim asked.

A sharp pull drew Aaron's attention toward his connection to the higher planes. The Eldarin were only moments away from his thoughts. He felt their unrest in response to one of their number being subverted with the Ryakul virus.

"I don't know," Aaron said finally. The others waited for him to continue. "I really don't know. One of their number is infected with the Ryakul virus, but the effect is more profound. The Eldarin are a higher-order life form. I don't know how to help them, and at the same time I don't want to put more of them at risk of infection."

Prince Cyrus frowned. "What makes their risk any greater than ours?"

"I don't mean to imply that. Colind told me that the Eldarin are able to traverse different dimensions. They are caretakers. My fear is if they all succumb to the Ryakul virus, then it would be disastrous for all life on this world and others. In essence, we're all connected on some level," Aaron said.

Gavril shared a glance with the others. "The Eldarin are an unknown quantity. We'll need to observe and react as best we can then. What about the contingency plan should the city fall?"

"I may be the commander of the FNA, but I believe this decision rests entirely upon you, my Lord," Aaron said to Cyrus.

The prince looked away from them, gazing out of the window to the palace grounds. "This fight we find ourselves in is bigger than any one nation. That much is clear. I will only give the order if all else fails."

King Nasim took his leave of them, and the holo display winked out.

"I hope it doesn't come to that," Aaron said.

Prince Cyrus nodded but didn't say anything.

Aaron left the prince and Gavril to look for Verona. He had been locked away for hours and felt that despite all their careful planning they didn't accomplish very much. Aaron's hands itched to do something tangible. He wanted to see the various battlements around the city for himself and judge their state of readiness. Aaron didn't want to think about all the lives that would be lost if the city fell, but couldn't help it. He needed to find a way to defeat the Zekara or stall their advance. He wondered where Sarah was and resisted the urge to trace her through the bond. Aaron knew she was alive, and that was enough.

A quick glance at the skyline told him the sun would be setting soon. He quickened his step, cursing inwardly for the lack of time they had to prepare for that attack. By Gavril's account, Shandara had almost sixty years to prepare for the Zekara to invade. In that time, the city was transformed to become something of a hybrid of Safanarion and Hythariam design. Even his ancestor, Daverim, had no idea how long the barrier he put in place would hold. Rexel had only six months to prepare with no confirmation that the Zekara would choose the city as a target. Not enough time by a long shot. The Hythariam's contingency plan for if the city fell was evidence enough of that. Should he tell Verona? Cyrus thought it best to keep it from him. Aaron had sworn to the prince that should the worst occur, he would get Verona to safety. Aaron shook his head and remembered that he also needed to speak with Tanneth about the Zekaran infiltrators.

CHAPTER 17
TRAP

The grandeur of the palace in Khamearra was well known throughout the land. Almost a city within the city proper. The proud gray walls could be seen from almost anywhere. Thick carpets and fine wooden furnishings (meticulously maintained) adorned the interior. Over hundreds of years, each successive ruler had contributed to the splendor of the palace. Nothing could compare to the magnificent views of the sprawling city and the countryside beyond. The dark cloud that had been her father's rule was gone. The servants and guards throughout the palace greeted their High Queen with heartfelt affection. So much blood had been spilled during her father's reign, and it was a cruel twist of fate that the peace that Khamearra deserved would need to wait a little longer. Nolan, the captain commander of the city districts, had made substantial gains in rooting out corruption. With her approval, Nolan had removed the more corrupt district captains while giving others a chance to change their ways. The people of the city were still haunted, and Sarah saw the echoes of fear mirrored among many faces.

The High Queen would be holding court this day at the great hall.

Isaac reminded Sarah that a High Queen didn't attend court in breeches with a sword at her hip. To make their trap convincing, Sarah had to look the part, which included wearing a gown and having servants attending to her appearance. She was no stranger to the formalities of court or any other time her father had paraded her around like a trophy piece to be auctioned off. Not this day. Today, she presided over the day's events of *her* kingdom. She would give her people the beautiful and strong High Queen they deserved. It was now well known that she was involved with the Resistance, which had stood against her father. She would bring honor back to the Faergrace name and restore Khamearra to the proud kingdom it once had been. The gown she selected was a velvety deep blue. Dark enough to conceal the breeches she wore underneath but fit well enough to hug her striking figure. Sarah stood before a large mirror. Her long blonde hair was braided into ringlets, setting off the angles of her face. If only Aaron could see her like this. He found her beautiful no matter what, but wearing a gown like this would steal his breath away. Her lips curved slightly, and her pulse quickened. She pulled in a small tendril of energy and felt for the bond she shared with Aaron. The bond had been forged when Aaron used his own lifebeat to bring her back from the brink of death. She knew he was alive and worried. He was always worried now. So much was riding upon his shoulders, and she knew there was only so much she could do to ease the burden.

She exhaled the breath she had been holding, and her gaze went to the window behind her. On top of a small wooden table, near the window, lay a purple travel crystal. She could be at his side in moments. Take off this foolish gown and fight by his side as she ought to. A slight flutter like the wings of a butterfly in her stomach reminded her of the lives growing inside her. Their children. She wanted to tell him, but this was something she wanted to do in person.

Sarah crossed the room and snatched the travel crystal from the table. After tempting fate for a moment, she stuffed the crystal within the hidden folds of her gown. She needed to be here. Her brother was desperate enough to align himself with the Zekara. It was something she had never considered. Rordan was foolish enough to believe whatever lies General Halcylon was feeding him.

Sarah pressed her lips together. There was a time when she thought that perhaps Rordan was different from her other brothers. He would listen and come close to breaking away from that malicious and cruel boy he had been. Goddess knows Aaron gave him the chance. Rordan had a taste of power and now craved it. If by some cruel twist of fate Rordan had become High King, then Khamearra would have sunk into open civil war. While blood had been spilled when she took the throne, it would have been much worse if Rordan had. He dealt out death and craved putting people under his power. *How like Father you've become, Rordan.*

She would stop him. The people of Khamearra must be united to face the Zekara. Halcylon wanted to punish the human race, and no one would escape his wrath. Roselyn had shown her records of what Halcylon had done on the Hythariam home world in the name of survival. He was a brilliant tactician and could give her father a few lessons in ruthlessness. She needed to stop Rordan quickly so they could focus on the real threat to them all.

Sarah turned in one swift motion and walked quickly to the door. She had an escort of twelve guards in total. One of them carried her sword for her. She may have been at court this day, but that didn't mean she wouldn't have a sword nearby. Isaac frowned at her.

Sarah leaned in so only Isaac heard her. "There is a place for it on the throne," Sarah said, smiling sweetly.

Isaac nodded, and they headed for the great hall. The palace was a buzz of activity. Knowing the High Queen was in attendance had everyone stirred up, and most rejoiced in having their beloved ruler safely within the palace. Only safety was far from Sarah's intention at the moment because she was here to set a trap for her brother.

People of all stations stopped what they were doing and bowed in respect as she passed. Their earnest and hopeful expressions warmed Sarah's heart, but there were still many who didn't know what to expect from her. She would make Khamearra great again, and they would know peace.

They came to the entrance of the great hall. Massive wooden doors, ornately carved by the finest craftsmen, swung silently open. There was another entrance near the throne more commonly used by Khamearra's rulers, but this was different. This occasion was more formal.

She knew the people had rallied behind her claim to the throne, and she wanted to be able to walk among them. It also presented Rordan with an opportunity if he was within the crowd.

Sarah opened herself to the energy. She could sense the former Elitesmen interspersed throughout the great hall. She had a general idea where they would be. The guards had simply been told to keep on the alert. They knew Rordan's face well and were ordered to signal for help rather than try and take him alone. The mirror shard was safely hidden within the folds of her gown.

She ascended the dais. The throne itself was carved from marble. The arms ended in two small Dragon heads with wings blending into the throne itself. The cushioned seat and back were wide enough to accommodate someone thrice her size. Laurel work adorned the top with rose petals gathered at the clawed feet of the Dragons. She had always thought the throne to be a beautiful piece of artwork and was delighted to find that it was comfortable to sit in as well.

The day drew onward as she listened to the petitioners. It was an unremarkably tame affair. Most still came to pay their respects. The sun made its trek through the sky, but of Rordan there was not a trace. Isaac kept a vigilant watch upon the crowd and occasionally caught her eye, shrugging his shoulders. More than once, her hand drifted to the mirror shard, and she'd even sent a tendril of energy into it, hoping for a glimpse into Rordan's whereabouts, but she heard nothing but silence.

The day was drawing to a close, and Sarah rose from the throne. Having sat for so long, she was surprised she wasn't stiffer than she was. Her retinue of guards gathered below the dais to escort her from the great hall. Sarah stepped down and took a few steps before glancing back at her sword. One of her guards detached himself from the group behind the dais and retrieved it. The guard carried the sheathed blade and held it out for her. As Sarah grasped the blade, the guard lunged forward, and she was sucked into a purple abyss.

***

Sarah gasped as they emerged inside a dark space dimly lit by the few orbs throughout the chamber they were in. The guard with the travel crystal quickly stepped away from her, taking her sword with him.

Sarah sucked in a torrent of energy, bringing a shield up around her. She raised the wrist her comms device was strapped around and pressed the button to activate it, but the device was unresponsive. Sarah pressed it again and saw the outlines of many shapes shifting just beyond the light.

There was a loud clapping sound as Rordan stepped away from the shadows. His deathly pale skin almost glowed.

"Oh, my sweet sister, I'm glad you could join us." Rordan smiled hungrily.

Sarah gave up on the comms device. There would be no signaling the others.

Rordan took a step closer. "Don't bother calling for help. Our new friend has blocked the signal, isn't that right?"

The lighted orbs grew brighter, pushing back the shadows. She was surrounded. They were in a warehouse. She could smell the dampness of Khamearra's river district. The wooden floor beneath her feet groaned as a Zekaran infiltrator rose above Rordan's ranks. There was a mechanical whirl as the infiltrator stepped forward. Its powered armor glowed cyan along the edges.

Sarah felt her heart sink into her rolling stomach.

"You're a fool, Rordan. You don't know what this thing carries inside it," Sarah said.

Rordan laughed. "You call me the fool, yet here we stand with you in my power."

If the Zekaran infiltrator released the Ryakul virus within the city, there would be chaos. Sarah made as if she were about to reply but instead leaped to the rafters high above them. The gown she wore was designed especially for her. The dressmaker had thought she was crazy when she requested a gown that could be removed quickly. Not to mention the additional cost, but it paid off today. She yanked the gown free, leaving only her dark breeches and shirt. Sarah tossed the gown aside and melted into the shadows. Elitesmen leaped to the rafters with their swords drawn, pressing in on her.

"No!" Rordan commanded.

The Elitesmen closing in on her retreated.

"Let's see what our new friend can do," Rordan said.

The infiltrator pivoted and raised its arm. The eye slots along the helmet gave off a greenish glow. The infiltrator scanned the ceiling and stopped on her position. A small shaft rose from its forearm and glowed orange before belching a bolt of energy. Sarah dashed away and returned to the ground. Pieces of the ceiling collapsed inside, and sunlight streamed through.

"You missed," Sarah called, before darting away.

Sarah charged toward the Elitesmen, who scrambled to get out of the way because the Zekaran infiltrator tracked her movements with its plasma cannon.

Come on. Keep firing, she urged in her mind.

The longer she could keep it firing, the greater the chance that the others would come investigate. She knew she couldn't take them all on. Though Sarah didn't carry a sword, she was hardly helpless. She was almost as deadly without a sword as she was with one. She twisted the arm of the nearest Elitesmen and forced him into the blast from the infiltrator. The blast incinerated a hole through the Elitesman.

"Stop firing!" Rordan howled.

Rordan bounded toward her with his arm outstretched. Sarah felt a massive force press in on her shield. The closer her brother came, the greater the pressure slowed her movements. Her legs tangled beneath her as she scrambled to get away, and Sarah went down. The mirror shard bit into her leg, and for a moment Rordan's attack dissipated.

Rordan came to a stop a few feet from her, his eyes growing wide.

Sarah regained her feet and charged. She spun, and the heel of her foot shot out like a coiled viper, tagging Rordan's chin. The force of the blow twisted his body to the side. Sarah swept out with her other foot, and Rordan's head smacked the floor. Sarah was on him instantly with a knife pressed to his throat.

"Back!" she shouted.

The Elitesmen came to a halt. The Zekaran infiltrator studied her as if deciding whether to shoot or not. She didn't like it. She knew the Elitesmen wouldn't take the chance. Not with her knife at Rordan's throat, but the infiltrator had no such issues.

Rordan coughed and opened his eyes. He looked up at her and chuckled. "Sweet sister," Rordan said.

Sarah pulled him up, keeping him in front of her, and cursed. If she killed Rordan now, they would attack.

"It's your move, Sarah. Kill me, if you dare."

Sarah stepped to the side, dragging Rordan with her. A trickle of blood ran down Rordan's throat. Her eyes darted around for a way to escape, but all she saw were Elitesmen closing in around her. She backed away, and the Elitesmen cautiously moved forward.

The infiltrator stood rooted in place. Its head swiveled back and forth from Sarah to the others. With a mechanical whirl, the infiltrator leaped back and bounded toward the wall. The wood shattered, giving way to the infiltrator's armor.

"You fool, Rordan. You don't know what you've unleashed in the city," Sarah hissed, and flung her brother forward, allowing her knife to bite farther into his neck, but she knew it wouldn't be enough to kill him.

Rordan stumbled into the pack of Elitesmen, and Sarah leaped up through the giant hole in the ceiling. She was out of the warehouse, and Elitesmen attack orbs burst through the ceiling, following her track. Sarah raced forward in the direction the infiltrator was heading. She felt the comms device buzz to life on her wrist and knew that help would soon be coming.

CHAPTER 18
FLAME

Aaron had spent the remainder of the day and most of the night reviewing the defenses in place for the city. With Gavril's Hythariam military experience and Prince Cyrus's knowledge of Rexel, it appeared they were in good shape. Their plans were brilliant, as were the people involved in prepping the city for attack. Aaron hated it. He felt like he was being cornered and there was no freedom to move. It was stifling, and he'd said as much to the others.

Gavril had talked him out of using his special forces to attack since they couldn't get reliable eyes on target. But being blind to the enemy's movements was too much a disadvantage, so he arranged for a few airships to make wide sweeps of the area north of Rexel. He had intended to be on board one of the airships, which led both Gavril and Cyrus to come down on him about the need to delegate. Even Verona's advice echoed their arguments. There was simply too much for any one person to do. Accepting the truth didn't mean that he didn't want to be on an airship looking for the Zekara or in a Hythariam flyer, for that matter.

His unit of elite special forces had swelled to over a hundred and fifty men and women. A drop in the bucket when compared with the FNA. They were volunteers from all corners of the world. There were former Elitesmen and members of the Safanarion Order along with Hythariam. There were also highly skilled soldiers from Rexel and Shandara. The De'anjard were missing, and that had been a tough call to make. Aaron could feel the waves of anger coming from Braden through the comms device. There were a few moments where Aaron thought that Braden would disobey and bring the De'anjard anyway. As much as Aaron would have preferred to have his friend fight at his side, he needed Braden to protect Shandara. Midnight had come and gone before Aaron slipped into a fitful slumber. If the same stale reports came in regarding the Zekara's progress, then he planned to take his men and do a bit of scouting on his own. He told his men to get what sleep they could, and he tried to do the same.

Later on, something nudged his shoulder.

"Human, the Zekara are here," Thraw whispered.

Aaron was instantly awake. Thraw's eyes bordered on the ferocity of a wild animal. The points of his teeth reflected the small amount of light from his partially opened mouth.

Aaron sat up. "How do you know?"

Thraw cocked his head to the side. "I can smell them—"

An alarm blared into the early morning hours. Aaron sprang to his feet and grabbed the rune-carved staff. As the rest of them came awake, Bayen caught his eye. He was on his feet only seconds after Aaron.

Verona was up as well and gave a few orders to the men nearest them. Word quickly spread.

They were a short way from the command center in the FNA encampment outside the city walls. Aaron and Verona were first to arrive. The command center was already a buzz of activity.

"Where are they?" Aaron asked.

The holo display came to life, showing a massive force only a few miles from the city. The Zekaran numbers were in the thousands. They had arrived in vehicles Aaron had never seen before. Aaron recognized the massive mobile command unit that cut a path through the forest. The rest of the Zekaran forces were obscured by the forest.

"Why would they stop at the forest line?" Aaron asked.

"It seems as if they are waiting for something, my friend," Verona answered.

What could they be waiting for? Aaron glanced at the tech who operated the display. "Show us the surrounding area. Start with east of the city."

The holo display zoomed back and panned around, but there was nothing.

"Gavril, are there any reports of the Forsaken?" Aaron asked.

"Not as far as we can tell," Gavril answered through comms.

"I don't like it. Why show yourselves and not attack?" Aaron said, his hardened gaze peering into the display as if it could give him some kind of insight that they didn't have before. "Inform the airship captains to report anything strange. Are the drones out?"

"The drones don't report anything," Gavril said.

"Do we have drones where we know the Zekara are currently at?" Aaron asked.

The Hythariam's fingers flashed through the holo interface, and he gasped. "Yes, we do, but they don't report anything either."

"Recall the drones if you can," Aaron said to the tech. "Gavril, we can't trust our sensors. The Zekara have compromised our equipment. They've blinded us. We can only act on firsthand accounts. Spread the word. I'm heading out to have a look."

They left the command center.

"Could this be a ruse?" Verona asked.

Aaron shook his head. "No, they're here."

They returned to the others, and Tanneth confirmed what Aaron had suspected. The Zekara had somehow infiltrated their systems. False reports were coming in all over. They were working on it.

"Whatever they do is going to be too late. One place we can be sure they're not going to attack is where they want us looking. At least not yet," Aaron said.

"How can you be sure?" Verona asked.

Aaron shrugged his shoulders. "It's a hunch. Misdirection."

There was a faint screech from far away. Aaron tilted his head to the side, straining to hear the sound again. Frowning, he drew in the energy, and his senses immediately sharpened. Aaron closed his eyes and knelt to the ground. The runes on his staff glowed faintly. Aaron placed his hand on the ground. He sent tendrils of energy out away from him. He could sense the faint cadence of an army of stomps through the ground. Aaron pushed farther along the line of energy to somewhere between where they were and where the Zekara appeared to be. The cadence grew more intense, as if many beasts were pawing at the ground. For a moment, Aaron thought he was just sensing the people in the city because there were so many of them. Aaron surged to his feet, brought up the comms device interface, and searched for the person he needed to speak to.

"Admiral Morgan, are you there?" Aaron asked.

"Aye, lad, we're here. Approaching the Zekaran line just beyond the main gates," Admiral Morgan answered.

"I need you to send a few ships in our direction fast. Fire on anything along the forest line," Aaron said.

Aaron heard Morgan bark his orders and imagined the sailors on the decks of the *Raven* rushing to obey the admiral.

"It's being done. Good hunting, your Grace," Morgan said.

"Thank you, and Morgan," Aaron said.

"Yes, your Grace."

"Tell your men to show them what we're worth."

Admiral Morgan gave a hearty laugh. "Will do."

Aaron opened a comms channel to the command center.

"Gavril, order the attack. Don't wait to engage. I think the Forsaken are massing southeast of their position," Aaron said.

Before Gavril could reply, the sky erupted into bright flashes of light. The Zekara were firing on them. The attack had begun.

"Travel crystals out," Aaron said, and the order was passed down the line. This was what they trained for. Within a minute, they had joined ranks and could travel wherever Aaron ordered.

An explosion sent a flaming plume billowing into the sky. Aaron drew his swords and the bladesong sparked inside him. He engaged the travel crystal, taking them to a secondary gate away from the main gate. The sky lit up as Hythariam weaponry was unleashed into the Zekaran line. Zekaran plasma cannons were chewing through Rexel's walls. Airships with their engines fully engaged zoomed across the sky, dropping their payloads. Halcylon was smart and had his forces concentrate their fire on select targets, destroying one airship before moving on to the next one. Aaron heard the flyer-class SPTs rocketing through the sky, being chased by a multitude of combat drones.

The sun was rising, but it was still dark near the forest. Aaron's force was a mixture of light and heavily armed soldiers and former

Elitesmen. Tanneth had his Hythariam powered armor on, with the helmet engaged. He peered into the darkened forest across the way and confirmed what Aaron already knew. The Forsaken were there. Aaron didn't know how Halcylon controlled them, but he did know if he unleashed the bladesong he would draw them to him.

Blinding lights suddenly came on from the forest line, catching them all in the open.

"Move!" Aaron shouted.

A barrage of plasma bolts fired at them. Former Elitesmen sent attack orbs racing back at the attackers. A screeching fireball blazed past them, slamming into the city walls. An explosion knocked Aaron and the others forward, and pieces of the city wall rained down around them. Ringing roared in Aaron's ears but slowly faded, and he scrambled back to his feet. Behind him was a massive hole in the city wall. Aaron helped Verona to his feet.

"Stand fast. They're coming!" Bayen shouted.

Aaron spun around, and a sea of shadows poured forth from the forest. The Forsaken bounded forth, using their clawed hands to propel them forward. Their mouths were gaping maws with elongated teeth. Nothing human remained of those who had been infected. Aaron raced forward, bringing his swords to bear. Notes from the bladesong trickled from the passing wind. A streak of white traveling next to him marked Bayen with his bladed staff. A volley of crystal-tipped arrows streaked by and blew the Forsaken back. Aaron growled, moving at blinding speeds, and met the frenzied attack of the Forsaken with his own fury. The Falcons cut through them, but still they came like moths to a flame. The Forsaken snapped and clawed their way to him despite his soldiers closing in. A few Forsaken broke off to attack the others, giving in to their thirst for human blood. The ground soon became littered with the twitching limbs of the Forsaken. Only hacking them to pieces seemed to slow them down. Hacking and flame, which kept them from rising again.

Aaron's sword bit into the nearest Forsaken, and its black blood hissed from the wound. He had seen the same before with the other Forsaken. Perhaps to fuel their frenzied attacks, the infected blood needed to be pumped at an equally rapid pace. It would explain the quickness with which the Ryakul virus spread through its victims.

Aaron leaped forward over the diminishing line of the Forsaken, and they followed him like the turn of the tide. His soldiers attacked them from behind, quickly dispatching the remaining Forsaken. Aaron crested the tree line, expecting to face the Zekaran soldiers, but the area was empty. He returned to Verona and the others. Some of their number had fallen to the Forsaken who hadn't killed their victims. A simple bite or scratch, and then they'd moved on. Within minutes, effects of the Ryakul virus were prominent in the victims. Death was the only release. Some had tried severing the infected limbs of their comrades, but the virus was too quick. It was like nothing Aaron had ever seen before. A nightmare come to life.

"Did any of them make it into the city?" Aaron asked.

The fighting in the distance, at the main gate, intensified as the FNA forces fully engaged the Zekara.

Verona shook his head.

"That's something at least," Aaron said.

Aaron's comms device buzzed on his arm.

"We've got Forsaken loose in the city. Multiple places."

Aaron's stomach clenched at the news. How had they gotten into the city? The message repeated, and Aaron shared a grim look with Verona. Aaron divided his forces to hunt for the Forsaken loose in the city. He glared toward the main gate, where the battle raged on. Halcylon had planned this perfectly.

Aaron and the others sped through the city, engaging pockets of Forsaken where they found them. The Forsaken seemed to be able to sense people nearby. They tore through buildings to get at them. The fighting grew worse because now they were facing newly infected Rexellians who still looked human. Cracks appeared along their ashen skin, with inky blackness visible beneath. Those who had been infected longer looked like something else entirely. Elongated hands ended in jagged claws, as if the process had been rushed. The claws cut through skin easily but were brittle against armor.

Smoke billowed into the air above the city, and the cycle continued. The airships hovering above would give the location of any group of Forsaken they saw. They, along with the city guards, would hunt them down. The groups they encountered increased in size, while they lost soldiers in the fight. By midmorning, they were already exhausted, with no sign of the fighting letting up. Rexellians, no longer feeling safe in their homes, were fleeing into the interior of the city.

Gavril had things in hand at the front, while Aaron was racing around the city, trying to prevent the Forsaken from overrunning them. General Halcylon kept his main force fighting at a distance, which forced the Free Nations Army to do the same. The FNA didn't have the ability to charge in and take the Zekaran army in a frontal assault.

Gavril contacted Aaron through the comms device.

"I need for you to take your soldiers and converge on the eastern gates. They're being overrun," Gavril said.

"By who? The Zekara are clustered at the western gates," Aaron said while signaling to the soldiers around him that they would be moving out. The FNA encampment was outside the eastern gates. If the gates were being overrun, then the FNA encampment was lost.

"It's the Forsaken. You must hurry," Gavril said.

Aaron glanced down the street they were on, looking for a tall building. He needed a better vantage point. *How could the Forsaken be overrunning the eastern gates?* Halcylon couldn't have infected so many people yet. The buildings in their immediate vicinity were only two stories high. Aaron leaped to the top of the nearest building and was quickly joined by the others. Hythariam strapped on gliders to their feet, and several FNA soldiers did as well. Former Elitesmen and those of the Safanarion Order with him had no need for the Hythariam machines. He peered to the east but couldn't see much through the smoky air.

"We go to the eastern gates," Aaron said.

Aaron leaped into the air, covering a massive distance. The bladesong churned inside him. He felt the others behind him, and he resisted the urge to help move them along. He had done small things during the fight today to help keep those with him alive. Every time he did so, he could almost hear the High King chuckling. Strengthening others' connection to the energy around them wasn't control. He reached out to the others and only those open to his touch did he help.

While former Elitesmen fought with them, many remained closed off. Surprisingly, Bayen was able to keep up with him without any help at all. The only other person who could do that was Sarah, and thankfully she was safe in Khamearra.

Hovering over the eastern walls of Rexel were eight airships unleashing hell's fury down at the clustering attack force below. A barrage of crystal-tipped arrows rained down from the airships. Aaron's breath caught in his chest at the sight of the FNA encampment beyond the wall. The encampment was a smoking ruin, as if a fiery tidal force had swept through the area, bringing destruction in its wake.

Tanneth hovered next to him on his glider, and Verona came to his side.

"Goddess be merciful," Verona whispered.

Hundreds of Forsaken threw themselves at the eastern gates. The smoke cleared, and Aaron got his first real look at the Forsaken attacking. His mouth fell open. They had been the remnants of Zsensibar's army. Aaron recognized the brown leather armor that left the wearers' arms exposed. Zsensibar was located far to the south in a much warmer climate. How could they have not been alerted that one of Zsensibar's armies had been consumed by the Forsaken? The ground lit up in a succession of explosions from crystal-tipped arrows that stalled the Forsaken's advance. The forces at the gate were barely holding. If this many Forsaken reached beyond the walls, then Rexel was lost.

"I'm going to give them something to chase," Aaron said.

Verona's crestfallen eyes wouldn't leave the crumbling line of defenders trying in vain to hold the eastern gates.

"It will buy you time to regroup," Aaron said, squeezing Verona's arm.

Verona's eyes blinked in rapid succession, and he snapped out of his shock. "We'll go with you."

Aaron shook his head. "Not this time. Once I see that you've regrouped on the wall, then I will return."

Bayen stepped closer. "I can keep up with you. You need someone to fight at your back," he said. His white armored shirt appeared unscathed much like what the Hythariam provided the rest of them. It couldn't do much against the impact of a blow, but it would prevent a sword from tearing into you.

Aaron gazed at Bayen, considering. He was right: Aaron could use the help, and Bayen had kept up with him before. "All right, you're with me," Aaron said.

Aaron sent the rest toward the gates while he and Bayen circled around. Aaron drew in the energy, aligning it inside him. Strengthening his muscles and bones. He could sense the lifebeat of everything around him except the Forsaken. They were the shadowy reflection of life. They sucked it in and snuffed it out. He clenched his swords and leaped into the air, streaking across the sky. He used the particles in the air to extend his jump. Aaron sensed Bayen behind him and was surprised that the youth allowed him to strengthen his connection to the energy. They came to a stop behind the line of Forsaken who were throwing themselves at the gates, desperate to get inside. Aaron wielded his swords, unleashing the bladesong. A sea of darkened figures perked up and spun around. Aaron bounded away, and the Forsaken charged after them. He pulled in the energy from the earth and pushed it through his swords. The crystals in the pommels glowed brightly, and Aaron slammed them down, sending a swath of pure energy tearing through the Forsaken.

Aaron leaped to the side, and the tide of Forsaken followed him, snapping at his heels. Bayen swung his bladed staff in wide arcs, cutting through a wave of attackers. They guarded each other's back, trusting each other with their lives. They settled into a deadly rhythm of attack, moving when the Forsaken mass grew too much to handle.

All the while they drew them farther away from Rexel's walls and into the encampment. The way Bayen fought echoed Aaron's own style, leaving Aaron to wonder who the mysterious Safanarion Order member that raised him had been. Aaron had been trained by his grandfather, Reymius Alenzar'seth, former ruler of Shandara and head of the Safanarion Order. Though that was not the man Aaron remembered. Reymius had fled Safanar, taking refuge on Earth with Aaron's mother. It was only when Reymius died that Safanar caught up with them and pulled Aaron, the last scion of the Alenzar'seth line, back to Safanar.

He and Bayen fought the Forsaken for a time, but there were limits that even energy enhancements couldn't overcome. Despite the numbers of Forsaken that lay burning upon the ground, more always came, as if the ones they dispatched were a mere drop in the bucket. They were about to jump away again when at the last second Bayen knocked him aside. Aaron tumbled and scrambled to his feet.

"Zekara!" Bayen hissed.

Several large objects shimmered in the air behind them, almost rippling along—the only indication a cloaked flyer would give before firing its weapons on you. Aaron gasped and shuffled back, pulling Bayen with him. They raced along the ground, taking smaller leaps along the mass of Forsaken that continued to rage for Aaron. Plasma blasts from the Zekaran flyers nipped at their heels. They were dead if they stayed out in the open, but the safety of Rexel's walls was so far away. A loud pop sounded through the air, and an airship streaked toward them with engines at full burst. Plasma blasts peppered in their direction from the airship, scoring a hit on the cloaked flyers.

Aaron extended tendrils of energy out from himself, weaving them together into a barrier. A plasma blast sizzled as its energy dispersed around the barrier.

"Get to the ship!" Aaron shouted.

"What are you going to do?" Bayen asked.

The snarling forms of the Forsaken were closing in on them.

"I'm going to give the Zekara something to shoot at and hopefully take a few of them out in the process," Aaron said.

Bayen shook his head. "I can help you."

"You already helped me. Get back to that ship, and tell the captain to return to the wall. I'll meet you back there," Aaron said.

Bayen frowned, pressing his lips together. "But—"

"The Dragons are coming. I sense them just beyond the flyers," Aaron said.

"I can't leave you like this," Bayen said, his voice choking and his eyes betraying something other than smoldering anger. The Forsaken slammed themselves against the barrier, trying to bash their way through.

Aaron stepped closer to him and grasped his shoulder. "I'm going to release the barrier. When I do, make for that airship, and tell the captain to turn around; otherwise, they *will* die."

With a final nod, Aaron released the barrier. Bayen waited for the last second and took off, leaping over the closing Forsaken. Aaron wielded the Falcons, allowing the pure notes from the bladesong to ride along the currents of air. This was his battle song, and it reached far and wide. The Forsaken fell to his blades, their black blood hissing from their bodies. Plasma blasts raked over the ground toward him, and Aaron dashed out of the way. The Forsaken scrambled to follow him, but Aaron outdistanced them in seconds. The glow of his swords streaked toward the flyers. Some had their cloaks down, exposing their golden hulls.

He felt the presence of several Dragons stealthily making their way through the tree line. They knew what the flyers could do and approached cautiously. The blasts from them could pierce even a Dragon's hide.

We will fight with you, Ferasdiam marked.

The Dragon's voice in his head spoke with fierce pride and strength. Aaron roared his battle cry, dodging plasma blasts. The Dragons launched into the air and pounced on the unsuspecting flyers. The flyers wobbled in the air for a moment as the Dragons tore through the ships' hulls. Several of them crashed into the ground while the others streaked away, making a beeline for the city. The Dragons flew after them but were soon outdistanced by the much faster craft. While the Dragons were indeed strong and fast, they were not Eldarin, who could outrun even Hythariam ships. The Dragons broke off their pursuit and flew high into the sky, taking cover in the clouds.

Aaron took a few seconds to search for any Zekaran soldiers that survived the crash, but nothing emerged from the smoking wrecks. Aaron brought out the travel crystal and returned to the city. The east gates were in ruins. While many of the Forsaken had followed Aaron and Bayen away, the newly formed Forsaken had remained behind and were pushing into the city.

The Free Nations Army, having lost the east gates, was trying to stall the Forsaken advance. Each soldier that fell eventually rose to join the ranks of the cursed Forsaken. The blaring truth was in front of him, and Aaron brought up his comms device, signaling to the command center at the palace.

"The eastern gates have fallen. The Forsaken are in the city," Aaron said.

"Understood," Gavril replied.

"They've hit the streets. Can you send in reinforcements? We've got to turn this—" Aaron began.

"The city is lost, Aaron," Prince Cyrus said.

"No! There has got to be something we can do."

"There is nothing we can do but ensure the survival of as many people as we can," Cyrus said.

Aaron's eyes scanned the city line. Fire and smoke wafted up from almost every corner. He heard the screams being snuffed out by the snarls of the Forsaken.

"We'll give them as much time as we can," Aaron said.

The comms device flashed blue and red, the signal to fall back to the palace. Aaron knew there would be keystone accelerators that held portals open to Shandara, but how many people would make it to them?

Screams from the streets below grated on Aaron's nerves, igniting the fires deep within him. His corded muscles rippled as he clenched his swords. He wanted to hurt the Zekara and make them pay for what they had done. Above all, he wanted Halcylon's blood. That twisted tyrant had conceived of this horrific plan, whose impact on the Safanarions was only just beginning to become apparent. Rexel may have been lost, but Aaron swore he would make Halcylon pay for it. First, he needed to help get the Rexellians to safety, then he would go after Halcylon.

The energy blazed through him. He raised his swords up and leaped down to one of Rexel's main thoroughfares. A small cluster of Forsaken was charging a group of fleeing people. Aaron attacked, cutting down the Forsaken and tried to ignore the FNA uniforms they wore. The bodies twitched as if the virus was trying some way to force the severed body parts to move. The sight of it made Aaron's skin crawl, and he forced the bile back down.

The street he was on was empty, and the abrupt silence seemed foreign to him. His mind flashed to a time when the streets had been lined with happy people and flags depicting the standard of Shandara, a Dragon cradling a rose within its talons. Verona had thought it gleefully ironic that fate had brought them to Rexel on eve of the feast of Shensharu honoring the Alenzar'seth.

Aaron called out, urging anyone hiding in the buildings to make for the palace. Soldiers joined him, and soon Verona and the others found him.

"They've ordered the retreat," Verona said.

"We need to get as many as we can to the palace. From there, they can escape through the portals to Shandara," Aaron said.

Verona stared at him in disbelief, and for once the faith his friend had in him cracked his heart.

"Isn't there something you can—" Verona started to say.

"I'm sorry, Verona. We need to save as many as we can," Aaron said.

They moved down the street, with the soldiers searching for survivors and urging them along as they made their way toward the palace.

Verona's mouth hung open as if he couldn't believe what he was seeing. "Call the Eldarin. They can help turn this around."

Aaron shook his head. "I can't summon them."

Verona's eyes flashed angrily. "Because one is infected with the Ryakul virus? Look around you. Thousands of people are going to die here today."

"I am," Aaron said. "Summoning the Eldarin will make it worse."

"You're Ferasdiam marked," Verona said, as if that could solve everything.

Aaron knew that his friend wasn't thinking straight, but the words stung him anyway. Alarms blaring from the palace snapped Verona's glare from him.

A building collapsed a short distance away, and Forsaken poured into the street. The FNA soldiers fired their weapons while Aaron lined up with the rest. Verona cursed, coming to his side and bringing his bow up. Crystal-tipped arrows took out Forsaken in small blasts. The Forsaken charging them wore the uniforms of fallen FNA soldiers. Aaron dashed forward, unleashing the bladesong and swirling into a whirlwind of death. Tanneth called for him to retreat, and Aaron slowly gave ground. The Forsaken never ceased throwing themselves at him. Tanneth screamed for him to move, and a blast took out the clustered Forsaken.

The Free Nations Army was in full retreat, sweeping through buildings and evacuating the citizens that had stayed behind. Those citizens who'd had faith that they would be protected were now fleeing for their lives. Aaron lost himself in the fight. He and the rest of his specialized squad went where the fighting was the worst. They were trying to keep a safe passage to the palace open, but more of the city was being lost. Desperation was spreading even faster than the Forsaken.

Just outside the palace walls, people were clawing their way to the portals. Gavril reported that things were unraveling fast. Aaron ordered the FNA soldiers that could use travel crystals to evacuate the people until there were none left. Some argued that their skills would be better served defending the way to the palace. These were former Elitesmen who had joined their cause and had a taste of a better world. The fact that they were volunteering to search for survivors should have made Aaron proud, but all he felt was the sting of defeat. He sent them out to make one last sweep of the city, giving people a way out if chance had denied them a way to the palace.

The Zekara hadn't moved into the city, and Aaron could guess why. Halcylon wouldn't waste a single soldier when the Forsaken were doing his work for him. The Zekaran weapons had demolished the western walls. Attack drones were being reported inside the city, but Hythariam flyers made short work of them. Halcylon had been methodical in his attack, accounting for their capabilities, including himself. Aaron suspected that Halcylon would order his troops in at any moment. Aaron was counting on it.

"Gavril, we're running out of time. Any minute now, the Zekara will push into the city and head for the palace. We need to set up more keystone accelerators outside the palace," Aaron said.

"If we set up accelerators outside the palace, then we risk one falling into their hands," Gavril said.

"Post soldiers with orders to destroy the keystone accelerators if they get overrun," Aaron said.

"Acknowledged," Gavril said. "Aaron, the prince would like to see you."

Aaron was about to refuse, but something in Gavril's voice gave him pause. He told the others he was heading to the palace and brought out a travel crystal. Tanneth placed his hand upon his arm and was quickly followed by Bayen and a few others. Verona sighed and reached out as well.

Aaron took them to the command center in the palace. All nonessential people had been evacuated. Gavril nodded to them grimly and returned his attention to the holo display before him.

There was a silent somberness in the room that made Aaron's gut clench. The people in the room knew the city was lost. Prince Cyrus's stooped form beckoned them over. Verona charged ahead.

"Uncle, the city is not lost. We can turn this around," Verona said.

"Peace, Verona. If this were a normal attack on the city, I would agree with you, but the Forsaken changed all that. They spread like wildfire. We weren't sure of their capability prior to this day, but we've taken precautions should the city fall," Cyrus said.

"Your Grace, I won't give that order," Aaron said.

"You won't need to. This is still my city, and I will be the one to see this through," Cyrus said.

Verona divided his gaze between them as if he had been betrayed. "What do you mean? What order?"

Aaron waited for the prince to answer.

Cyrus took a long swallow from the tankard he had on the table. "What Aaron is reluctant to do, but has agreed with the rest of the council about, is that should the city fall, it will be destroyed. At first, the idea was to capture the Zekara inside the city and then trigger its destruction, but now with the Forsaken... We have no choice. The army of the Forsaken must be stopped, or all of Safanar will pay the price."

Verona's mouth hung open. "Destroy the city? Uncle, this is our home. What about the people? I won't leave."

Aaron reached out and put his hand on his friend's shoulder. "I'm sorry."

Verona sank into a chair. "How is this even possible?"

"The Hythariam have a bomb with enough power to level this city," Aaron said.

Verona's breath came in gasps. "Then use it on the Zekara," Verona

said.

Aaron shook his head. "We can't. They are too close. We need to hold them off as long as we can."

Verona sprang to his feet, crying out his defiance. Aaron went to follow him, but the prince motioned for him to stay. Tanneth said he would check on Verona. Aaron wobbled on his feet, his knees going weak. He grabbed a tankard off the table. Rexellian ale burned its way down his throat.

"He will understand, given time," Cyrus said.

Aaron felt a lump grow in his throat. "If there was something I could do…"

"There is: Promise me you will get Verona to safety. I know my nephew. He will not leave," Cyrus said.

"I swear to you that I will get him out alive."

"One more thing," Cyrus said, his cold gray eyes regarding Aaron for a moment. "Learn from this. It's up to you to save the rest, Aaron."

Aaron's eyes widened. "You're not leaving?"

Prince Cyrus shook his head. "Rexel has been ruled by my ancestors for almost as long as Shandara. I won't leave, but I'll make sure I can take out enough of our enemy to see that you have a fighting chance."

"You don't have to stay," Aaron said.

Cyrus regarded him for a few seconds. "Yes, I do, Aaron. For the same reason you had to go through that portal to Hytharia. He would have been proud of you, you know, Reymius."

Aaron's throat grew thick, and he was about to reply to the prince when the windows along the far side of the main hall shattered and the floor shook beneath Aaron's feet. An explosion filled the view outside the gaping hole where the large windows had been. Chatter from the comms device confirmed that Zekaran attack drones were making runs toward the palace.

Aaron ran toward the opening to get a better look. He stopped along the way to help people regain their feet. Thankfully, no one was hurt too badly. He was joined by Gavril and Bayen. The portals were easy to spot, their silvery glow looked like pools of moonlight cast across the water. Several portals were open on the palace grounds and one beyond the walls. People were running through the portals at breakneck speeds. All semblance of order was disintegrating. Attack drones kept close to the buildings, avoiding the plasma cannons on the airships above. The portal beyond the palace walls flickered and then went out.

"The Forsaken have reached the palace walls," Bayen said.

Gavril glanced at Bayen as if seeing him for the first time. The Hythariam's eyes slid down Bayen's white armor, and his gaze narrowed.

"Order the evacuation. Get everyone in the palace out of here," Aaron said, and returned to the holo display.

Gavril came to his side. "What are you looking for?"

"Halcylon," Aaron said. "Look, the Zekaran troops are now entering the city."

The holo display showed the troops in their dark armor marching through the remnants of the western walls.

Gavril's hands swiped at the display. "He would be close to their mobile command center," Gavril said.

Aaron nodded. "Keep looking for him, and send me his coordinates through comms. I'll see you in Shandara."

"What do you intend to do?" Gavril asked.

Aaron hefted the rune-carved staff. "I'm going to take him out if I can. We need to get the Zekara to go to Shandara. It's where this war was meant to be fought," he said, heading back to the gaping hole where the windows had been.

Gavril looked as if he were going to protest but shook his head. "When Cyrus sets the self-destruct, you will have seconds to use your travel crystal to get away. Not even you are fast enough to outrun the blast. Your comms device will let you know."

Another portal went out. Aaron felt the energy gather in the rune-carved staff. Within the furthest recesses of his mind, he heard the low rumblings of the Eldarin. They were close. The airships hovering above fired into the Forsaken, giving the people precious time to get through the portals.

"I'm going to buy them some time," Aaron said, and launched himself out of the opening, with Bayen close on his heels.

Aaron landed near the closest portal and jumped into the air again. He had to get closer. FNA soldiers fought to stem the advance of the Forsaken, buying time for people to get to safety, to perhaps escape with their lives. Aaron closed in on the front line and drove his staff into the ground.

"Fall back!" Aaron shouted.

FNA soldiers retreated, and the Forsaken pressed forward, coming to a halt and slamming themselves into a barrier. Aaron kept his hands upon the staff and used it to merge the energy from the soil into the barrier. He expanded the barrier as the Forsaken continued to throw themselves at it, howling as they tried to claw their way toward him.

"Go through the portal. I'll hold them off for as long as I can," Aaron said to the soldiers fanning out on either side of him.

The soldiers around him saluted with fists across their hearts and headed back toward the three remaining portals. Bayen came to his side, holding his bladed staff at the ready.

"You mean to take out Halcylon?" Bayen asked.

Aaron kept his attention focused on the barrier but nodded.

"Is this wise? He created the Forsaken. How do we know that Halcylon can't unmake what he's done?" Bayen asked.

The Forsaken strained against the barrier, and Aaron felt the pressure in his mind. This barrier was fueled by the energy he continued to gather around him, with the staff working to amplify its effectiveness. It wasn't tethered to the land as the barrier had been in Shandara. He couldn't risk it, or the travel crystals wouldn't work properly.

"I'll ask him just before I kill him," Aaron said through clenched teeth, straining to keep the barrier up. His breath came in gasps, but still he held on.

Bayen glanced behind them. The portals outside the palace were being shut down. Bayen put his hand on Aaron's shoulder. Aaron released the barrier and engaged the travel crystal and took them to the nearest guard tower. Catching his breath, Aaron looked back at the palace. There were still defenders shooting crystal-tipped arrows at the charging Forsaken. He brought up the comms device and saw Halcylon's coordinates. He'd stayed in the Zekaran mobile command center.

"You should go with the others," Aaron said, but Bayen shook his head.

Aaron engaged the travel crystal and took them within sight of the Zekaran mobile command center. The thing was immense, like a floating fortress with turrets and observation decks. With the Zekaran forces focused on the burning city, no one noticed them slip near the massive craft, unobserved.

"What are you going to do now? We can't get inside," Bayen said.

Aaron smiled hungrily. "I'm going to call in some friends."

Bayen's eyes widened. "The Eldarin, but you said it was too dangerous to call upon them."

"I did, but we're surrounded by the enemy and... I can feel them. It's like they are anticipating the call. It's getting harder to resist," Aaron said.

Bayen didn't say anything else but waited for Aaron. He gathered the energy and fed it into the rune-carved staff. They launched into the air, and a few Zekaran troops took a shot at them as they zoomed overhead. They circled around and landed atop the mobile command center. Aaron slammed the staff into its hull, unleashing all the energy in a single blow. Bolts of energy extended out from him, and the vehicle stopped. The turrets nearest him spun around, targeting his position, but he was already moving again. Bayen tossed a small cube at the turret, and after a few seconds it exploded.

"Tanneth gave a couple to me. I only have two more," Bayen said.

Aaron summoned the energy and slammed the staff into the armored hull again, harder than before. A fissure opened, exposing the inner hull. Bayen dropped another cube inside, and they sprinted away.

Bayen pointed to a small tower-like structure. "That's their comms array; if we take it out, it will cripple their communications for a time."

Aaron narrowed his gaze and stepped away from Bayen. "No former member of the Safanarion Order would know this. Are you working for Halcylon?"

Bayen kept his halberd to the side. "I fought at your side most of today, and you doubt me? No, I don't work for Halcylon. Time is short; we can sort this out later."

Bayen was right about that. Time was something they had little of. Troops mustered outside on the ground, with some cresting the roof of the mobile command center. Aaron charged toward them, moving at speeds the Zekara in their powered armor couldn't hope to match. They veered to the side, closing in on the smaller comms tower. Bayen raced ahead and tossed his last explosive cube at it. The cube adhered to the base, and they raced away with the flames of the explosion licking their heels.

Hythariam were a tall race, and the Zekara were a military faction of the same race. A Zekaran soldier in full power armor easily reached a height of seven feet. The cyan lines of their powered armor could be seen through the smoke. The black armor reminded Aaron of when he faced the Drake. Instead of one there were multitudes of them on the field.

"They're weak on the back of their helmets and behind the knees," Bayen said.

Aaron nodded and accepted the young man's knowledge of the Zekara. They raced forward, zigzagging across the massive vehicle. Aaron could sense the lifebeat of the Zekara within the armored hull. He searched, looking for the one Hythariam he had held by the throat while imprisoned on their dying planet. He should have killed Halcylon then. His own life be damned. It would have prevented all of this. *That's not true,* he told himself. The Zekara would have reached Safanar even if he'd traded his own life for Halcylon. They moved on to another comms tower, and Aaron unleashed the pent-up energy from the staff, leaving the tower inoperable. A cluster of soldiers emerged on the roof, and even without sensing the lifebeats of those around, he knew Halcylon was with them. The Zekara charged forward, firing their weapons. Aaron and Bayen weaved through the deadly barrage of plasma bolts. Aaron swung his staff, slamming the end behind the leg of a Zekaran soldier, forcing him to his knees. He followed up with a blow behind the neck, and the soldier went down. Aaron glanced to the side and saw that Bayen had taken out a soldier as well. The Zekara focused their fire on Aaron, and he dashed to the side. On instinct, he reached out and took hold of their lifebeats with tendrils of energy, freezing them in place. They resisted at first, and Aaron drew in more energy from the staff. The Zekara stopped firing their weapons. Aaron closed in on them, with Bayen on his heels. He reached out for the center Zekaran soldier, who had a red slash down his armor, and engaged the travel crystal. The three of them emerged just outside the city walls, well away from the Zekaran army. They stumbled away from each other but quickly recovered.

The Zekaran soldier looked down at the rifle he carried and tossed it to the ground. An armored hand lifted and touched the side of his neck. The helmet retracted, revealing the sneering face of General Halcylon. The Zekaran general withdrew a thick shaft from his back. The shaft extended to the length of a staff, with twin blades on one end.

"Come face me, human," Halcylon said.

Aaron drove the rune-carved staff into the ground and drew his swords. He charged forward and swung his blades. The big Hythariam quickly blocked Aaron's blows, moving with blinding speed. Aaron focused, augmenting his strength and speed that should have overwhelmed Halcylon, but the general was able to stand his ground. Halcylon bounded forward, swinging his bladed staff in wide arcs. Aaron ducked under a deadly swing, trying to move in closer, but as he did so, Halcylon's staff deflected his blows. The Hythariam bared his teeth, with a wicked gleam in his eyes as if he were toying with him.

Aaron stepped back and focused. He wielded the Falcons, forming the bladesong. He no longer heard the whisperings of souls past, as he had melded their influence into his own. He was one. A clear head could mean the difference between survival and death. Aaron darted in, his blades lashing out, driving the Hythariam back. Aaron rained down the blows with blurring speed, working his way closer. He kicked out with an energy-enhanced blow to the side of Halcylon's armored knee. Armor or not, you couldn't protect against the physics of the blow. Aaron spun and back-kicked Halcylon, sending him back several feet. The Hythariam rolled and was instantly on his feet. Halcylon regarded Aaron for a moment.

"What's the matter? We're not as weak as you thought?" Aaron taunted.

"Your city lies in ruins, human." Halcylon smirked.

Aaron leaped forward and shifted his momentum at the last moment, bringing his swords down upon an armored forearm. Halcylon attempted to shove him back, but Aaron stepped to the side and landed another blow. Halcylon grunted under the force of the blow, but Aaron's swords didn't pierce the armor.

Halcylon stepped back, bringing up his staff, aiming it like a rifle. Aaron dodged to the side, avoiding the plasma blast, and dashed forward. The Hythariam smoothly transitioned his fighting form to meet Aaron's attack. The combination of powered armor and Nanites gave the Hythariam super-quick reflexes, but Aaron was faster. He beat Halcylon's staff to the side and slammed the pommel of his sword in the Hythariam's face. The force of the blow left the Zekaran general wobbly on his feet. Aaron yanked Halcylon's staff from his grasp and plunged one of his blades through the Hythariam's midsection. Halcylon's golden eyes widened in disbelief. Aaron lifted his other sword, intent on taking the Hythariam's life, but at the last moment his blade was blocked.

"No!" Bayen cried. "I won't let you," he said, and shoved Aaron back.

Halcylon crumbled to the ground, holding his bleeding stomach.

"Get out of my way, Bayen."

"If you kill him, you'll doom us all," Bayen said, his breath coming in gasps. He hunched for a moment as if he were in pain, then straightened.

Aaron's surroundings became apparent in a rush. The rumbling of the Eldarin grew more intense. The runes on the staff flared to life, and a beam of light shot forth from his medallion to the staff and lit up the smoke filled sky. Aaron felt as if electricity were charging through his skin. Above them a fissure opened in a bright flash of light. Aaron looked up expectantly while at the same time hoping it would close before the Eldarin came through. A wave of darkness plunged through the opening. The beast that flew through dripped inky blackness from its wings, and the great form of what had once been an Eldarin Dragon lord slammed into the ground. The once-vibrant hide had become a shadowy gray. The Ryakul-infected Dragon lord breathed a great sigh and opened its deep red eyes. Those eyes caught sight of Aaron in a mask of pure hatred. Aaron's mouth hung open at the sheer size of the Dragon lord. This was the same Eldarin that had cradled him in its wings while the Zekara and

Ryakuls attacked it. The fallen Eldarin raised its massive head and roared. The force of it hit Aaron like a blow. After a few moments, Aaron heard answering cries, not from any Ryakul, for there were none in the area, but from the Forsaken. Aaron glanced behind him and heard the Forsaken closing in, answering the call of the fallen Eldarin.

The Eldarin lunged forward, snapping at him. Aaron zipped to the side and kicked off from the Eldarin's body, barely missing its claws. The Dragon lord circled around and was on his tail faster than anything he had ever seen. It was all Aaron could do to dodge the massive jaws. On a hunch, Aaron came to an abrupt stop and brought up a barrier. The Eldarin stopped its massive form at almost the same instant that Aaron did. It swiped at Aaron with its claws, but the barrier brushed off the attack. The Eldarin spun, using its tail. Aaron winced as the armored tail slammed into the barrier, but still it held. The Dragon lord reared back, and Aaron felt the waves of energy gathering into it. From behind the barrier, Aaron wielded his Falcons, and the pure notes of the bladesong pierced the air. Aaron pushed out with the melody, sending it to the Eldarin. Tendrils of energy seeped up from the ground, reaching hungrily for the Eldarin. For a moment, the Dragon lord faltered. It shook its massive head to clear it. Those piercing red eyes regarded him, and for an instant they recognized him. The Eldarin's eyes grew wide, losing some of their menacing glare. Aaron released the barrier and reached across the expanse. The lifebeat of the Eldarin was eclipsed by swirling shadows, but Aaron knew that something of its old self was still there. The Ryakul virus hadn't completely vanquished the Eldarin's former self. The Eldarin shook its head, its eyes darting around. The snarling growls from the Forsaken came closer as their blackened forms poured through gaps in the city walls.

The comms device buzzed upon Aaron's wrist, and he risked a glance at it. There was a brief flash of a blue and green light, signaling Rexel's destruction was imminent. A dark shadow swooped down, and a Dragon slammed itself into the disoriented Eldarin. The Dragon was much smaller than the Dragon lord, but with the Ryakul virus present in the Eldarin's physical form, the Dragon attacked on instinct. The Eldarin snapped out of it, and its lifebeat went dark. The Eldarin seized the Dragon by the throat and gouged at its underbelly, then flung the much smaller beast back. Aaron closed the distance to the Dragon and brought out the travel crystal. He didn't know whether he could successfully take the dragon with him, but he would be damned if he wasn't going to try. A blinding light turned the sky from purple to orange, and the ground shook beneath him. Aaron reached out and touched the Dragon's hide and engaged the travel crystal. He pulled in all the energy he could muster and pushed in through the crystal. For a moment, nothing happened. Smoldering heat blasted the side of him closest to the walls, and then they were gone. Aaron and the Dragon emerged many miles away from Rexel. He collapsed to the ground. The searing heat blistered his skin. Aaron's breath came in gasps, and he tried to focus his mind. He needed a clear head if he was going to be able to channel the energy to heal his wounds. The armor the Hythariam had provided him with protected much of his body, but still the pain was almost overwhelming. Aaron closed his eyes and blocked out the pain. His breath evened out, and he focused on drawing in the energy, urging his body to repair itself. Burned skin fell away from the side of his face and neck—that was a mix of pain and itchy relief. Aaron opened his eyes and touched the side of his face that had been burned. It felt just like his other side, down to the stubble of his beard from lack of shaving.

He slowly came to his feet. The Dragon that came to his aid lay next to him, its body quivering, and its breath seemed to come with a slight wheeze. The Dragon's bluish hide had deep gashes from the Eldarin's claws. Aaron surveyed the wounds grimly, and the Dragon's tired eyes opened.

She still lives, Ferasdiam marked, the Dragon spoke in his mind.

It took Aaron a moment to realize that the Dragon was referring to the Eldarin.

She hasn't fallen fully into the abyss.

The Dragon's eyes squeezed shut, its blood soaking the ground at its feet. Aaron drew in the energy and pushed it into the Dragon, trying to repair the wounds, but the damage was too much. The Dragon opened its eyes that were once fierce and vibrant but were now only moments from death.

You must save her...

I will. I promise, Aaron said.

The Dragon's final breath was released in a great sigh, and the vibrancy of its hide faded to a misty gray. Aaron felt a presence almost tease along the edges of his senses, and then it was gone. He had felt this before in Shandara, when his grandfather's soul at last came to rest. The soul of the Dragon had left its broken body, which rapidly diminished until a vague impression in the ground was its only mark. The Dragon had confirmed what Aaron had suspected. The Eldarin had not fully succumbed to the Ryakul virus. There was still hope of beating it.

Aaron searched the ground for the travel crystal and found it shattered to pieces. It was his last one. He scanned the skyline and saw smoke rising in the distance. He brought up the comms device, but it wouldn't respond. It wasn't dead because he saw the tiny glow of power inside, but the screen was still blank. Aaron glanced at the smoke. It was the middle of the afternoon. If the travel crystal worked properly, he should only be a few miles from where he was supposed to meet the others. He hoped they escaped the destruction of the city. The rune-carved staff must have been destroyed in the blast. Hopefully the explosion took out a good chunk of the Zekara. Maybe even Halcylon as well. Thoughts of the Zekaran general made him think of Bayen. He had stopped Aaron from killing Halcylon. Why would he do that? *You'll kill us all,* Bayen had said. He hoped Bayen made it out of there. Bayen had fought at his side only to betray him at the last instant. Aaron didn't know what to make of it. He wanted answers, and he hoped the mysterious young man was still alive to give them. Aaron started walking, preferring to go at a normal pace so he could collect his thoughts. Rexel lost. People dying or being turned into the Forsaken. The day's events were the stuff of nightmares. He felt the weight of all those deaths of the people he failed to protect. Aaron pushed his scattering thoughts to the side of his mind while his body went into the rhythmic pace of traversing the land around him. He needed to focus on solutions, not the problems. In his mind, he started making mental lists, breaking down the destruction of Rexel, trying to glean what they could have done differently. Halcylon had masterfully played his hand. Even though they had sacrificed the city in hopes of weakening the enemy, the sting of defeat was a bitter pill to swallow.

Halcylon counted on their dependence on Hythariam technology. He had used it against them. They needed to find a way to turn the tables.

Aaron's thoughts turned to the Eldarin. The Forsaken had responded to the fallen Eldarin. It was something he hadn't considered. He knew that the Forsaken would throw themselves at him, but with the Eldarin it was something different. The Forsaken by themselves were perhaps a step or two beyond mindless aggression.

At least Rexel's sacrifice had done one thing: The rising number of Forsaken had been halted for the moment. Aaron silently cursed Bayen for keeping him from taking Halcylon's life. If they couldn't stop the Zekara the next time they met, then all of Safanar would pay the price.

CHAPTER 19
CAPTURE

Sarah's footsteps pounded along the flat rooftops of the warehouse district near the river. The Zekaran infiltrator was barreling along the street below her. She pulled in the energy and closed the distance between them. Over the years, she had found that few could match her speed, and Beck, the rogue Elite Master who trained her, had said speed was something you were born with. You either had it, or you didn't, and Sarah had it in abundance. The only one to match her was Aaron, whom she enjoyed testing whenever the chance presented itself. Here and now, her speed was an asset to her and a source of frustration to Rordan and the Elitesmen who chased her. She collected the energy into an orb in her hand and sent it streaking ahead. The orb slammed into the back of the infiltrator, but its armor shrugged off the blow.

Sarah leaped down to the street and closed in on the infiltrator. She heard the mechanical whirl of its powered armor. Another of her attack orbs demolished the ground at the infiltrator's feet, causing it to stumble. Sarah pounced on it, kicking the infiltrator into the building. The infiltrator stumbled and fell, then quickly regained its feet and charged ahead. Sarah heard her brother call out from behind her. She wasn't sure of the range of his attack, but she knew she must be beyond it because he hadn't attacked her as he had done in the warehouse. A faint ache in her chest pressed in on her lungs. She was tiring. So quickly? How could that be? Then she remembered. Roselyn had warned her that her pregnancy would leave her feeling tired. Gritting her teeth, Sarah pushed onward. The infiltrator was heading to a more populated district to spread the virus. Where were Isaac and the others? They should be here by now. The stone archway separating the districts was just up ahead. She caught up to the infiltrator, and it immediately shot a few plasma bolts at her. Sarah yelled out for the gates to be closed, but as the guards ahead moved to carry out her orders, the infiltrator killed them with its cursed plasma pistol. The denizens of the district passing the archway ran out of the way. The infiltrator burst through the archway into the crowded district beyond.

Sarah grabbed a sword off a dead guard. As she went through the archway, she found the Zekaran infiltrator leveling its pistol in her direction. She slid down by its legs, lashing out with her sword as she passed. Sarah quickly got to her feet, spun around, and slammed her sword down upon the infiltrator's armored hand. She kicked the plasma pistol away.

The infiltrator grabbed for Sarah, but she deftly leaped back. She shouted for the people in the streets to get back. The infiltrator spun around as it scanned the area. Sarah didn't give it any more time before she attacked. She had to keep it busy. The others were coming, but so was her brother. Dark-clad Elitesmen came through the archway, but Sarah focused on the infiltrator. The infiltrator kept trying to maneuver her into Rordan and the others, but Sarah wouldn't oblige it. The Elitesmen closing in faltered. Sarah risked a glance up and saw Free Nations Army soldiers crest the top of the buildings surrounding them all. They fired their weapons on the Elitesmen, scattering them. Rordan darted from the ring of Elitesmen and dove for her. Sarah sidestepped out of the way and snatched at the chain around his neck. She yanked the amulet as hard as she could, snapping the chain. Rordan stumbled toward the infiltrator. Hythariam soldiers with the FNA surrounded the Zekaran infiltrator, lashing out with their blades at different armored parts. Sparks burst from the infiltrator's powered armor, and it sank to its knees. The infiltrator raised its arm, and a panel opened. Yellow gas shot toward Rordan and Sarah. An Elitesman leaped forward, trying to pull her brother from the path, but instead was pulled in by Rordan's flailing. The breath caught in Sarah's chest, and she stumbled backward, desperate to get away. The yellow substance billowed against an invisible wall. Sarah glanced up and saw Isaac standing there with an outstretched hand, his face a mask of concentration. Sarah and the other humans backed away, allowing the Hythariam to move in and finish off the infiltrator.

Sarah kept waiting for the infiltrator to self-destruct, but all it did was collapse. Rordan and the other Elitesmen were writhing on the ground. The yellow substance dissipated from within the confines of Isaac's shield. A Hythariam soldier motioned for Isaac to release the shield so the others could get close to Rordan and the Elitesmen. They restrained Rordan first, with bands that held his arms and feet tightly together. As they turned over an Elitesman, Sarah gasped as she saw his face. The other man exposed to the Ryakul virus was Darven, Mactar's apprentice. It all clicked into place. Darven was the experienced leader that guided Rordan.

The Hythariam finished restraining Darven. She stepped closer to Rordan, who was straining against his bonds, with his head shaking violently. He kept growling, and Sarah lifted her sword. Rordan deserved death for all the people he murdered.

"Your Grace, we need to get them back to Hathenwood. Roselyn needs live specimens in order to find a cure," the Hythariam soldier said.

Sarah stared at the Hythariam for a moment and then back down at Rordan, inching closer. She wanted to kill him. They could take Darven back with them to find a cure. As the seconds dripped by, the virus took a firm hold of her brother.

"Your Grace, please. We must get them into the capsule and move them, or it will be too late."

At last, Sarah nodded, and the Hythariam looked relieved.

"Soldier," Sarah said.

"Baylor, your Grace."

"We have travel crystals," Sarah said.

Baylor shook his head. "We don't want to risk it. We brought a keystone accelerator to open a portal for us. We'll signal ahead so they can prepare."

The Hythariam loaded Rordan and Darven into separate capsules that hissed shut. After a few moments, all movement ceased from within them.

Isaac approached her. "Are you all right, my Lady?"

Sarah surveyed the area and took a deep breath. "It was a close thing, Isaac. The infiltrator was trying to reach a more crowded area to release the virus. How were they able to take it down before it destroyed itself?"

"We only found out that they could do it moments before we

reached you. I was contacted through that comms device, and Baylor told us not to engage the infiltrator. He and his people would handle it. I'm glad they were here," Isaac said.

"Make sure our people know how to take those things down. We can't afford even one of those things loose in the city," Sarah said.

The FNA soldiers activated the keystone accelerator, and a portal sheared open. The FNA soldiers went through, and Sarah followed. Isaac didn't even question her but simply followed her lead. It was as it should be. Rordan had taken so many lives in his attempt to draw her out, and she didn't want to let him out of her sight.

CHAPTER 20
THEORY

Halcylon rose from the ground. The Nanites worked to repair the wound in his stomach. Twice now that human, Aaron Jace, had held him by the throat. The first time on Hytharia, he'd known the human would attack. He'd goaded Aaron into it. He should have killed the human then and been done with it.

What he hadn't counted on was the human's restraint. The human had some intelligence, Halcylon admitted, but his enemy suffered no such restraint today. He had been a soldier for hundreds of years. Defeated the mighty to become leader of his race. Survived years of bloody conflict where so many others had perished. Halcylon glanced down at the fibered layers of his armor that stitched itself back together. The human's sword should not have been able to pierce his armor, yet his newly healed wound contradicted what had been fact before. His irritation was compounded by the fact that if it weren't for the other human's interference, his life would be over. Halcylon pressed his lips together in thought. The human in the white armor. Bayen is what Aaron had called him. Halcylon's wounds had already begun to heal when the explosion leveled most of the city. This Bayen had dragged him beyond the blast and for a moment looked as if he too would try to take Halcylon's life. Instead, the young human left him and disappeared. Halcylon returned to the mobile command center. His soldiers saluted him as he passed, a hungry gleam to their eyes. They had performed flawlessly. The victory over the humans was nearly perfect except for the bomb. He hadn't accounted for anything like that in his plans. Halcylon entered his quarters and gave the command for his armor to remove itself. He wanted a full diagnostic run on the armor and the combat AI. He needed to understand how he was beaten in order to assure victory at the next confrontation.

Halcylon headed through the narrow corridors to the operations center.

"Situation report," Halcylon ordered as he entered.

Chinta, his second in command, saluted him. "The explosion leveled most of the city. Most of our troops were still in the outer recesses and suffered some bumps and bruises. Those closer to the blast weren't so lucky."

"What about the infected? Do we have any prisoners?" Halcylon asked.

"The blast centered from the palace, which was where the infected had converged. So far, we've only found pockets of humans and infected. Repairs to our vehicles are underway. Our enemy had a few surprises for us, but up until the blast the battle pretty much went as we expected," Chinta said.

"Except for the bomb," Halcylon said, and an uneasy silence descended upon them.

Chinta nodded. "We also believe they know we've tapped their communications."

Halcylon shrugged. "They were bound to pick up on it sooner or later."

Chinta eyed him for a moment. "They? Don't you mean Iranus?"

"The scientist, no. Iranus may be among the leaders of the traitors, but he wasn't of the military. The name that keeps cropping up on their comms channels is Gavril Sorindal," Halcylon said.

A coldness swept through the room. Gavril had been one of them before the portal to Safanar had been shut. Halcylon had discovered that Gavril had been aiding the traitors and was among those directly responsible for stranding their race on Hytharia. Gavril had been the head of his intelligence operations, and his betrayal had been a surprise. Halcylon would have his reckoning with him and all the rest of the traitors for the crimes they'd visited upon the Zekara.

Halcylon scanned the faces around him until he found who he was looking for. "Ronin, I've observed some odd behavior from the infected humans. There is a creature just outside the city walls. It's a mix of a Dragon and a Ryakul but much larger. The infected humans seem to be drawn to it. It was overriding the expected protocols."

Ronin pursed his lips in thought. "The virus at its foundation is the same. We may have modified it for humans, but we didn't change the underlying core. Perhaps it saw a kindred spirit. One of the same, but an alpha in the hierarchy."

"I've also seen reports of many of them being drawn to the human," Halcylon said. There was no need for him to be specific. Everyone around him knew which of the primitive species he was referring to.

"I've seen the same reports. That I can't account for at the moment, but I do have a theory if you're interested," Ronin offered.

"This should be interesting," Chinta murmured.

"Proceed," Halcylon ordered.

"The two appear to be natural enemies. One of the core functions of the virus is to spread itself in order to thrive. Perhaps it senses something different about Aaron," Ronin said. The others around began objecting. "Oh, don't be so ridiculous, the humans, as primitive as they are, have names. You must admit the human was able to achieve things that we're only able to do assisted with our technology. So in keeping with the virus's core functions—to spread itself—presents a strong correlation to why it targets Aaron above all other humans."

"Which is?" Halcylon asked.

"Because it believes that he represents the best way for it to spread itself," Ronin said.

"And the Dragon hybrid?" Halcylon asked.

"I believe it could be something similar. I will examine the creature if I can get close enough," Ronin said.

"Take a squad with you. As far as I know, it hasn't moved. If I had to guess, I would say it's in the middle of its transformation, which should have been completed by now. You're dismissed, Ronin," Halcylon said.

"There is another matter I'd like to bring to your attention," Chinta said.

"Proceed."

"We've found further evidence of soldiers' death from wounds that could only be inflicted by a maul-cat," Chinta said.

"When were they killed?" Halcylon asked.

Chinta frowned, glancing at the report in front of him. "Just after the battle. They were found inside the city. They were searching through the wreckage for anything we can use."

Halcylon nodded. "We have a bigger problem than one maul-cat. Our enemy has perfected the use of the keystone accelerator. It is the only reason so many were able to escape. We need to figure out where they went. We also need to build up the number of infected humans again before the next phase of our attack."

What Halcylon said was true, but the presence of the maul-cat did worry him. He couldn't let on how much it concerned him because he needed for his people to focus on the tasks he set for them.

"How many infiltrators can we bring online?" Halcylon asked.

"We have only twenty more units, sir," Chinta replied.

"Deploy fifteen of them, and save the remainder for the attack on Shandara. I want the remains of the city searched for any of our technology. The keystone accelerators would be a valuable addition for our resources," Halcylon said.

They had their orders. Now Halcylon wanted to take a look at the remnants of the city for himself. The next battle would be harder for them. A smart enemy would study his opponent, and he was willing to bet that the human... Aaron... had learned a great deal by this encounter. No matter. The human race was finished. They just didn't know it yet. Once he conquered Shandara, the power issues for his machines would be resolved, and that would allow them to build more of a tech base from which to rule this planet. Halcylon left the mobile command center and headed toward the smoky remains of the first Safanarion city to fall to them. It wouldn't be the last.

CHAPTER 21

RUSE

Aaron was still piecing the battle together in his mind and would need to consult with Gavril to be sure about how they were defeated. They had been blindsided. What would it take to defeat Halcylon? The Zekaran general had shown a level of ruthlessness that rivaled that of the High King. Is that what was required of him so they could survive? Could he become that person?

He kept seeing the faces of the dead. Aaron's brow furrowed as he lost himself in his thoughts. His breath caught in his lungs, and he felt a great weight press down upon his chest. Aaron blew out his breath and let his gaze drift skyward. He shook his head and kept going. A soft breeze blew along the grass, and he inhaled the sweet smells of wild flowers. Aaron could smell the faint odor of cook fires from a camp up ahead. He quickened his steps, believing that he would reach the camp just over the next hill. The closer he got, the more he realized that it wasn't the FNA encampment. Gleeful shouts of children playing seemed foreign to his ears and stood in stark contrast to the horrors he had witnessed this day.

Aaron came over the hill and stopped. Below was a camp mostly made up of brightly painted wagons constructed as small houses on wheels. People went along doing their daily chores. Clothes hung drying along the lines between the wagons. The place was so calm and serene that just the sight of it made Aaron think he had strayed into a dream. An older man came from behind a wagon and greeted Aaron with a warm smile.

"Tolvar," Aaron whispered.

The bald man in a gray shirt and brown trousers waved at him. "We meet again," Tolvar said, and glanced up at the sky. "No Ryakuls following you this time?"

Aaron closed his mouth and felt the edges of his lips curve. "Not this time," Aaron replied.

Tolvar made a show of looking past him and tilted his head in mock disappointment. "No princess this time either." Tolvar sighed.

Aaron chuckled. "I'm afraid not. Should I turn around and leave?"

Tolvar laughed and put a companionable arm around Aaron's shoulder. "Don't be silly, my boy. You are exactly where you need to be right now."

"Is that right? Truth be told, I don't know where I am," Aaron said, and glanced down at the comms device on his wrist.

Tolvar followed his gaze. "Not to worry. Your friends will be joining us soon enough."

Aaron frowned. "How do you know?"

Tolvar chuckled again. "Some of us see with eyes beyond that of ordinary men."

Aaron sensed the energy swirling around Tolvar, strongly rooted to the ground. "I remember," Aaron said, some of the somberness returning to his voice.

Tolvar glanced at him. "Come, I've just the thing to lift those with a heavy heart."

"But, Tolvar. Rexel... Prince Cyrus..."

"Come, we will take our ease by the fire, and you can tell me what has happened," Tolvar said.

Tolvar guided Aaron through the camp, and many stopped what they were doing to offer a quick greeting. They were joined by Tolvar's son, Armel, a grizzly-looking man with a burly brown beard that reached down his broad chest. He flipped a small ax in his beefy hand as he walked.

"Care for another go?" Armel offered, but Aaron shook his head.

Tolvar took him to a basin of water so he could wash. Aaron wished he could soak for a few hours in a tub of hot water, but this would have to do. When he was finished, he was amazed at how dirty the water was.

'There, that's better. Have some of this," Tolvar said, and offered him a tankard. "It's our dark ale with a little something extra. Speaking of extra, I really do wish that princess of yours was here."

"You and me both. She's the High Queen now," Aaron said.

Tolvar nodded. "She'll do well, and so will you."

Aaron thanked him and took a long swallow. Whatever Tolvar had put in the ale blazed a path down his throat. He felt waves of warmth spread out through his core, and some of the tension drained away from between his shoulders. Tolvar and Armel took a sip from their tankards and waited for him to begin. Aaron told them of the events that had taken place over the past few days. From their first encounter with the Zekaran infiltrator and the Forsaken to their defeat at Rexel.

Tolvar exchanged a few glances with his son. "Cyrus was a good man. I'm truly sorry to hear of his passing," Tolvar said.

Aaron raised his tankard in a silent toast for those who had fallen today and took another long swallow.

"Halcylon is going to spread the Ryakul virus. No human is safe. The battle at Rexel was something out of a nightmare. Friends and comrades who fought at your side rising again only to turn on you. No one was spared, and nothing we did could stop it. He defeated us so utterly."

Tolvar frowned. "War is a nasty business."

"I don't know how to defeat him," Aaron admitted.

"The same way you defeated the High King. With heart, faith, and skill. And certainly not alone. I know Reymius taught you that half of the battle is here," Tolvar said, tapping the side of his head. "You carry a great many burdens, but I get the sense there is more."

Aaron set his tankard down and paced for a few steps. The energy sparked within him. He hadn't realized he had seized it and quickly let it go. In the brief moments he held the energy, he sensed the presence of the Eldarin. They were restless, waiting for his call, but the risk was too great.

"What good is being Ferasdiam marked if I can't help them?" Aaron said.

"Who?" Tolvar asked.

"The Eldarin. One is infected with the same virus that turns Dragons into Ryakuls."

"Do you know what it means to be Ferasdiam marked? One who has been marked by fate?"

Aaron met Tolvar's gaze but didn't answer.

"Because you were born different. You are the bridge across all life forms," Tolvar said.

Life's champion. The Dragon's words echoed in Aaron's mind.

"Colind warned me of the danger of being Ferasdiam marked. How I could traverse to the higher planes where the Eldarin reside, but I wouldn't be able to come back," Aaron said.

"Colind is correct in that you possess within you the potential to cast away your physical form. Returning is completely up to you."

Aaron tilted his head in thought. "Not just me."

Tolvar smiled. "Your assertion that the potential is with us all is correct. But you are more in tune with our realm than anyone else. Even now, I bet you can sense the lifebeat of every living creature in this camp without any effort at all."

He could, and in a place such as this, his gift drove the point home just how precious life really was. "The High King used his power to control everyone. He said it was the destiny of the Ferasdiam marked. I swore it was something I wouldn't do, but during the battle…"

"Amorak's heart was black long before. He may have been a good man once, but power has a way of corrupting a person," Tolvar said.

"That's why I'm afraid. I won't become like him. But I can feel it inside. The ability to control things. I'm afraid I could become exactly like him. What if the only way to defeat Halcylon is to become like the High King?"

"You are wise to fear your power, and the same holds true for anyone regardless of their abilities. That's what makes you better than the High King could ever be. Has it occurred to you that the energy you use is inside everything around us?" Tolvar asked.

Aaron glanced around him. "You mean living things?"

"Not just living things as you think they are," Tolvar said.

Aaron bent down and scooped up a stone. "Are you saying this rock is alive?"

Tolvar shook his head. "Of course not, but it does have an energy all its own. Can you feel it… vibrating?"

Aaron looked at the stone but didn't sense anything. "I'm not exactly sure what you mean. I used the bladesong to lift one of the boulders in Colind's prison."

"You're on the right track. You used the actual sound that your blades emit to move the boulder. Now try it without your blades," Tolvar said.

"But the sound is how it worked the last time," Aaron said.

Tolvar just nodded toward the stone. Aaron took a deep breath and quieted his mind. He drew in the energy and sent a tendril around the stone he held in his hand.

"Just explore it. Feel what it's made off. How it holds together," Tolvar urged.

Aaron probed the rough surface of the stone. He allowed the tendril of energy to become infused into the hard surface. The rock warmed in his hand. The deeper he probed, the hotter it became. Aaron gasped and dropped the stone to the ground.

"That was wonderful," Tolvar exclaimed. "I told you he was a quick learner," Tolvar said to his son.

Aaron tore his eyes from the stone. "It got so hot."

"To be expected."

"Thank you for showing me this, but I'm not sure how useful it will be."

Tolvar waved his comment away. "One more tool in your arsenal. Regardless, I'm sure you'll see the benefits of this knowledge very soon," Tolvar said.

"We've been rebuilding the Safanarion Order. Some of the old members have returned. We would be honored if you could help us."

Tolvar frowned. "To fight the Zekara?"

"How you help is up to you. Just sharing some of your knowledge would help," Aaron said.

Armel shifted his stance and stared pointedly at his father.

Tolvar took a draining swallow from the tankard he held. "The things I have to teach can't be learned in a few days."

"But it could mean the difference between life or death for some," Aaron countered.

"Father," Armel said. "I will help them."

"Armel—"

"Not this time," Armel said. "This is different, and you know it."

Tolvar frowned but didn't say anything.

"What's different?" Aaron asked.

"We've taken an oath not to do battle unless we're defending ourselves," Tolvar said.

Armel grumbled something under his breath and stalked away from them.

"Oh, I didn't know," Aaron said, and paused. "I don't mean to cause you and your people trouble."

Tolvar shook his head. "It's not you. When Shandara fell, we lost a number of our people, and Armel has never forgiven himself for not being there."

The fall, Aaron thought. So many lives had been ruined when Shandara fell.

"Shandara is being rebuilt—" Aaron started to say but was cut off by Armel calling for them.

They headed to the far side of the camp. Hovering above the ground was the *Raven.* His heart leaped in his chest. The airship was battered and beat up, but it was such a welcoming sight. The holes in the dark hull and the gaps along the railings only hinted at the battle the ship had been in.

Verona leaped down from the deck.

"Well, look who we found," Verona said, and pulled him in for a bear hug. "I'm glad I told Morgan to bring us to that column of smoke."

Aaron was too startled by the greeting to say anything. When last they spoke, Verona had blamed him for the city falling. Aaron knew Verona hadn't meant what he said, but the words still stung. He should have been able to do more.

"My friend, I must apologize to you. I had no right to place Rexel's destruction at your feet," Verona said.

"You don't need to apologize to me. I'm just glad you made it out of there alive," Aaron said.

They didn't say anything for a few moments. "I'm sorry about your uncle. Cyrus was a good man," Aaron said, trying to keep his own emotions in check.

Verona drew in a shaky breath and nodded. "Nathaniel and I spoke at length after we were clear of the city… I just can't believe Rexel is gone. When you spoke to me about your home being gone, I was sympathetic, but I had no idea what it was like to lose everything you've ever known."

"We'll rebuild it. I'll help you," Aaron said.

Verona nodded. "I'll hold you to that, my friend."

"Tell me what happened to you. How you ended up on the *Raven*," Aaron said.

"I will, but first, who is this with you?"

Aaron was confused for a moment and followed Verona's gaze. Tolvar stood a few feet behind them and gave them a friendly wave. Aaron apologized and made the introductions.

"I'm glad to finally meet you, Tolvar. Aaron has told me quite a bit about you," Verona said, giving a small bow.

"You're a friendly sort. We'll share some ale with you, but I will tell you: you're no princess," Tolvar said.

Verona chuckled and looked at Aaron. "That reminds me. Is your comms device working? Sarah is in Hathenwood with Roselyn. She threatened all of our hides if we didn't find you."

"It stopped working. If Tanneth is with you, I'll get him to look at it."

"He's with us and should be along any moment," Verona said.

"What's Sarah doing in Hathenwood? She was in Khamearra, hunting her brother."

"She captured two of the Forsaken and brought them to Roselyn to examine," Verona answered.

Aaron's gaze hardened for a moment, and then he let his angst go. She was safe now, and that was all that mattered.

"You should speak to her," Verona said.

"I will."

"No. You really need to speak to her. The sooner, the better," Verona pressed.

Aaron frowned. "Okay."

Admiral Morgan came down the gangplank and gave Aaron a grim nod. "You have no idea how relieved we are that you're all right. Sarah assured us that you were alive, but—"

Aaron was about to respond when he saw a familiar figure in white armor.

"You!" Aaron shouted, taking several strides.

Bayen glared at Aaron, and though he held his bladed staff loosely in his hands, Aaron knew Bayen was ready to use it at a moment's notice.

"What is it?" Verona asked. "He retrieved your staff from the battlefield. We escaped the blast because of him."

"He's a traitor," Aaron said.

"I'm the traitor?" Bayen asked. "It's you who act without thought of consequence."

"I had Halcylon by the throat. I was about to finish him off until you stopped me," Aaron said.

The others all turned to Bayen, with some placing their hands on their weapons.

Bayen sprang forward, grabbing Aaron by his shirt. "I'm not gonna let you do it," he sneered. "I'm not going to let you doom us all."

Aaron shoved him back, and Bayen brought his bladed staff up. The others drew their weapons. He needed answers. Bayen was hiding something, but what?

"No," Aaron said to the others, and drew his own swords, facing Bayen. "What happened to you? Did I wrong you in another life?" Aaron asked.

Bayen glared at him, his face a mask of some inner torment. His blue eyes, like liquid lightning, bored into him, full of hate. He growled and swung his halberd. The bladed end met the Falcons in a harsh metallic clang.

"Come on, Bayen. Let it out. You can do better than that," Aaron taunted.

Bayen howled and threw himself at him. Aaron gave himself over to the rhythmic dance, taking everything that Bayen could throw at him and more. This was the only way. The others backed away, giving them room. Bayen charged. His attacks were precise and powerful at first, but the longer they fought, the more Bayen gave over to his emotions. Aaron needed to wear him down.

"What was done to you that made you this way?" Aaron asked.

Bayen kept charging at him, his eyes blazing. "Choices," he snarled.

Aaron trapped Bayen's blade with his own and kicked out, knocking Bayen to the ground. Aaron let his swords fall. Bayen abandoned his weapon and came at him with clenched fists.

The FNA soldiers that came from the airship kept their distance but watched intently, waiting to see if they were needed.

"What choices?" Aaron asked.

Bayen swung and missed. Panting and exhausted, he still came. Bayen no longer had his rigid control, and his focus slipped.

"Choices were stolen from me. I deserved the right to choose for myself. It's my life, but you stole it from me."

Me?

Bayen's blows pounded upon Aaron's defenses. He grabbed Bayen's wrist and pinned his arm behind him. Bayen struggled at first but eventually relented, his breath coming in harsh gasps. Then he stepped back while driving his body forward, tossing Aaron forward, too. The two them rolled forward and were on their feet in almost perfect unison.

"Tell me the rest," Aaron said, waving him on with leaden arms.

Bayen was silent, his body rigid with cold fury.

"If it's me you want, come on," Aaron said.

Bayen strode up to him and swung his fist. Aaron let himself be hit. Blow after blow, they came, but Aaron didn't stop him. He had to take what Bayen could give. It was the only way.

"He stole my life away. I should have been there!" Bayen shouted.

"Who? Tell me who stole your life away."

His lips trembling, Bayen glared at him with bloodshot eyes. "*You* did. While everyone else died, *you* kept me locked away. Safe while Safanar burned around us. The Ryakul plague is your fault. Safanar dies because of your thoughtless actions." Bayen collapsed to his knees, holding his chest. His face crumpled in pain.

"Me?" Aaron asked, kneeling in front of him.

"Warning. Temporal matrix is below 50 percent and falling," a voice said, coming from Bayen's bracer.

Whatever was causing Bayen's pain lessened, and he opened his eyes.

"Who are you?" Aaron asked.

Bayen's breathing evened out, and he leveled his gaze at Aaron. "I'm your son. You sent me back through time to prevent the Ryakul plague from happening. Only I keep failing," Bayen said, biting off the last words.

Aaron's eyes widened. "My son? That's impossible. I have no son."

The silence dragged for a few moments until he heard Verona curse from behind him.

"Aaron," Verona said softly as he came next to him. "There is something you need to know."

Aaron tore his eyes from Bayen.

"Sarah didn't want to tell you because of everything else going on, but Roselyn sent word that I should tell you if the situation warranted. I believe this qualifies. Sarah is pregnant, " Verona said.

Aaron's mind raced to oblivion. *Pregnant? Sarah? A son... Bayen is my son? Impossible.* He stood up and called out to the nearest FNA soldier. "I want him bound and under guard. Take that bracer off, and have it analyzed."

Verona's eyes widened in shock. "Why?"

Aaron glared down at Bayen. "Because he's a spy for Halcylon."

Verona glanced between Aaron and Bayen. "How do you know?"

"This is something Halcylon could put together to fool all of us. He created a clone of me to fool all of you, remember? What's to prevent him from creating another clone that's a little bit different and with an imprint of false memories? It's a little too convenient. Bayen shows up just when we first encountered the infiltrator, exposing us to the virus," Aaron said, his mind racing as he stared down at Bayen. "No, this is exactly what Halcylon would do to spin us in circles. I won't have it."

"But Aaron," Verona began, "what if he's telling the truth?"

"He's not," Aaron said.

Verona reached out to him. "Hear me out. What if he is who he says he is? Just for a moment."

"Those things overran Rexel. Before long the countryside could be crawling with the Forsaken. And Halcylon is going to head to Shandara next. If Shandara falls, there is nowhere else for anyone to fall back to. I could have killed Halcylon at Rexel, but Bayen stopped me."

"That's it," Verona said. "Bayen stopped you. How could that be? My friend, as a warrior, you have no equal that I've seen. Yet here we have Bayen, who was able to go toe to toe with you. He fought at your side this whole day, and for what? You're Ferasdiam marked. Elitesmen and the like have thrown themselves against you. The only way I can see it is that Bayen was able to stand against you because he knew how to face you. He was able to keep up with you? Now, how could that be?"

Aaron felt his breath catch in his throat. *Sarah pregnant. Bayen is my son?* His eyes darted around as he came to grips with what Verona was telling him. *The Ryakul plague is your fault. Safanar dies because of your thoughtless actions.* Bayen's words played in his mind.

"There is only one answer, and you know it, my friend. He was trained by you. I could tell by the way he fights. This isn't something that Halcylon could copy," Verona said.

Aaron felt his stomach turn to lead. *Could it be? No, this is a trick.*

Aaron waved for the soldiers to bring Bayen's body; it was slumped forward. "You said that I sent you back in time to prevent the Ryakul plague? How were you going to do that? How would you know if you succeeded?"

Bayen's eyes were distant for a moment, and then they locked on Aaron. "Because I would cease to exist."

"Warning. Temporal matrix is at 47 percent."

"What is that?" Aaron asked.

"It's the AI that I brought with me. It's warning me that time is running out," Bayen said.

"How is keeping Halcylon alive going to prevent the destruction you've described?" Aaron asked.

Bayen glanced at his bracer, and Aaron nodded for the soldiers to let Bayen go.

"Sam, what is the greatest probability for preventing the Ryakul plague?" Bayen spoke into his bracer.

"Keep General Halcylon alive. 55 percent success probability rate," a monotone voice said from Bayen's bracer.

Aaron glanced at Verona and Tanneth, but both were at a loss for words. "You're basing your actions upon what a machine is telling you?"

"Do you have a better suggestion? Your actions led me here, and Safanar is upon the brink of destruction," Bayen said.

"So you say," Aaron said, unimpressed.

Bayen took a steadying breath. "The AI in this bracer represents the last-ditch efforts to save our world. The last remnants of the Safanarion Order poured their resources into creating this to help them cure the virus."

"The virus only affects humans. How will curing it save the world?" Aaron asked.

Bayen sank to his knees, shoulders slumped. "The virus spread. Nothing was beyond its grasp."

"The Hythariam are immune to it," Aaron said.

Bayen shook his head. "Not in my time. Nothing is immune, and there is no cure. That's why I was sent. To prevent this from happening in the first place."

Aaron rubbed his eyes with his hand, thinking. "What about the Eldarin? They are tied to this."

Bayen frowned. "Sam, what is the probability of the Eldarin and cure for the plague?"

"The Eldarin represent an unknown quantity, and therefore their influence on the course of events is inconclusive," the AI answered.

"I still don't know if I believe any of this," Aaron said.

Tanneth stepped forward. "Computer, who inputted the parameters for probabilities concerning the Ryakul plague?"

"Aaron Jace of the House Alenzar'seth. Leader of the Safanarion Order and chancellor of the Free Nations," the AI said.

Aaron glanced at Tanneth. "We can't trust this thing. This could have been coded into the AI."

"Perhaps," Tanneth said. "Computer. Identify the man standing to Aaron's right."

The holo display glowed upon Bayen's wrist, and a beam of light scanned Verona.

"Verona Ryder, nephew of Prince Cyrus, the last ruler of Rexel. Current status: deceased," the AI said.

Verona frowned. "I'm very much alive, thank you very much."

"Of course," Tanneth said. "The AI is referring to the current status in the future. If we asked it all of our statuses, it would likely say we are all dead. Aaron is right; we're dealing with a machine. If I were to make my guess upon the facts before me, I would wager that Bayen is who he says he is."

"How can you be so sure?" Aaron asked.

"As resourceful as Halcylon is, there is no way he would know so much detailed information about Verona. I would continue to wager that the AI has detailed information about most of us, and there is no way Halcylon could know about that."

"But time travel?" Aaron asked.

Tanneth shrugged. "That is beyond my expertise," Tanneth said, and knelt down to examine Bayen's bracer.

"What's the problem with time travel?" Verona asked.

"It's impossible," Aaron said.

Verona laughed. "You've traveled to two worlds through a portal, and yet time travel is where you draw the line of what is possible."

A small smile lifted the edges of Aaron's mouth. "It's not that simple. I understand the concept of what the keystone accelerator does. What it doesn't do is enable someone to travel back almost twenty years in the past."

Verona pursed his lips together and stepped closer to Aaron. "I don't think he's lying. Something in my gut tells me that he's telling the truth."

Aaron frowned. "Bayen seems to believe what he's saying. I'll give you that. But that doesn't mean it's the truth. Sending him back through time to prevent me from killing Halcylon? How does that make any sense?"

"Aaron, you're gonna want to hear this," Tanneth called. "Listen to this. Sam, what is the current status of Aaron Jace?"

"Aaron Jace is currently alive," the AI said.

Aaron shared a look with Tanneth.

"Of course he's alive," Verona said, and glanced at Aaron and Tanneth. "What is it?"

"The AI believes I am alive. A few moments ago, it reported you as dead," Aaron said.

Verona's eyes widened in understanding. "That's a good thing though. It means you are alive."

"He is the only one that the AI reports as alive," Tanneth said. "Every other name I try, the AI says is dead."

Aaron stared at Bayen, considering. He knelt with his eyes downcast upon the ground. Verona's comms device chimed, and Aaron heard Sarah's voice asking for him.

Bayen's head snapped toward Verona. "*Mother*," he whispered.

Halcylon was a master at manipulation. This was something he could pull off to spin them in circles to put them off balance. "I want him bound and kept under guard. Put him back on the *Raven*," Aaron said to the FNA soldiers.

Verona handed Aaron his comms device. Aaron thanked him and stepped off to the side to speak with Sarah.

"Are you well?" Sarah asked.

In spite of his anger, Aaron was glad to hear the sound of her voice. "I think I should be asking you that, but I'm fine."

He didn't feel fine. In fact, he felt as far away from fine as a person could get, and he knew that Sarah could tell the difference.

"I'm sorry about Cyrus. He was a good man," Sarah said.

Aaron was silent for a moment. There was so much he wanted to say, but the words wouldn't come. He wanted to see her. Hold her in his arms.

"Talk to me, my love," Sarah said.

Though he couldn't see her, he built a perfect picture of her in his mind. *Pregnant? They were going to have a child.* The world seemed to spin around him, and he shut his eyes. A stifled cry escaped his lips. The fall of Rexel. Halcylon's manipulation. Bayen telling him that his choices had laid waste to the world. A child… their child… it was all too much.

"I'll come to you—" Sarah began.

"No!" Aaron said. "It's not safe. Please stay where you are. I need to know that you're safe. Verona said you were in Hathenwood with Roselyn."

There was a moment's hesitation, and then Sarah began telling him of the events in Khamearra. As she spoke, Aaron drew in the energy and sought out his connection to her. The connection they shared ever since he had used his own lifebeat to save her life. He focused inward and followed the shimmering translucent trail to Sarah. He felt as if he could almost reach across the expanse and touch her. The golden glow of her lifebeat pulsated with the rhythm of her beating heart. This time, there was an additional pulse that flashed in between her heartbeats. Aaron gasped. Sarah stopped speaking in the middle of what she was saying.

"Oh, Aaron," Sarah whispered. "I'm sorry I didn't tell you sooner, but with everything that was going on…"

Aaron felt his lips curve into a smile, but he remained focused on Sarah's lifebeat and that of their child.

"It's all right. I understand," Aaron said. He drew back to himself and wondered why he hadn't sensed the change in their connection before. For a moment, he pushed all other thoughts from his mind but for the two most important things he counted himself fortunate to have. Sarah was safe, and they were going to have a child.

"How do you feel?" Aaron asked.

"A little tired, but Roselyn says that is normal," Sarah said, and Aaron heard the relief in her voice. "I know this isn't the best time. Believe me, I do, but I want this."

"So do I," Aaron said, and felt his heart fill his chest and a small lump grow in his throat.

He glanced at the *Raven* hovering nearby and decided not to tell Sarah about Bayen. They spoke for a little while longer, and then Aaron closed the comms device. Having seen so much death and destruction, he had never considered that life would have its presence on a day like today.

Tolvar was among the first to congratulate Aaron. The word spread among the people around them like wildfire. Tolvar opened a cask of ale set aside for special occasions. Every now and again, Aaron glanced up at the *Raven*, where Bayen was being held. Tolvar, who was standing next to him, caught his line of sight.

"What do you think?" Aaron asked.

Tolvar ran his hand over his bald head and sighed. "The boy believes wholeheartedly in what he's saying, but there is more at play here than the events that have transpired."

"Is it possible to travel through time?"

Tolvar shrugged his shoulders. "Anything is possible. We have always believed in infinite possibilities. The knowledge of such a thing is beyond me."

Aaron nodded. "Given everything that Halcylon has done. This is something that he could do."

"Indeed, but you need to focus on why he would do such a thing. Based upon what I've heard, this General Halcylon is logical almost to a fault. Cunning and ruthless. It begs the question as to why he would put together such an elaborate ruse," Tolvar said.

"That's the question," Aaron said.

"One that I would like to know the answer to. For that reason," Tolvar said, and glanced at Armel, "we will join you in Shandara."

"Thank you," Aaron said, sounding relieved. They could use any advantage they could get. "I'm sure we have a keystone accelerator on board the *Raven*. A portal would be able to get everyone through."

Tolvar chuckled. "I appreciate the offer, but I think we'll manage. We have ways to make the journey quickly."

Aaron nodded; he should have known. Tolvar took his leave of him and went to make preparations for his people to leave.

Aaron turned, and a few feet away the ground looked slightly off.

Thraw opened his eyes. "You almost had him."

"I'm glad to see you made it," Aaron said.

"Oh, I managed to take more than a few of the Zekara with me, but I will have no rest until Halcylon is dead."

"Halcylon isn't going anywhere," Aaron said.

Thraw stalked off and headed back to the *Raven* with no one the wiser. It was easy to see why the Hythariam feared the maul-cat. Aaron headed toward the *Raven* with the others, and as he walked up the gangplank, it almost felt like he was coming home.

Chapter 22
TESTS

Sarah closed the comms device with shaky hands and took a steadying breath. When did they start keeping secrets from one another? She knew there was something Aaron wasn't telling her. He carried the weight of the dead with him. It was hard to believe that Rexel was gone. Roselyn had shown her. The refugees from Rexel had found a haven in Shandara. She knew it wasn't lost upon the people of Rexel that twenty-five years ago they gave refuge to the Shandarian survivors. She was glad that Aaron at least had Verona with him.

Roselyn called her name and asked her a question. It took Sarah a few moments to catch up. They were in a laboratory in Hathenwood. There were few humans in Hathenwood, so it was less of a risk to bring her brother here than Shandara.

"They're on board the *Raven* and heading to Shandara," Sarah said.

The Raven, Sarah mused, remembering their journey on board that airship. It seemed as if they had come full circle.

"Then they should reach Shandara in about five hours' time," Roselyn said.

Sarah nodded. The first time they journeyed to Shandara had taken weeks with the Drake and Ryakuls dogging their every move. Now the time was cut down to hours instead of days. If a Hythariam flyer was dispatched, the journey would take even less time. There were other methods of travel, but Aaron needed this time. They all needed a moment to catch their breath.

"Does he know yet?" Roselyn asked.

Sarah nodded. "He knows."

"How did he take the news? Sometimes, men can be funny about such things," Roselyn said.

"Quite well, considering. I'm sure he's still in shock, but after everything that's happened, I think it helped him," Sarah said. She needed him near her now. Out of danger. She wanted all this to be over so they could live out their lives in peace.

There were two large capsules in the room, and Roselyn went around them making notations. They had frozen Rordan and Darven to slow down the infection. There were other Hythariam in the room, monitoring from their stations. The only person out of place was Sarah, but she couldn't bring herself to leave.

Roselyn walked over to her. "We're going to open one of them up now. It's the only way to get the samples I need. Perhaps it would be safest if you were to watch from the observation room?"

"What about you? Proximity would put you in danger as well," Sarah said.

The metallic door to the lab hissed open, and two black armored Hythariam soldiers entered. They nodded in greeting to them and stayed just inside the doorway.

"I'll be well protected," Roselyn said.

"You'll be even better protected if I remain," Sarah said, with her fingertips grazing the handle of the long knife on her belt.

"I would never doubt your prowess as a warrior. I was thinking that the virus is designed to infect humans so…" Roselyn said.

Sarah smiled. "I can create a shield if it comes to it."

Roselyn nodded, letting the matter drop.

"What do you need to get from Rordan that you don't already know?" Sarah asked.

"The samples collected so far contain dead versions of the virus. Or the change is so far along that it hinders our efforts to create a cure. Rordan and this other man were newly infected before they were captured. We can get much more information this way," Roselyn said.

The capsule with her brother inside was moved to the central table. As soon as the capsule was locked into place, several holographic monitors came online. Each showed different sets of information. Roselyn entered a few commands and watched the capsule expectantly.

The capsule slowly hissed open, a misty vapor escaping from the edges. The top slid halfway down, exposing Rordan's upper torso. Sarah grabbed her knife as she leaned over to get a better look. Rordan's pasty-white skin almost glowed under the lighting. His features were smooth as if he was asleep. She saw the slight flicker of his pulse on his neck. Roselyn used a long needle to extract Rordan's blood, and for a moment Sarah thought she saw his fingers move.

"Are you sure he won't wake up?" Sarah asked.

The two soldiers moved to the end of the capsule.

Roselyn filled up two more vials with Rordan's blood. "No, he's still in cryostasis."

Sarah could barely take her eyes off her brother. She tried to convince herself that he was just asleep and continued to watch the pulse in his neck. She had gambled that removing the amulet would diminish his powers, but she didn't think they were completely gone. Some doors, when opened, couldn't be shut again.

Roselyn carried the vials away and returned with another device. It was some type of scanner, Sarah recalled. The skin on Rordan's torso darkened like a storm cloud.

"Increase the dose," Roselyn said to one of the other scientists in the room.

Sarah drew in the energy, heightening her senses. "I don't like this. Something isn't right. Can you close it back up?"

Roselyn put the scanner down and retrieved another instrument from the tray nearby.

"I just need to collect a skin sample and a culture from inside his mouth, then—"

Rordan's eyes flicked open. His irises were completely black. Rordan's hand shot forth, grabbing Roselyn's outstretched arm. Roselyn cried out as Rordan let out a guttural roar. One soldier tried to pin Rordan's flailing body down while the other grabbed his arm. Sarah was there in an instant, her long knife out, and slammed it down, severing Rordan's hand at the wrist. Metallic bands stretched across his body, restraining him. Snapping his teeth like a wild animal, he jerked his head toward Sarah. The soldiers released him, and the capsule shut. After a few moments, sounds of Rordan's struggling ceased.

Roselyn blew out a breath and thanked her. A Hythariam came and retrieved Rordan's severed hand and placed it on a tray, then loaded it into a small clear container.

"I thought you said he couldn't wake up?" Sarah asked.

"The virus must work faster than we thought. Did he get you?"

Sarah shook her head. "He went for you. The reports from the battlefield were that they all but avoided Hythariam."

"I think I just happened to be in his way. Come on over here. Let's see what we have," Roselyn said, some of the shakiness leaving her voice.

The soldiers stood guard on either side of the capsules now. Roselyn loaded the vials, and they emptied into a machine. Sarah glanced back at Rordan's capsule. The sight of his black eyes made her skin crawl.

They both sat down at one of the large holo displays while Roselyn worked her magic.

"This will allow me to take a closer look at the blood. I have some theories on how the virus works, but this will help me understand it better," Roselyn said.

"Is Iranus still angry with you for giving the Nanites to Verona?" Sarah asked.

"He can be angry for as long as he wants. Those Nanites saved Verona's life. That in and of itself is enough justification in my mind. Without them, we wouldn't know as much as we do now. Verona was lucky to only be partially exposed."

Sarah pursed her lips in thought. "I wouldn't want anything to happen to Verona, but I agree with Iranus: our world isn't ready for the Nanites."

Roselyn was silent as she worked through the data in front of her. "People like Halcylon made a perversion of their intended purpose."

"Once you release something into the world, you need to accept that the intended purposes of that something is bound to change," Sarah replied.

"Regardless, the Nanites aren't a viable option. We don't have the means to distribute them to every human on the continent anytime soon," Roselyn said.

Sarah frowned. "What about a cure? Will you be able to distribute that?" she asked.

Roselyn's face lit up. "Oh, yes. There are a lot of ways to distribute a cure. It doesn't need to go everywhere at once. We can address the most immediate threat first and then work our way out."

Sarah smiled. She like the simplicity with which Roselyn set about what others would consider insurmountable tasks.

"This is interesting," Roselyn said. "Once introduced into a host, the virus becomes more aggressive. It's almost like it doesn't fully engage until it finds a viable host. Halcylon had to modify it so it would be compatible with humans."

Roselyn kept working, and Sarah felt a slight flutter in her stomach. She smiled slightly while caressing her stomach.

Roselyn turned toward her. "Oh, did you feel them?"

A giggle escaped Sarah's lips, and she nodded. They shared a quick hug, and something chimed on the holo display.

"The simulations are done," Roselyn said.

"I thought you said it would take a while."

"Normally they would, but we're patched into the systems in Shandara. Those systems did all the heavy lifting for us," Roselyn said.

The door to the lab opened, and Iranus stepped inside. He stooped more now when he stood, and the lines showed on his face. His hair was completely white. Sarah rose from her seat to offer it to him, but he waved her back down with a smile.

"I see you've gotten your samples," Iranus said.

"I may have a solution, and it has to do with blocking what

Halcylon has done to adapt the virus to humans."

Iranus rubbed his chin as he read the information on the display. "You're looking to prevent the infection."

"Correct. Once they are already infected, I can't reverse the infection. I think prevention is our best option. Essentially, I'm hoping to convince the virus that it is in an incompatible host, which would cause it to go dormant. I will keep working on it, but given the time we have, I think we should move forward with this," Roselyn said.

"The results look promising," Iranus agreed, studying the screen for a moment.

"I want to run a few physical tests, with the samples we've collected," Roselyn said.

"Assuming all this works," Sarah said. "How will you distribute it? We should protect our soldiers and other essential people first, as there is greater risk of exposure for them."

Iranus nodded. "Once we confirm what the simulations tell us. Then there are a number of ways we can distribute. We might even consider using a method that the Zekara have already proven to be an effective way to distribute the virus. Only we'll be distributing the cure."

"Great news. We should tell the others," Sarah said.

Iranus shook his head. "We can't. Not something this important. We need to keep this a secret for as long as we can."

"Why?" Sarah asked.

"The Zekara are able to listen to our communications. Gavril has been using codes to keep communications going, but I'm willing to wager you understand how important something like this could be," Iranus said.

"I see," Sarah said.

"We won't know if this works until we test it on someone who has been exposed," Iranus said, and nodded to the capsules behind them.

The interior of the capsules showed up on the display, showing Rordan's and Darven's faces. Seeing Darven's face with the scars that marred one side triggered a memory. Darven had been among those that they had fought at Shandara before the Drake captured her. Aaron had singled him out. The two had met before. Sarah gasped, her eyes widening. Iranus and Roselyn stopped speaking and looked at her.

"What is it?" Roselyn asked.

Sarah pointed at Darven's face on the display. "That's the man who murdered Aaron's mother."

Roselyn and Iranus looked at the display, their mouths agape.

"He was with the attack force that went to Earth," Sarah said. "Darven held his mother captive to get Aaron to surrender."

"We have him now, and he won't escape," Roselyn said.

Iranus sighed. "We will need to test the cure on him."

Sarah was about to protest, but she knew Iranus was right. "Fine. Cure him, and then I will have him executed." Darven was a citizen of Khamearra and subject to the justice that Sarah would visit upon him.

Iranus left them to make arrangements for synthesizing the cure. This way, they would be ready if Roselyn's tests were successful.

Roselyn's eyes were locked on the screen as she continued to work. They were both warriors of a different sort. Both of them dangerous in their own ways. The capsules behind them were quiet, but Sarah had to suppress a shudder whenever she glanced back at them. When she had been captured by the Drake and was surrounded by Ryakuls, she had felt the presence before. Not since then had she experienced the feeling she got when she looked upon Rordan's capsule. Nothing living was inside. She reached out with the energy, immediately sensing the lifebeats of those around her, but from inside the capsule that held her brother there was not a trace of life.

"Who does this?" Sarah asked.

Roselyn gave her a bewildered look.

"I've been witness to all manner of cruelty done by my father and the Elitesmen, but what Halcylon and his Zekara have done is just so… evil," Sarah said.

Roselyn placed her hand on Sarah's shoulder. "We'll stop them. All of us together. You've got to believe that."

"Rordan would kill everyone in this room without a moment's hesitation, but he doesn't deserve this. No one does," Sarah said.

"Halcylon is consumed by hate."

"How can anyone follow such a person? They're here and free, yet they still follow Halcylon to war."

Roselyn turned back to the screen. "We'll see how many follow him when they're defeated. You're right, no one deserves this, but at least some good will come from Rordan's death."

Sarah nodded and remained quiet with her thoughts while Roselyn worked. This war couldn't be over soon enough.

CHAPTER 23
LEAP OF FAITH

Aaron stood staring at a large map in the navigation room on the *Raven*. After briefly speaking with others, he asked for some time alone. His gaze slid across the map. The continent stretched before him, and a section had been replaced since he was last in the room. Shandara was no longer in a blackened area marked *Land of Shadow*. Instead, Shandara and the White Rose Palace were clearly defined with fine gold lettering. He reached out and traced the script with his fingertips, admiring the work of the cartographer that made this map. Aaron felt a slight shudder beneath his feet as the engines were engaged. The engines could run a full burst longer, but there was a need to rotate their use to prevent overheating. Leaning against the wall was the rune-carved staff. The dark wood with the strange runes lay seemingly innocuous. The ghost of his great-grandfather, Daverim Alenzar'seth, had more or less thrust it into his hands. He had needed a good walking stick, Aaron mused. The rune-carved staff had been retrieved from the battlefield by Bayen, the man who claimed to be his son.

Retrieving the staff was hardly the work of a spy, Aaron argued to himself.

The most convincing infiltrator of your ranks would be the one who didn't realize he was, in fact, a spy. It wasn't that long ago that Halcylon had used the Nanites to erase Aaron's own identity. Aaron's recollection of his time as Len was foggy at best. A few strange images and scattered emotions mostly surrounding Sarah. The Nanites had nearly been successful, and only the intervention of the Eldarin had saved him.

Verona entered the room and was followed by Admiral Morgan.

"Your Grace," Morgan said with a salute.

"If you start doing that, then I'm going to start calling you admiral," Aaron said.

Morgan chuckled. "Would commander be better?"

Verona grinned and glanced at the map, noticing the new section.

Morgan rested his hand upon a wooden chair. He wore a dark blue coat with silver buckles along the front. Most of the sailors on board had them to keep warm against the cool temperatures felt at high altitudes. "You're going to have to make your peace with titles. Like it or not, you are royalty. The Alenzar'seth is the ruling house of Shandara, and that mantle falls to you. With Sarah as the High Queen, that makes both you and her among the most powerful people on Safanar."

Aaron frowned and then nodded. "One of the things Cyrus called me was a bridge between the races. The Free Nations Army is bound together by me."

"And he was right," Morgan said.

Aaron saw the pain ringed around Morgan's eyes. The admiral had served Prince Cyrus for most of his life. It was a quite a surprise when Morgan announced his intention to retire from service to Rexel in favor of serving Shandara.

"Sarah is pregnant," Aaron said. It was the first time he had said it out loud, and doing so made it more real to him.

Morgan let out a hearty laugh and gave him a slap to match on his shoulder. "Good for you, lad. Nothing like having children to put things in perspective for you."

"You don't have any children," Verona said.

Morgan nodded. "That's why things are never out of perspective for me. Just wait until it's your turn."

The color drained from Verona's face, and Aaron chuckled.

"You two are like peas in the pod. What makes you think that you're not half a step behind him?" Morgan pressed, gesturing with his hand toward Aaron.

"Well, I, uh… I'm not sure," Verona stammered.

"Are they friends?" Morgan asked.

Verona was too flustered to give Morgan more than a bewildered expression.

"Sarah and Roselyn are indeed friends," Aaron said.

Morgan shrugged his shoulders and laid a companionable hand on each of them. "Welcome to fatherhood, Verona. You're next."

At this, they all laughed. Aaron wished the others were with them to share the moment. Braden and Sarik were in Shandara along with Vaughn and Garret. He missed Eric's playful banter and Colind's wise counsel. How many more would not be present before this was over? Would the ghosts of those who had passed always stand in silent judgment of his deeds? Aaron prayed he would be worthy of their sacrifice.

"We need to get the Zekara to face us at Shandara. If we fail to defeat them there, then the other nations will quickly fall," Aaron

said.

"What do you want us to do?" Verona asked.

"I'm not sure. Halcylon has a lot of pride. He believes humans are beneath him. I'm trying to think of a way to use that," Aaron said.

"Best way to deal with a bully is to hit him back," Morgan said.

"Eloquent as always, but yes, I'd say Morgan hit the nail on its head," Verona added.

"I was thinking along similar lines. We'll regroup at Shandara and plan our next move," Aaron said, and glanced out the window. "Excuse me, but I need to get some air."

Admiral Morgan headed for the wheelhouse, and Verona followed him on deck. Aaron recognized many of the sailors they saw on deck. They offered a friendly greeting before going back to their duties. The air was crisp and clear. At the bow of the ship were shields for blocking the wind. Something the sailors needed now more than ever with the new engines. It wouldn't be long before airships themselves were nothing more than relics. Despite that, Aaron found that being on deck set his mind at ease. There were a lot of memories for him here, from his humbling first attempt at jumping great distances to Zeus, his grandfather's wolf half-breed that helped guide him to Safanar.

"Are you afraid?" Verona asked.

"Of what?"

"Becoming a father."

The question caught him off guard. "I haven't had much time to think about it."

"Fair enough, my friend. Tell me what your father was like."

"My dad—" Aaron took a second to collect his thoughts. "Was much like Morgan or your uncle in a lot of ways. You always knew where you stood with him. He liked to work with his hands and enjoyed building things. He was extremely patient, though I didn't realize how much at the time. God knows I tested his patience a lot growing up. I'm not sure he saw eye to eye with Reymius, but where my mother was concerned they were united."

"And your sister?"

"When I left, my sister was planning her wedding..." Aaron said, thinking of Tara for the first time in weeks. "She should be married by now."

"One of the reasons you came here was to keep her safe. She's safe now," Verona said.

Aaron shook his head. "From Mactar, yes, but not Halcylon."

"What do you mean?"

"When I was prisoner on Hytharia, they probed my mind. Halcylon knows about Earth. He even asked why they couldn't go there when they put me before a tribunal," Aaron said.

Verona shook his head. "Beings like Halcylon will never stop. War is all they know. It's a cycle the Zekara know well. Why do you think that is?"

"Because his heart rages for the one thing he can't have: his home world back. I doubt even he realizes it. You would think that given the lifespan afforded to them by the Nanites, that a race of beings would be better off for it. Hythariam and humans are more alike than they are different," Aaron said.

"A lot of people would be tempted by eternal life. Wouldn't you?"

"Forever is a long time. Right now, I can't see past the next few days," Aaron replied.

"There is something we should talk about," Verona said.

"All right," Aaron said. With Verona, it really could have been anything.

"I think you need to reconsider your stance on Bayen," Verona said.

Aaron sighed heavily. "What do you want me to reconsider, specifically? That he could be my son who came here from the future, or that my actions will mean the end of life as we know it?"

"You're so hell-bent on what Halcylon has done that you're letting it cloud your judgment," Verona said. "My friend, I would follow you to hell and back, but in this instance you're wrong to dismiss this so quickly. You need to look at it objectively. If Sarah were here—"

"I don't want Sarah anywhere near Bayen."

For a moment, the two friends traded hardened glances at one another.

Aaron pounded a fist on the railing. "I'll give you this. Maybe you're right, and I do need to think more about what Bayen has said, but he's listening to a machine. For all the Hythariam technological advancements, they aren't infallible," Aaron said.

"Right, but don't you act like a machine by not listening at all? Now, Tanneth wanted the two of us to go to where they are holding Bayen. Let's go down there and see what we can learn," Verona said.

"All that just to get me to go down there?" Aaron asked.

"You can be quite bullheaded at times, my friend."

Aaron chuckled and followed Verona belowdecks. There were two FNA soldiers posted outside the room where Bayen was being held. One opened the door for them, and there were two more soldiers inside. There was a small wooden desk with Bayen sitting on one side and Tanneth on the other. Bayen's hands were bound, but Aaron suspected that if Bayen wanted to free himself, he would have little difficulty doing so.

Bayen looked up at them when they entered. There was no accusing glare, only exhausted resignation. Perhaps Bayen revealing himself had eased the burden he carried. Aaron looked into Bayen's eyes. Were they reminiscent of Sarah's eyes and he had been too blind to see it, or was he struggling to see a connection that simply wasn't there? Bayen was tall and broad shouldered, approaching Aaron's own six-foot-four-inch frame. Bayen had stayed with him throughout the battle. He fought well. Neither of them said a word, with each taking a few moments to study the other.

"I've come to hear what you have to say," Aaron said, breaking the silence.

"Nothing has changed in the past few hours," Bayen said.

Tanneth was about to speak, but Aaron held up his hand. "Let's start from the beginning. What do you remember?"

Bayen looked at his hands for a moment, his eyes growing distant. "I woke up in a cryogenic chamber on an island a few hundred miles off the western coast. I don't know which one, and I only looked at the map for a few seconds. We were being attacked. The facility was being overrun."

Aaron glanced at Tanneth.

"There are islands off the western coast," Tanneth said.

"That would mean they might have left from Khamearra then, since that would be the closest city," Verona said.

"What happened after you woke up?" Aaron asked.

"Like I said, the facility was being overrun. We were being attacked," Bayen said.

"By who?"

"All manner of creatures, but the biggest shockwaves came when the Eldarin attacked."

Aaron's gaze darted to the others. "The Eldarin are allied with us."

Bayen shook his head. "They became infected just like everyone else."

"Then what happened?"

"We took an elevator down into a hollowed-out chamber deep beneath the surface. They were tapping into the energy and feeding it into a prototype keystone accelerator. The war lasted years. The FNA moved from place to place. We fought, and the Ryakul virus continued to spread across multiple species. Each time there was talk of a cure, it would fail. Each failure supposedly brought us closer to a more permanent cure."

"You were put into cryostasis. How long did you expect to be asleep?" Aaron asked.

"It was only supposed to be for a few weeks, perhaps a month at most, but instead it was closer to twenty years," Bayen said.

Aaron fought to keep the doubt from showing on his face, but Bayen must have sensed it.

"You don't have to believe me."

"I'm still trying to understand why you would voluntarily go into cryostasis. That doesn't add up for me," Aaron said.

Verona pursed his lips, and Tanneth nodded.

Bayen gave him a long look before speaking. "It's because I was infected."

Aaron's eyes widened. "Are you infected right now?"

"Yes," Bayen whispered.

The others in the room shifted their stance. They had all fought the Forsaken in the battle and knew the stakes.

"It's contained," Bayen said.

"How?"

"With this," Bayen said, holding up the bracer that housed the AI.

Aaron looked at Tanneth. "Are are you able to detect anything in his system?"

Tanneth shook his head.

"He can't. Passive scans won't work. I will need to grant you access," Bayen said.

"Please do so," Aaron said.

"Sam," Bayen said, "please allow passive scans and reporting from the Nanites in my system."

"Sir, I'm unable to comply with this request," the AI replied.

Bayen frowned and looked up uncertainly at the others. "I'm giving you a command. Why can't you comply?"

"You don't have the necessary privileges to allow me to grant the request," Sam replied.

Aaron's lips curved into a smile.

"What is it?" Verona asked.

"It seems as if our young friend here doesn't know all there is to know," Aaron said. "Sam, would you accept such a command from me?"

"Affirmative, granting limited access to requested data now," the AI replied.

Bayen looked at him, understanding registering in his eyes.

"How did you know?" Tanneth asked.

"Earlier the system said it was designed by me. Perhaps some information is restricted," Aaron said.

"If you accept that, then do you accept the rest of Bayen's story as well?" Verona asked.

"I'm not sure. This could be an elaborate script the AI was tasked to follow," Aaron replied.

"I had no idea you were this slow to trust," Verona said.

"It's not a matter of trust. The AI, while lifelike and intuitive as it is, is still a machine bound by specific protocols for which it was specifically designed. We've witnessed the effects of that," Aaron said.

Verona nodded. "The Drake."

"Exactly," Aaron said, and turned to Tanneth. "Do you think we can remove the bracer?"

Tanneth tore his eyes from his readout. "No. It's just as he says. The bracer is more than a comms device. It's also managing his Nanite protocols to contain the infection. If we remove the bracer, then those will fail."

Aaron frowned and leveled his gaze at Bayen. "And expose us all to the virus." After a few moments of silence, he continued. "Why help with the infiltrators? You gave us a way to stop them."

"I was trying to prevent the outbreak of the virus," Bayen said.

"I understand that. Why did you try to hide the fact that you were helping us? They've used the process you've sent in Khamearra and Lorric. It saved a lot of lives," Aaron said.

Bayen held up his bound hands. "This was one reason."

Despite himself, Aaron chuckled and then said, "You blame me for things that I haven't done yet."

Bayen's gaze immediately hardened. "For as bad as the battle at Rexel was, it gets much worse. My life was stolen from me. I wanted to fight alongside the others. Die if that was my fate. But you took that away from me."

Aaron took a breath and glanced at the ceiling, collecting his thoughts. "Maybe it was for your protection. Or perhaps having lost everyone else, he needed something kept safe for the future." As Aaron said the last, he thought of his grandfather leaving Safanar behind to keep his mother safe.

Bayen's eyes locked with his own, and for a moment the anger was replaced with something else that Aaron had scarcely thought he would see from the youth. Understanding and acknowledgement. Aaron knew because he had to endure similar trials when his grandfather, Reymius, died. It was a hard burden to bear, and if Bayen was indeed his son, then not protecting him from this burden was one of Aaron's failures as a father. There was one way he could confirm who Bayen was. It involved the bladesong and tapping into the energy. Aaron wasn't sure what he was more afraid of: if Bayen was telling the truth or if it was all a lie.

Tanneth gasped and exclaimed something that Aaron didn't understand. "Since you instructed the AI to allow us access, I've been scanning it for information. What I've found are the keys to the Zekara's military apparatus. We can use this to level the playing field. Tap into their communications and perhaps turn the tide of this war."

"We'll need to test it, but with the Zekara listening to our communications, let's hold off from informing the others at this time," Aaron said.

"I'll come up with some small things we can try without alerting the Zekara," Tanneth said, and moved over to the corner of the room.

Verona pressed his lips together in thought and looked at Bayen. "You seem as surprised as Tanneth by this discovery."

"I didn't know any of that was in there," Bayen said.

The door opened, and a sailor poked his head in. "Admiral Morgan requests that Aaron and Verona join him at their earliest convenience."

"We'll be up in a few minutes," Aaron said.

Verona left the room, but Aaron stayed behind for a moment.

"Untie him," Aaron said. It was a gesture of good faith and one that wasn't lost upon Bayen.

The soldier removed the bindings around Bayen's wrists. Bayen rubbed the circulation back into his hands and looked up at Aaron.

"Can you work with Tanneth to see what else the AI has been hiding?" Aaron asked.

Bayen said he would, and Aaron left the room.

In the hallway, Verona waited for him.

"Well, that was a leap of faith, my friend."

Aaron nodded. "Tanneth is pretty smart and will be studying Bayen as closely as he is studying that AI of his," Aaron said.

"I still sense some hesitation," Verona said.

Aaron sighed. "It's a lot to take in. Either we have to trust everything that Bayen is telling us, or we can't trust any of it. There is no middle ground for this. It puts us in a rather precarious position for the next battle. Don't you think?"

"Agreed," Verona said.

Truthfully, Aaron was a bit relieved that Morgan summoned them. He wanted to get away from Bayen and everything he represented. This war had reached across worlds to pull him into this fight, whether it was the High King or actions stemming from General Halcylon. Now, someone or something was reaching across time to help avert disaster on an unimaginable scale. But a nefarious force could just as easily be leading them to certain doom. It was enough to give anyone pause. He needed a little bit of time to get his bearings, to center himself, and make the best decisions he could with the information available. It was how a leader should behave, but he worried it wouldn't be enough. Bayen's presence was testament that in the very near future Aaron's best wasn't enough and all of Safanar would pay the price for his failure.

CHAPTER 24
RETURN

The great towers of Shandara stretched toward the sky. Some were in a state of repair with scaffolding built around them. Approaching by airship allowed Aaron to appreciate all of the changes to the immense city and the green and lush land surrounding it. From this distance, the city walls appeared smooth and white, glistening in the sunlight. The Alenzar'seth family sigil alternating with a massive tree adorned the city walls. When they had first come to Shandara, it had been little more than a graveyard, dark and forbidding. Now it was growing into a city reborn. The breaches in the walls had all been repaired with the only evidence of their existence firmly in Aaron's memory. Airships dotted the sky above the city and the surrounding area. A Hythariam flyer rose into the air and sped north, heading to Hathenwood. The De'anjard manned the walls and the towers between them. Many wore golden armor found in the weapons caches hidden throughout the city. Though the armor appeared golden, it was not made out of the soft metal. The armor was stronger and lighter than steel. According to Braden, they were as effective as the Hythariam light-armored shirts. There was no lack of volunteers to join the De'anjard, stemming from descendants of the original guard to those coming from the Free Nations Army. Braden had been adamant that the De'anjard needed to be reborn to protect Shandara as a separate entity from the FNA. Aaron saw his point, and he couldn't see standing in the way of the honored tradition of the Shields of Shandara's rightful place. Aaron let his preference be known that he wanted only men and women of integrity to be part of the De'anjard, but it was Braden who pointed out that sometimes the people you want fighting at your side could be a bit rough around the edges.

Aaron had only spent a handful of weeks in Shandara and hardly any of that time at the palace. The time he had spent there had been in the encampment or the command center, familiarizing himself with the city's defenses. It seemed that many of the systems required a member of the Alenzar'seth line to activate and grant access. Iranus had told him that his great-grandfather, Daverim, was fiercely protective of Shandara. The Hythariam had some redundancies put in place, but they never had the opportunity to try any of them out. When Shandara fell, the Hythariam looked for other ways to prepare against the threat of the Zekara. Aaron wasn't convinced that alienating themselves, by way of restricting all Hythariam to Hathenwood, was the best course of action they could have taken. Even if it was put to a vote. He wasn't shy about letting Iranus know his thoughts. Granted, living under the threat of the High King and his Elitesmen was no inconsequential thing. Still, Aaron hoped they would make better decisions in the future.

As the *Raven* flew over the city, there was a section set aside to bring the rubbled remains of the old so it could be fashioned into something new. Significant progress had been made restoring the city, and the Hythariam had some ingenious ways of dealing with the large fissures that snaked their way through parts of the city. But it was the old members of the Safanarion Order that were able to repair the damage. While the Elitesmen had been primarily an order that focused upon martial skills, the Safanarion Order was comprised of many different focuses. Not all of the Order were warriors. Many had chosen to focus their efforts in a capacity for which they were suited. Promoting such a diverse pursuit of knowledge spurred innovation and was one reason the Hythariam had aligned themselves with the Shandarians.

Tanneth came on deck with Bayen following him. Four FNA soldiers trailed in their wake. Bayen's mouth hung open as he took in the sight of Shandara. He caught Aaron watching him.

"Shandara was destroyed when I was young," Bayen said.

His skin was ashen, and there were signs of strain showing around his eyes. The clone of Aaron that Halcylon had used had deteriorated rapidly, which was one of the ways Roselyn had known that the clone was an imposter. Bayen's state could be the result of a rushed cloning process rather than the temporal matrix coming out of alignment. Aaron had sent a sample of Bayen's blood to Roselyn a short time ago for her to test. One way or the other, he would know if Bayen was a clone or not.

The *Raven* descended into the courtyard of the White Rose. The palace had been home to the Alenzar'seths for generations and dwarfed the palace at Rexel. The sheer size rivaled the palace in Khamearra, but the architecture was radically different. Aaron saw the Hythariam influence in various parts that held technological advances that were beyond anything else on Safanar. Verona occasionally commented that the palace now belonged to him, and Aaron supposed he was right, but it didn't feel like home. Aaron found the whole place intimidating.

The gangplank automatically extended to the ground, where a large company of De'anjard waited to welcome him home. They lined a path and stood with rigid attention. At their head was Braden, who carried his Warden's hammer. His armor did little to hide the bulging muscles underneath. His dirty-blond hair was tied back with a black leather cord.

Admiral Morgan barked an order, and the sailors and FNA soldiers alike formed ranks along the deck. As one, they saluted with fists across their hearts. With his head held high and his shoulders back, Aaron returned the salute and walked down the gangplank. As his feet touched the ground, Braden shouted a command, and the palace grounds thundered with armored fists striking armored chests as the De'anjard saluted the Heir of Shandara.

Aaron inclined his head, and Braden walked next to him while Verona followed. They headed just inside the palace walls and took the cleared path down to the command center.

"You've been busy, my friend," Verona commented to Braden as they went.

"They're good men. I'm only sorry I couldn't have brought them to Rexel," Braden said.

Verona nodded.

"Gavril has kept me up to speed," Braden continued. "When do you think the Zekara will strike?"

"Soon," Aaron said. "Are the De'anjard ready?"

"All you need to do is give the order. But there is something else," Braden said.

"What's that?" Aaron asked.

"Since you've been away, I've had several requests of former Elitesmen to join the De'anjard. It's strange. I would have thought they would join the Safanarion Order after their service in the FNA was up. There haven't been many, but enough for me to notice," Braden said.

"What did you do with them?" Aaron asked.

"I put them to work and told them I would discuss it with you. What do you think?"

"We're giving them a second chance. Let them earn a place just like anyone else would. We'll need everyone we can get our hands on for the battle with the Zekara," Aaron said.

Braden nodded. They made their way through the underground passages to the command center. The heart of Shandara's defenses were there. Gavril met them as they entered. He was one of the few Hythariam with green eyes, which marked him as being of the military back on Hytharia. The tall Hythariam wore black armor with a few lines of cyan running along the edges, indicating that it was powered.

"Have the Zekara compromised these systems?" Aaron asked, gesturing to the room.

"No," Gavril said. "Remember, the systems in Shandara are closed off. We ran communications from Hathenwood, and it was there that the Zekara were able to tap into our communications. I've instituted some coded messages, but otherwise we haven't let on that we know they're listening."

"I want to go over the city's defenses. We need to adapt them for facing the Forsaken," Aaron said.

"Don't we want to talk about what Tanneth has discovered, and Bayen—" Verona began.

"We will," Aaron said.

Gavril led them over to a small group gathered around a holo display of Shandara. Vaughn came over and gave Verona a firm hug. Grief still shone around his eyes at the loss of Rexel and its prince, but relief also shone as Vaughn had also been tasked with watching over Verona. The two were close.

"We do have some good news," Gavril said, drawing their attention. "This is something that doesn't leave this room, but we may have found a way to prevent the infection of the Ryakul virus among humans."

Aaron and Verona exchanged glances, which Gavril didn't miss, but he continued.

"We'll be distributing it to the troops here first and other essential personnel. After that, it will be released to the general population. There is one catch though," Gavril said.

"There is always a catch," Aaron said.

"In Hathenwood, they are working as fast as they can to make it, but not everyone will get it in time if the Zekaran attack sooner than expected," Gavril said.

Aaron's mind flashed to battling the Forsaken on the streets of Rexel. The ear-piercing screams of those falling victim to the virus. "We don't have the luxury of time. The more time that passes, the more Halcylon will rebuild his Forsaken army. There is something else. The Eldarin that is infected with the Ryakul virus is in Rexel. She is on the brink of fully succumbing to the virus."

"I knew you faced the Eldarin, but I didn't know it stayed after the battle," Gavril said.

"She's not like the others. She attacked, but part of me thinks she is looking for a way to die," Aaron said.

"Is that even possible? Killing an Eldarin?" Verona asked.

"They are a higher-order life form. I'm not sure what the natural order of things are where they are involved. Nothing lasts forever. Why would it be any different for them?" Aaron said.

"What will you do if that Eldarin comes to Shandara? You said the Forsaken were drawn to it in Rexel," Gavril said.

Aaron had been racking his brain on that very question since Rexel. If the Eldarin attacked Shandara, he would have to defend the city.

"What is it?" Verona asked.

Aaron sighed. "If the Eldarin attacks, we will have no choice but to defend ourselves."

"You make it sound as if that's a bad thing," Verona said.

"It is. They are an old race. They can traverse among realms and understand more of the great mysteries of the universe than any of us do. They've been protectors of this world. Is there a chance that the cure Roselyn has come up with would work on the Eldarin?" Aaron asked.

Gavril's face drew down in regret, and he slowly shook his head. "Unfortunately, no. What Roselyn was able to do is reverse what the Zekara did in order to adapt the virus for humans in the first place. Calling it a cure is not entirely accurate. It's more of a prevention."

They spent the rest of the time going over the city's defenses. A number of years had already been spent preparing Shandara for invasion before the city fell. A good portion of those defenses were being brought back into full service. Hythariam weapons had been built into the walls of the city and on the rooftops of various buildings. The natural terrain surrounding the city prevented an enemy from attacking from behind. At least not with any sort of real numbers.

Aaron, wanting to clear his head, left to take a walk. Verona came with him. They emerged to a starlit sky. Safanar's moons shone brightly, making it easy for them to see.

"How come you didn't tell them about Bayen?" Verona asked.

"I'm not sure it would help anything. Everyone in that room needs to focus on the battle with the Zekara," Aaron said.

"I see your point, but surely Gavril should be brought into the fold."

"Maybe you're right," Aaron said.

They left the palace grounds and came onto one of the main thoroughfares of the city. It was a wide-open street lined with large statues. The statues alternated between male and female, all depicting different stances of the slow-fighting forms. Sarah had brought him here. It was where they had found the first weapons caches. The place was quiet, almost serene. Aaron felt more centered here, under the watchful eyes of the statues lining the streets.

"If we tell everyone about Bayen, it will scatter them. Our alliance could come undone. Instead of uniting to face the Zekara, we will be driven apart. That's why I want it to stay between you, me, and Tanneth," Aaron said.

Verona's eyes widened. "Doesn't Roselyn know?"

Aaron shook his head. "She only knows that I wanted the sample I sent to her to be checked for signs of cloning."

"I don't know," Verona said.

"Me either. If everything that Bayen says is true, will it change whether we fight the Zekara?"

"No, I suppose it won't. But that AI was pretty clear about how keeping Halcylon alive was our best chance to cure the plague," Verona said.

"Fifty-five percent probability rate. Hardly conclusive evidence. I still think this is tied to the Eldarin," Aaron said.

"Perhaps it's both."

"You could be right."

"It doesn't make me feel any better."

"Me either, but can you give me your word that you won't say anything about Bayen?" Aaron asked.

"I told you I would see this through with you to the end wherever our road takes us. You have my word that I will not reveal anything about Bayen," Verona said.

"Thank you."

"You don't need to thank me, my friend."

"Yes, I do."

Verona blew out a breath and let his gaze drift to the moonlit statues lining the street. "What should we do now?"

"I need to think of a way to pick a fight," Aaron said.

"Normally, I'd think that this would be the fun part, but don't you think we should wait a few days? Give us a chance to regroup and catch our breaths?" Verona asked.

"It has to be tomorrow. With each passing moment, the Zekara grow stronger. They surprised us with an army of Forsaken at Rexel. I don't want to give them a chance to do the same thing again. We need to draw their attention because we have the best chance to defeat them here," Aaron said.

They decided to head back. Aaron took one last look at the majestic statues lining the streets of Shandara. He drew in the energy, and his perceptions sharpened. He sensed Verona's lifebeat and those of the De'anjard nearest them. Aaron sucked in a breath. Coming from each of the statues was a soft azure glow. The effect was so subtle that you could miss it. This was no trick of the light. He sensed tiny energy sources within each of the statues. It wasn't anything Hythariam made but something that matched the crystals inlaid in the pommels of his swords. Aaron's gaze slid down to his swords, and in the moonlight there was a soft glow. He let the energy go and saw only the vague impressions of what was so vibrant before.

"Did you see something?" Verona asked.

Aaron glanced at the statues. "I'm not sure, but I don't think it's anything to worry about."

"Perhaps it's Thraw stalking us," Verona quipped.

Aaron had little doubt that the mysterious maul-cat was close by. He seemed to always be in the background and would make his presence known when Aaron looked for him. Thraw had helped him escape the destruction of the Hythariam home world, but Aaron still didn't know who had freed the maul-cat in the first place or why.

Instead of going to the palace, Aaron led them to a grove of trees. In the center of the grove were the remnants of a massive white tree. Reymius's soul had returned here after his death on Earth. The majestic glow surrounding the tree was gone, but Aaron could still feel whispers of energy surrounding it. He sat down and leaned against the massive trunk, the past few days finally catching up with him. Verona sat next to him, just as tired. Aaron rested his head against the tree and gazed up at the night sky. Nighttime critters sang their songs into an otherwise normal night. The sound of deep breathing next to him told Aaron that Verona was already asleep. His thoughts drifted back to Bayen. Was he his son? If some future version of himself did send Bayen back through time to prevent the Ryakul virus from spreading, why would he give Bayen so little information to go on? Unless after all that time there simply wasn't anything else that they knew. Sending Bayen back through time was a last-ditch effort at saving their future. The fact that he could think of a counterargument for everything that proved Bayen's story was, in fact, the truth didn't sit well with him. Halcylon could have conceived this and sent Bayen into their midst to throw them off balance. It was a leap of faith no matter which Aaron chose to believe. Before a numbing sleep finally swept him away, he heard the rumblings of the Eldarin. The Dragon lords watched and waited. Aaron knew that whatever he did next would have lasting effects upon all of Safanar. It was the duty of the Ferasdiam marked to defend the lives of this world. In defense of this world, could he strike down an Eldarin, the purest of creatures he had ever encountered, and one he didn't fully comprehend? There must be another way. His eyes heavy, he let a numbing, dreamless sleep take him.

CHAPTER 25
SABOTAGE

General Morag Halcylon walked among the ruins of the desolated city. Without his armor, his skin would have blistered in seconds from the searing heat that still clung to the rubbled remains of Rexel. He was impressed that his enemies had thought to use such a bomb. These many years hadn't softened his old student in the least. Gavril was a grave disappointment since he chose to stand with the traitors and would die a painful death like the rest of them. This world would be cleansed of their taint so that it could be remade for his Zekara. His internal helmet display showed ten of his soldiers with him. None of the senior leadership was allowed to travel alone since the presence of the maul-cat had been detected. It wasn't until after the battle that seemingly random acts of sabotage formed a pattern. The maul-cat was patient. It struck seemingly innocuous blows from the shadows, and before you knew it, you were hemorrhaging uncontrollably. Only this time the beast struck them where they were weakest. Their power supplies were draining fast. The maul-cat had been his blind spot, just as the Forsaken had been the humans'. Diagnostics of his powered armor and combat AI showed no defects at all. In the most simplistic terms, the human had defeated him just as surely as the Zekara had been victorious on this battlefield. Nanite augmentation, powered armor, and the most sophisticated combat AI created by the Hythariam should have been enough to handle one human. Should have been...

Ronin had sent a message. It seemed the Forsaken were becoming more of a problem. Halcylon gestured to the others, and they set off to where the Forsaken had gathered. Outside the walls, the temperature was much cooler, and they didn't require armor to protect them. Ronin and his science team stood dozens of yards from the clustering forms of the Forsaken. There weren't as many as he would have liked since most had been destroyed in the explosion.

Ronin saw them and walked over.

"What is your team doing just standing around?" Halcylon asked.

"We can't get close enough to finish our examination of the Dragon hybrid. I did some preliminary analysis and returned with my team. By then, the Forsaken had gathered around it and wouldn't budge," Ronin complained.

"Why didn't your escort make a path for you?"

"They tried," Ronin said, and gestured to four bodies off to the side. "At first, it appeared as if they were going to get through, but then something changed. The Forsaken turned and attacked. Only when we retreated did they stop. Also, the soldiers were reporting some sort of interference with their armor."

Halcylon looked at the dark shapes clustering around the Dragon hybrid. They were all in the final stages of infection and barely looked human anymore. Their skin had blackened to form a toughened hide that stretched over the elongated bones. A thick yellow drool gathered around their mouths. He brought up the comms device and engaged the signal used to control the Forsaken. Many of them shifted on their feet, and their heads jerked from side to side. After a few more seconds, Halcylon turned up the frequency, and the Forsaken's agitation grew. The Dragon hybrid shot to its feet and turned its massive head toward him. Eyes full of hate peered through him as if the beast knew he was the source of the disturbance. The soldiers around him readied their weapons. Halcylon stopped the signal, and after a few moments the Forsaken settled down to their former catatonic state.

The Dragon hybrid stood poised, its muscles straining against an unseen force.

"It's fighting the infection," Ronin said, sounding amazed.

The Dragon shook its head and let out an ear-piercing roar. Halcylon ducked his head down at the sound with the others doing the same. The Dragon spun around and slammed a great clawed fist into the ground, leaving a small crater.

Halcylon gestured to the others to back away, and they slowly retreated. "This isn't good. We're losing control. Perhaps we should take out the hybrid?"

Ronin's mouth hung open in shock. "And lose such a magnificent specimen? It won't do if they all turn on us."

"We need to move out soon. Our power supply issues are becoming critical," Halcylon said, and studied Ronin's reaction. His chief science officer simply nodded. There was a traitor in their midst. He could feel it. Who else could have unleashed the maul-cat? He needed Ronin to manage the Forsaken. If he failed in that task, then he was no longer useful and would be dealt with accordingly.

"I've run the numbers. We can't make it to Shandara and fight a battle there," Ronin said.

Halcylon smirked. "It amuses me that you think we're going to march all the way there. We have a keystone accelerator of our own that is able to open a portal big enough for us to march through easy enough."

Ronin pursed his thin lips together in thought. "How did you reconfigure them? The calculations involved—"

"Weren't your concern. We'll open up a portal in the heart of their precious city and lay waste to it."

The comms device chimed, and Halcylon opened the line.

"Sir," Chinta said, "I have an update on the deployment of infiltrators. The two we sent to Khamearra have gone offline without delivering the payload. Same for the one other sent to a smaller kingdom. More reports of the same in other places. It seems that our enemy has devised a way to take them out and prevent the self-destruct."

"Which was supposed to be impossible," Ronin said.

Halcylon ignored the jibe. "Recall them at once. I'll be back at the command center in a few minutes."

Halcylon cut the line and turned to one of the nearby soldiers. "I want a battalion of troops brought here. Keep your distance. When it's time for us to move out, if that thing interferes then kill it."

Halcylon stormed off. They needed to strike soon, while they still had the advantage. Defeating the infiltrators was expected. However, incapacitating them without them delivering their payloads shouldn't have been possible. Not even his own people knew how it could be done. So how did a group of what was essentially non-military personnel figure it out? He felt his emotions churning within him and knew that rash decisions never panned out. He was anxious to meet the human again on the battlefield. He would see them all begging for mercy before he was done.

He called for Ronin to walk at his side as they made their way back to the command center.

"The hybrid. When do you think it will succumb to the infection?" Halcylon asked.

"It's tough to say. We've never encountered a species that was able to resist it this long, but I would say any time now. I've reviewed some of the drone's feeds, and the hybrid attacked Aaron. Perhaps if we put the two together, both problems will take care of themselves," Ronin said.

Halcylon had similar thoughts and cursed himself for a coward at the same time. "Perhaps," Halcylon said.

"We have other means to distribute the virus if you still wish to pursue that path," Ronin said.

"As a backup. We have enough infected at the moment. Once Shandara falls, I think we'll find the rest will fall with minimal effort. It's time to use the rest of our arsenal on them," Halcylon said.

Ronin didn't reply, and Halcylon kept a watchful eye on the science officer. He was capable of ruthless pragmatism just like the rest of his senior staff, but at times Halcylon suspected that Ronin's heart wasn't in it. Ronin just wanted to experiment and be left to his own devices. It just happened to be that Ronin's devices were extremely useful.

CHAPTER 26
TRUCE

The old man knelt amid the wreckage in the bowels of the base. Q34B Alpha Base was their last hope. The bronze holo displays had long since gone dark, their individual power sources depleted. The only indication of power was from the dimly pulsating crystals within the chamber. His eyes were shut, but he was focused upon maintaining the barrier that kept hordes of infected life forms at bay. The Ryakul virus held the world by the throat. With the failure of the holo displays, he had lost all semblance of time. All his focus went toward the barrier and keeping it strong. He just needed to hold on longer, or all hope would be lost. For a moment, he opened his eyes and shifted his attention to the energy bands that connected to the keystone accelerator. Only a few pylons remained. When they were gone, the connection would be severed forever.

Hurry, Bayen, he urged, knowing that the path his son had to walk would be the hardest for him to accept. At the same moment, the beings that had been Eldarin pressed their attack, driving the barrier back.

* * *

***

Aaron woke to the comms device buzzing from his wrist. The sun had only just risen, and he heard Verona stir next to him. They had passed out from exhaustion the night before.

"Bayen is awake," Tanneth said, his voice coming through comms. "I've been working with Sam through the night, and there is a lot more in there than we originally thought. This could give us a decisive advantage over the Zekara."

Aaron wiped the sleep from his eyes and was a bit envious of the fact that the Nanites reduced the amount of time needed for sleep in Hythariam. They still needed rest, but they could put it off for a while if they needed to.

"We'll be right there," Aaron said. He rolled his shoulders and stretched his neck. He had needed the rest, and his mind was clearer for it.

"I needed that," Verona said, stifling a yawn. "I swear I feel as if I slept for a week upon the feather mattresses that Vaughn is always going on about."

Aaron helped his friend to his feet. "No offense, but if I were on a feather mattress, I would much rather have Sarah at my side than you."

Verona grinned.

Aaron felt better too and wondered if the energy left in the white tree had somehow seeped into them while they slept. The comms device chimed again, and this time it was Sarah. Verona went on ahead, giving Aaron some privacy.

"My Queen," Aaron greeted.

"Good morning," Sarah said, and Aaron heard her smiling though he couldn't see her face. "You sound better," she said.

"I feel better. We camped out in the grove," Aaron said.

"Couldn't make it back to the palace?"

Aaron frowned. The palace was his, which was what everyone else more or less implied, but it wasn't home. Not yet at least. He had been taken through the palace and seen his mother's rooms. A small part of him still clung to his ties to Earth and had trouble imagining his mother growing up here. He had no such issues with his grandfather. Perhaps it was because he had seen his ghost when he first came to Shandara.

"I hate the comms device," Sarah said.

"So do I sometimes, but it's safer for you in Hathenwood," Aaron said.

"We'll get to that in a moment. I do have news. I assume that Gavril filled you in last night on the progress we've made with the cure," Sarah said.

"Yeah, he mentioned it. He said you had two people who were exposed to the virus. How do we know if it really works?"

"The virus is in full remission on one of them," Sarah said.

"And the other?"

"He was too far gone," Sarah said.

Something in her voice piqued his interest. "What is it?"

"The person that we were able to cure is Darven," Sarah said.

Aaron's teeth clamped down for a moment, and his eyes bored into the comms device. "Mactar's apprentice?"

"Yes," Sarah answered softly.

Aaron glanced to the north where he knew Hathenwood would be. *Darven!* The former Elitesman had been among those who had attacked his family on Earth. It was Darven's knife that had taken his mother's life. His hand locked around the hilt of his sword. Their paths crossed briefly at Shandara, but with battling the Drake, Darven was able to get away. The old anger rose up in him. Darven deserved death, but Aaron had seen so much of it lately that part of him was sickened at the thought. If he blazed a path to Hathenwood to take Darven's life, nothing would change. Halcylon would still be poised to attack, and those who had died would still be dead.

"Talk to me," Sarah said.

"I appreciate you telling me," Aaron said.

"I had thought to keep it from you, but I don't want there to be any more secrets between us."

A pang of regret seeped into Aaron's stomach because he hadn't told her about Bayen. "I want him dead, but I'm so tired of the killing. If it weren't for this war, I'd be perfectly happy to hang my swords up and never use them again."

"I know what you mean. I have an idea that I think you will approve," Sarah said.

"What is it?"

"Death doesn't have to be the only answer, though I agree in this case it would be well deserved. Let Darven stand trial after all this is done," Sarah said.

Aaron was silent for a moment, allowing his mind to come to grips with Sarah's suggestion. He took a firm hold of the voice inside him that cried out for vengeance. He would lead by example and trust in the rule of law to see justice done.

"Okay. Hold Darven, and he will be tried like anyone else," Aaron said.

"If he tries to escape, the guards will kill him, but I don't think he'll try. He was exposed to the virus, and though he was cured, he seems to be a bit less of himself than before. Roselyn explained that the cure works to prevent the virus, so we'll be coming to Shandara to distribute it shortly," Sarah said.

"Please stay in Hathenwood. I need to know that you're safe," Aaron pleaded.

"*I* need to know *you're* safe, which is why I will be at your side," Sarah replied.

"What about—"

"Don't you dare! You and everyone else thinks I should stay where it's safe because I'm pregnant. I won't do it. Not while you and everyone else will be fighting around me," Sarah said.

"But—"

Sarah cut him off again. "It's not up for discussion. No one controls my destiny. I will go where I choose, and I choose to fight at your side."

Aaron was silent for a moment, trying to think of a way he could get her to stay away from the fighting.

"If you die, and I were to live—left alone to raise our baby—how would I explain to them that I stayed idly by while their father died in battle? No. I'm coming, and that's final."

Aaron knew that tone. There was little he could say or do at this point to sway her, and the part that irked him most was that she was right. It was unfair of him to ask this of her, but he sure as hell didn't like it.

"Fine," Aaron said.

In his mind he was already planning his next move, and it didn't involve Sarah fighting at his side. She would be furious that he planned to go off without her, but at least she would be alive to be furious with him. That's what mattered.

"Gavril has kept us informed of what you're planning. Don't even think of charging off without me, Shandarian," Sarah warned.

"The thought never crossed my mind," Aaron said, but he knew she wasn't fooled. Instead, she closed the connection, leaving him to imagine her shouting for them to move faster. At some point, she would realize that her travel crystal was missing and trace that back to him as well. He had friends in Hathenwood.

Something Sarah had said stood out in his mind. *Death wasn't always the answer.* Her words repeated in his mind. It wasn't the first time she had said something along those lines. Aaron's thoughts raced away, chasing an elusive idea that remained stubbornly out of reach. He quickened his pace to the command center to meet up with the others.

Aaron entered the command center and found Gavril speaking with a host of others.

"Where did the intel come from?" Gavril asked Tanneth, who looked relieved as Aaron joined them. Gavril followed Tanneth's gaze to Aaron and frowned. "I see, care to enlighten me?"

"About what exactly?" Aaron asked.

"This new intel that allows us access into the Zekaran computer systems," Gavril said.

"Do you trust me?"

"Of course," Gavril answered.

"Then trust that the intel is good, but don't make it the foundation for our strategic defense or attack. We're not even sure it's going to work," Aaron said.

Gavril frowned. "Can I speak with you privately for a moment?"

Aaron nodded, and they moved off to the side.

"I don't like being kept in the dark. Especially where it involves our enemy. I can help you if you will let me," Gavril said.

Aaron didn't like keeping Gavril in the dark about this, but the less people knew, the more they would be able to concentrate on other things. "Please believe me when I say this, but this isn't a matter of me not trusting you. We've stumbled onto something that we might be able to leverage in the battle with the Zekara."

"That's great. Why the secrecy?" Gavril asked.

"Because if it doesn't work then we've lost nothing," Aaron said.

Gavril looked away for a moment and then turned back to him and saluted with a fist across his heart. "You are our commander," Gavril said, and let the matter drop.

Aaron reached out to Gavril. "I promise I will tell you everything."

Gavril nodded, and they rejoined the others.

"What I'm about to say doesn't leave this room and certainly not on any comms channels. Is that clear?" Aaron asked. The people in the room all nodded. Some faces were familiar, and others Aaron didn't recognize. Anytime he met with the FNA, he made it a point to get to know the people he was working with when time permitted. "At any moment, the Zekara will attack Shandara. They will bring the full force of their army against us and use every means at their disposal. It's doubtless you've heard rumors about the new intel we have about the enemy. What I'm willing to share with you is that we do have something in the works, but it may be a farce. At this point, we're not sure yet. Many of you know Tanneth. He's working on something that may give us an advantage in the next battle with the Zekara. He may come to you with a request in the near future. If this occurs, I need for you to give it your highest priority because it could mean the difference between victory and defeat."

"How do you know the Zekara will attack?" Braden asked.

"Because I'm going to take a small force and vehemently ask them to," Aaron said.

Many in the room nodded in approval, but some had their doubts.

"Shandara is where this war was meant to be fought. Even in its current state, we stand the best chance at defeating our enemy here than anywhere else. I'm not eager for another battle, but the more time we give the Zekara, the more the advantage swings in their favor. The Forsaken will be a factor in this battle. They caught us off guard at Rexel. We fought in the streets and on the battlefield. We will be better prepared this time. Another reason to attack them is that right now the Zekara have the offensive. They know the taste of victory. We need to hit them back just like we did with the High King. Make no mistake. The Zekara will offer no quarter, and we need to be ready to fight a battle on those terms," Aaron said.

The horrors they faced at Rexel shone on the faces of anyone who had been there. For everyone else there was a heated desire to even the score.

"What if they surrender?" Verona asked.

"If it comes to it, then we let them," Aaron answered. "We're not barbarians. We're better than they are. If they surrender, we disarm them and take them into custody."

There were many challenging glares in the room, and Aaron met all of their gazes. If they didn't like that, then it was too damn bad. He would never sanction wholesale murder of a foe who would surrender.

"Are we not men of honor?" Aaron asked, his gaze sweeping around the room.

There were a few moments of silence before a grim-faced officer wearing Rexel's colors stood. Aaron had seen him before in the company of Prince Cyrus. Wallis was his name. Lines of grief and smoldering anger rolled off the officer in waves. The pristine gray uniform of the Rexellian corps was faded and bloodstained.

Wallis lifted his head, and the shadows of grief burned from his gaze. "Honor won't win us this war," Wallis said.

"Honor is what will allow us to hold our heads up after the war is over and know that we didn't sacrifice our own souls for the hollowness of victory," Aaron said firmly.

"I don't want honor. I want all the Zekara dead for what they've done."

"I want them to pay for what they've done too. Never believe otherwise, but I won't fight this war without mercy. The order stands. If any of the Zekara surrender, then we take them into custody," Aaron said.

"What about justice for my family, my prince, our homes..." Wallis said.

Aaron knew all too well the pain that was upon the survivors of Rexel. He too had lost a home and a family. Aaron walked in front of Wallis and spoke softly. "You can never kill enough to fill the void that's in you now. It will only make it bigger, until the darkness consumes you. Honor their memory with the actions you take. Fight as if they stand at your side watching your every move."

The fight left Wallis's eyes, and the good man that he was returned. This would be a constant struggle, and the effects of this war would be felt long after they quit the battlefield. The meeting went on for a short while longer, until Aaron dismissed them. The forces gathered in Shandara had already maintained a state of readiness since the High King had attacked them.

"I'll make sure our group is ready," Verona said.

Aaron nodded and approached Tanneth. "Where is Bayen?"

""He's down the hall, waiting for you," Tanneth replied.

Aaron nodded and glanced at Gavril, who stood before several bronze holo displays. "Bring Gavril into this if you need to. Tell him about the AI if it becomes an issue. I don't know if I would tell him all the details because it sounds crazy."

Tanneth grinned. "I mean no disrespect when I say this, but crazy and you go hand in hand."

"It would appear that way," Aaron said.

"Oh, here, take this," Tanneth said, and handed Aaron Bayen's halberd.

It was an exquisite weapon that was extremely well balanced. At the end of the haft was a Dragon carving with flames spewing from its mouth that extended into the bladed end. The rest of it was red mixed with gold. The blade was sharp and despite the heavy use the past few days, showed little signs of wear.

"Oh, and this," Tanneth said, handing Aaron a small metallic sphere.

"What does it do?" Aaron asked.

"It will be quicker to try and access the Zekaran systems with this. It's a reconnaissance drone. I've upgrade it with the information from Bayen's AI. If it works, then we'll know that much more about their systems," Tanneth said.

Aaron nodded and stuffed the small drone into his pocket. A few minutes later, Aaron stood in front of the door to where Bayen was being held. He nodded to the two FNA soldiers that stood guard and went through. Bayen sat on the floor, leaning back against the wall. He looked at Aaron and then at the halberd. Bayen slowly rose to his feet. He looked calmer than he had been yesterday.

"Let's take a walk," Aaron said.

He went through the door first, and Bayen followed. The FNA soldiers waited for a few moments and followed as well. They left the command center through the elevator that would take them to the grove. Aaron led him to the remains of the white tree and leaned the halberd against it. Bayen kept looking around, failing to keep the awe from his face. When Bayen noticed Aaron watching him, he closed his mouth and waited.

"I've been watching you since you joined us," Aaron said. "I've seen you fight alongside the rest of us. Saved lives, been helpful, and shown kindness…" Aaron paused and smiled slightly. "Well, to most of us."

A slight smile tugged at the edges of Bayen's lips. "Does this mean you believe me?"

"I'm not sure," Aaron said. "I believe that you did what you believed to be right. Just because our paths crossed doesn't mean there was malicious intent. But I didn't bring you here to talk about whether I believe you or not."

"Why did you bring me here?"

Aaron extended the halberd toward Bayen. "I brought you here to ask for your help in the coming battle."

Bayen's mouth fell open. He slowly reached for the halberd. "You never asked for my help before. You always commanded."

Aaron suppressed a shudder. The thought of becoming so cold frightened him. He didn't want to become the hardened man that Bayen had known. He saw some familiarities in Bayen's mannerisms that reminded Aaron of himself and Sarah, but he wondered if they only appeared because now he was looking for them. Despite all his doubts, Aaron found himself believing what Bayen had told them.

With a story like that you couldn't pick and choose the parts you wanted to believe. Verona was right: it was a leap of faith.

"Let's see if we can change fate," Aaron said.

Bayen's chin trembled, and he looked away. "I tried so hard to hate you. I did hate you. I even thought about killing you to avoid what is to come."

"What stopped you?"

"The AI said it wouldn't stop the Ryakul virus from spreading and I... couldn't."

Aaron watched Bayen for a moment. *His son?*

"You were different than what I remembered. So young. This place was gone, with only whispers to mark its passing," Bayen said.

"We're still here. The future is not set. There is still time," Aaron said.

Bayen winced and collapsed to his knees, clutching his chest.

"Warning. Temporal matrix is at 15 percent," the AI said.

Aaron tried to help Bayen back up, but he collapsed again.

"It hurts," Bayen cried.

Aaron seized the energy and extended it toward him. Bayen's lifebeat rippled before him as if it were out of focus. Aaron had never seen anything like it. It was like some unseen force was tearing Bayen's lifebeat away. Aaron reached out and found the pattern beneath the ripple. He extended the energy across, saturating Bayen's lifebeat, bringing it into alignment, and the rippling diminished. Bayen sighed, his breathing returning to normal.

"I don't know what you did, but thank you," Bayen said.

"I just tried to reinforce the pattern that was already there," Aaron said.

"I don't have much time. I'm not sure what you intend to do, but I will help however I can," Bayen said.

"Thank you," Aaron said. "Let's get to it. Verona and the others are waiting for us."

"What about Halcylon?" Bayen asked.

Aaron pressed his lips together in thought. "We'll try to take him alive if we can. That's the best I can offer."

Fifty-five percent probability wasn't conclusive as far as Aaron was concerned, but at the same time he wouldn't put it past the ruthless general to unleash something horrible in the event of his death. As he turned to head toward Verona and the rest of the men, Aaron noticed Thraw's cold green eyes watching him. The maul-cat kept close because he believed that Aaron was his best chance for putting him near Halcylon. He hoped the recon drone that Tanneth gave him worked. Aaron glanced at Bayen as they walked. It was hard to believe that this was his son. Bayen was only a few years younger than Aaron was now. He decided not to dwell on it. They caught up with Verona and the rest of their forces. Interspersed throughout them were armored domes that had a small protrusion.

"These were all we could salvage," Verona said.

"What are they?" Bayen asked.

"They house focusing crystals that can shoot bursts of energy. They have limited range, so we'll need to get in close to use them," Aaron said.

Bayen frowned. "They won't last long against the Zekara."

"They don't need to. We need to get them into position at key locations. Take a few shots and get out again," Aaron said.

"All at once?" Bayen asked.

Aaron shook his head. "No, in succession. I want to pull their attention into as many directions as I can."

"There are still Forsaken there," Verona said.

"I'm counting on it. Let's keep this simple. We get in and out quickly. If we can do that and salvage this equipment, great; if not, we'll leave it. The focusing crystals have a full charge," Aaron said.

Verona leveled his gaze at him. "Is the Eldarin still there?"

Aaron nodded.

"That's the part that worries me, my friend," Verona said.

"Let me worry about the Eldarin," Aaron said.

They split into six groups, each with their own keystone accelerator. The men with them were all battle hardened and ready to go. They would take some time to get into position and then strike. He glanced at the palace, and his thoughts went to Sarah. She was on her way here, bringing the vaccine against the Ryakul virus. *Forgive me.* Aaron gave the command, and the portals opened up. Aaron took a deep breath and charged through.

CHAPTER 27
BELIEF

The Zekaran mobile command center lurched forward. The bronze holo displays flickered for a moment, which was a subtle reminder to Halcylon of their depleting power. Chinta waved him over to the private display he was working from.

"Sir," he began quietly, "I have the results of the investigation you ordered. They found that some records have been deleted, but the guilty party had to rush and didn't cover their tracks very well. You were right. Someone released the maul-cat while we were still on Hytharia."

Halcylon nodded. The doors on the opposite side of the operations center opened, and Ronin entered, leading a small team of scientists. They were preparing to go back out to study the Dragon hybrid.

"Were you able to get an ID?" Halcylon asked.

"Not from the actual holding areas, no, but we did find them in the entrance logs," Chinta said.

The display showed encrypted characters. Halcylon authenticated and was immediately granted access. His gaze narrowed as he quickly read through the log entries. Halcylon spun around, and for a moment he and Ronin locked gazes.

"Stop him!" Halcylon shouted.

Surprise didn't register on his science officer's face. Just resignation that his gambit was finally up and the betrayal had finally come to light.

Alarms blared, and the lighting inside the operations center shifted to red. They were being attacked. The military operations staff immediately went to work. Halcylon looked back where Ronin had been, but his chief science officer was gone.

Chinta glanced at the log display. "It was him? This whole time he was right there. Why would he betray you?"

Halcylon slammed his fist onto the table. "Because he's loyal to the traitors. I want him found."

A Zekaran soldier approached. "Sir, FNA forces are attacking us. We have three marks—no, make that four marks and counting. Ground assault only," the soldier said.

"On-screen," Halcylon ordered.

The main holo display showed an aerial display from the drones they had deployed. The soldiers were using some sort of energy weapon. Halcylon clenched his teeth, searching for the one human he was sure would be there. The beams were wreaking havoc on the smaller units. Smoking wrecks were evident across the display. To the untrained eye, the attacks appeared to crop up at random, but Halcylon knew better.

"Have them fall back to the away points. Operation Trident authorized. We take Shandara now," Halcylon said.

***

"They're retreating," Verona said.

Moments before, the Zekara had been attacking in force. Aaron narrowed his gaze, following the Zekara's retreat. He engaged the recon drone only a few minutes ago. The small metallic drone zoomed away from them. To minimize the chance of drawing the Forsaken, he had purposefully not used his swords. They hadn't seen any so far, which Aaron didn't like. He knew they were somewhere close by.

"What now, my friend?" Verona asked.

"Have the men fall back to Shandara. We don't have enough to go toe to toe with them," Aaron said.

Verona gave the orders through the comms device. These had been secure against the Zekara. The FNA started falling back, but only after taking a few more shots with the Khamearrian focusing crystals. Very few were intact and would not be brought back to Shandara.

Tanneth's signal came over Aaron's comms device.

"The drone is working. I'm in their systems. They just sent a signal about something called Operation Trident," Tanneth said.

"They're falling back here. If I had to guess, I think they're getting ready to leave. Tell Gavril I'm sending the rest of the men back to see if they can slow them down a bit," Aaron said.

Verona and Bayen looked at Aaron expectantly.

"Let's go start some trouble," Aaron said.

"You know I'm in. What is it you intend to do?" Verona asked.

"Make the Forsaken work for us. We find where they are and lead them to the camp," Aaron said.

"Simple enough plan. Just don't let them catch you," Verona said.

Aaron drew in the energy and sped off with Verona and Bayen close on his heels. He drew his swords, and a few random notes from the bladesong could be heard. Aaron extended tendrils of energy to Verona and Bayen, strengthening their own connections so they could keep up with him. When they first arrived, it was hard to see the smoldering remains of Rexel. The only thing worse than that sight was the stricken look on Verona's normally happy face. He promised Verona he would help rebuild the city with him when this was all done. They sped along the ground, which blurred by. If he had been alone, he might have risked a jump, but soaring through the air might prove too tempting a target for the Zekara.

They circled the remains of Rexel's walls, covering the long distance in minutes, closing in on what remained of the eastern gates. Hundreds of dark shadows were clustered together so tightly that they formed a large mound. Aaron came to a stop a few hundred yards away. There was hardly anything left even remotely human in the Forsaken's appearance. The clothing of their human hosts was little more than rags all stretched and torn. Blackened skin stretched over elongated bones that poked through in harsh spikes. Great clawed hands dragged on the ground by their slumped forms.

"Goddess be merciful," Verona gasped.

"No, let the Goddess lend us her speed. Here they come," Bayen said.

Aaron wielded his swords, and the pure notes of the bladesong pierced the air. A rage filled howl spread across the Forsaken. They rose up, forming a massive dark wave pierced by yellow eyes that barreled toward them. The ground rumbled beneath their feet, and the great mound shifted.

"Go!" Aaron said.

Verona and Bayen sped off toward the Zekaran encampment. Aaron stayed a few more seconds to be sure the bulk of the Forsaken were coming. An enormous head poked through the dark forms that dropped off it like a shroud made up of bodies. The mound that the

Forsaken had clustered around was the Eldarin. The Dragon lord stirred in response to the bladesong and fixed Aaron with a baleful glare. The Forsaken moved quickly and were almost upon him. Aaron spun, taking in a torrent of energy, and darted away from the horde.

Come on, Aaron urged in his mind as he sped forth.

He quickly caught up to Verona and Bayen and slowed down to match their pace. They were closing on the Zekaran encampment with a horde of Forsaken on their heels. The Zekara began firing their weapons at them. They dodged plasma bolts as they raced by. The Forsaken shrieked as they closed in on their quarry. Aaron reached out, grabbed the others, and engaged the travel crystal. They emerged at Shandara and skidded to a halt, barely keeping their feet beneath them.

"That was close," Verona gasped.

Aaron gulped mouthfuls of air and nodded. Towering over them were statues honoring the Safanarion Order.

Bayen collapsed to the ground, clutching his chest.

"What's wrong with him?" Verona asked.

Aaron seized the energy. Bayen's lifebeat was a spinning mass of gold and black. He tried to bolster the pattern as he had done before, but it didn't work. It was like trying to capture running water. Aaron reached out and took Bayen's hand. Bayen's eyes were a mix of pain and terror.

"I'm not gonna let you go," Aaron said.

Bayen struggled to speak but couldn't.

Aaron looked at Verona. "The staff," he said, and gestured with his head toward the rune-carved staff that leaned against the fallen white tree.

Verona raced to get it.

"What's this?" a voice said, approaching them from the opposite direction.

Aaron turned and saw Tolvar racing toward them.

"Please, Tolvar, I don't know how to help him," Aaron said.

Tolvar knelt down next to them, his eyes going from Aaron to Bayen in shock. The lines along his forehead seemed more pronounced on his bald head.

"Here is the staff," Verona said.

Aaron grabbed the staff, and the runes flared.

"Bind him to you," Tolvar said.

"I don't know how," Aaron said.

Tolvar smiled at Aaron sadly and mouthed a single word.

Aaron closed his eyes, focusing on Bayen's lifebeat. The arguments rallied up inside him, and he swept them aside. He had to believe. He opened up his lifebeat and extended a golden tendril that came from his core. He urged it toward Bayen, and it latched onto his chest. The spinning core of Bayen's lifebeat slowed down, and he sagged in a great sigh. His breathing returned to normal. Bayen squeezed Aaron's hand, and he let go. The glowing runes of the staff diminished.

"You're all right," Aaron said.

Bayen nodded and slowly sat up. His ashen face still remained pale, and Aaron didn't know what to do.

"The time lines are separating. I don't know how much time I have left," Bayen said.

"Verona, warn the others that the Zekara are going to attack," Aaron said.

"Would either of you care to explain to me what's going on?" Tolvar asked.

Aaron was about to answer when several people came from around the fallen tree. Sarah rounded the corner, looking none too pleased with him. Her golden hair hung in a braid, and her hand rested upon the hilt of her sword.

"Well, don't keep us waiting, my love. Answer the question."

CHAPTER 28
BATTLE

"They're attacking us," a tech said. Despite years of training, he couldn't keep the surprise from his voice.

The main display showed the Forsaken barreling toward their encampment. Halcylon frowned at the screen. *Well played, human.* Halcylon thought.

"Let's play, human," Halcylon muttered. "Send in a squad with the secondary keystone accelerator, using these coordinates."

The tech's fingers flew over his console. "Orders given, sir."

Halcylon nodded. The humans believed they were safe behind their walls. They would soon learn that there was nowhere safe from him.

"Sir, main keystone accelerators are ready."

Halcylon checked the coordinates. "This ends now. Operation Trident is go."

His orders were repeated and confirmed. A bright curtain of light stretched between two pylons. He was draining the reserve power but knew that there was a power source in Shandara that would last hundreds of years. The Zekara in the mobile command center cheered. They were hungry for this fight just as he knew they would be. They were the finest army from their beloved home world. He would resurrect Hytharia from the ashes of Safanar and make the humans pay for daring to rise up against their betters.

***

A squad of former Elitesmen formed a perimeter. They were young and eager to prove themselves. Aaron recognized Isaac, who nodded in greeting. The old Elitesman was ever watchful and would protect Sarah until his dying breath. Aaron met Sarah's icy gaze. He couldn't help the slight tug of his lips or the softening of his face as he took in the sight of her. Though their time apart had been short, so much had changed, which made his heart ache at the sight of her all the more. Her gaze softened for a moment and then resumed its frosty demeanor. Sarah was right, comms was a terrible way to communicate with the ones you love. She looked at Bayen, who stood with his mouth agape.

Alarms blared through Shandara. The city was under attack. Messages began spewing forth over comms. The Zekara were outside the city walls. They'd used a massive keystone accelerator to move their entire army. Thousands were pouring through. Not giving the Zekara any breathing room, Gavril immediately ordered the attack.

Aaron stepped before Sarah and took her hand in his. "I promise I will explain everything to you."

Airships raced overhead, engines firing at full burst. Hythariam flyers zipped past the much slower airships. The skies over the walls in the distance flashed as the fighting began in earnest.

"We're right behind you," Sarah said. Her eyes dared him to ask her to stay behind.

"Aaron, we have a secondary portal signature coming from the heart of the city," Tanneth's voice said over comms. "Forsaken are pouring through."

Aaron's gut clenched. It was Rexel all over again. *No!* They were better prepared. Most people who couldn't fight were sheltering at the palace and in various strongholds throughout the city. Aaron glanced at Sarah, and the same look of horror reflected in her eyes.

The cure.

"We were distributing it to the people. There are lines of them waiting outside the palace and near the command center," Sarah said.

"Tanneth, we need soldiers at the distribution points for the cure," Aaron said, and paused, pursing his lips in thought. "Have them bring keystone accelerators." Aaron looked at the others. "I have an idea."

***

The western gates to Shandara opened, and Braden led a legion of De'anjard through. Hythariam cannons belched plasma bolts into the Zekaran forces still coming through the portal.

"Shields!" Braden shouted, and his command was echoed down the line.

De'anjard in bronze colored armor engaged their Shandarian shields. The shields fanned out from the rods, forming large ovals. Braden activated his shield and knew that if it could repel an Elitesman's attack orb, then it should repel the plasma bolts from the Zekaran weapons.

Braden raised his Warden's hammer into the air. "Forward!"

The legion of De'anjard charged forward with shields in front.

Maintaining the line, they closed in on the black armored Zekara. The Zekara fired their weapons, and the plasma bolts bounced harmlessly off the shields. The De'anjard pushed faster, screaming their battle cries. The front line of Zekaran soldiers changed weapons for close-quarters fighting.

Now it was a fight, Braden thought, and slammed his hammer down upon the first Zekara he met with an energy enhanced blow.

***

"Here we are again," Verona said, racing along next to Aaron.

They had found the Zekaran portal in the city square located in the center of Shandara. Hundreds of Forsaken poured through. Knowing the Forsaken threat, the remaining people scrambled into the stone buildings, seeking shelter. Aaron and the others arrived just in time. He raced ahead and engaged the bladesong, drawing the attention of the Forsaken. He cut through their front line and wheeled around, darting away from them. Their savage roars filled the street as they focused in on him. The others were on sides streets, enticing the Forsaken to chase. They worked in teams with one being the bait while the others cleaned up any stragglers.

"Is it ready?" Aaron spoke into his comms device as he ran.

"Almost," Bayen answered. "We'll have it up by the time you get here."

"Verona, take some of the men and circle back. We can't afford to have any stragglers loose," Aaron said.

Verona nodded and sped off with several former Elitesmen following. Sarah moved in next to Aaron, easily keeping his pace. The Forsaken snarled as they gave chase. Aaron and Sarah slowed enough to encourage the Forsaken to keep following.

"I hope this plan of yours works," Sarah said.

"So do I," Aaron replied. If it didn't work, they would need to fight the Forsaken up close.

This part of the city was still being rebuilt. Remnant buildings from the fall still lined the streets. They rounded a street corner to a narrow alleyway. A curtain of light opened in front of them. Aaron and Sarah leaped over it, and the Forsaken poured through the portal, unable to stop themselves. Aaron stayed just beyond the portal on top of a pile of rubble and kept the bladesong engaged. As the last of this group of Forsaken went through, the FNA soldiers deactivated the keystone accelerator.

"Where did you send them?" Sarah asked.

"Someplace where they can't harm anyone. About a hundred miles straight up," Aaron said.

The Forsaken would emerge on the other side, in the vacuum of outer space. If they fell back toward the surface, they would burn up in the atmosphere first. FNA soldiers reported in that the portal tactic was working elsewhere. Aaron wished he had thought of it sooner. The Forsaken threat was contained for the moment, but this battle had only just begun. They headed toward the city walls where the Zekaran army was still coming through the portal.

***

Airships fell from the sky in flaming husks. They were outmatched by the more advanced Zekaran flyers and combat drones. FNA soldiers riding on gliders swooped in, trying to rescue as many as they could. Sections of Shandara's great wall slid away, and gun turrets emerged, firing into the enemy.

Braden and the De'anjard fought toe to toe with the Zekaran soldiers. The Zekara were a strong enemy and fought well. For all their advanced technology, they hadn't lost their ability for close-quarters combat. There was still the underlying dependency upon their technology, and it was this that gave Braden and the De'anjard a slight edge. They kept the Zekaran ground force from entering the city. The Zekara regrouped to make another push, and the De'anjard used the opportunity to cluster together to form a shield wall. Braden put himself at the point and slammed his Warden's hammer upon his shield. He used the energy to fuel the vibrations in the shield, and the charging Zekara slammed into an unseen force that flung them back. Braden braced himself to counter the forces from his shield and was reinforced by the men at his back. He pivoted to the side, and more of the Zekaran soldiers were sent flying. The De'anjard fought with renewed vigor.

Behind the Zekaran line, something massive burst through the portal. Huge cannons emerged from the rooftop of the largest vehicle that Braden had ever seen. A glowing point appeared in each of the cannons as they primed to fire. Plasma bolts the size of airships lanced into Shandara's walls, leaving craters where they hit. Then they started targeting the De'anjard. Each blast blazed through the men, leaving nothing left.

"Get your men out of there," Gavril's voice said over the comms device. Turrets along Shandara's walls returned fire, but nothing was penetrating the hull of the Zekaran mobile command center.

"Fall back!" Braden bellowed.

The remaining airships of the Free Nations Army air corps crash landed between the two armies. Braden recognized the burning black hull of the *Raven*. They were sacrificing the ships so the De'anjard could pull back. Braden ordered a small detachment to make a quick sweep for survivors and bring them back inside the city walls. Then he turned and headed for the smoking wreck of the *Raven*. The De'anjard with him scrambled to help the sailors get off the ship.

"Where is the admiral?" Braden asked a sailor being carried off the ship.

"He was in the wheelhouse," the sailor said.

Braden didn't hear anything else as he charged onto the ship. Hythariam flyers swarmed overhead, giving them cover fire. Braden knew he had minutes before the focusing crystals in the ship's engine blew. Nearby explosions shook the hull beneath his feet. He crossed the deck and came to the shattered remains of the wheelhouse. Braden screamed Morgan's name and heard a slight response from inside. He scrambled to the side, where a support beam stuck out of the pile. Drawing in the energy, Braden fed it into his muscles and bones. He squatted down and braced his shoulder under the beam and heaved with all his strength. Grunting with effort, Braden lifted the roof of the wheelhouse several feet into the air. Bloodied, but very much alive, Admiral Morgan began to pull himself from the wreckage. Several Zekaran soldiers hauled themselves over the side and trained their weapons on them. Braden tensed up, anticipating the blast, but couldn't let go or Morgan would be crushed. As a Zekaran was about to fire, something silver flashed into the soldier's chest. The soldier's shot went wide, and the soldier went down. A man in white armor, similar to that of the Hythariam, landed between Braden and the soldiers. He wielded a bladed staff and made quick work of the opposing troops. More Zekaran soldiers pulled themselves over the side. Braden heard the melodious tune of the bladesong and felt his heart lift. Aaron was near. The Heir of Shandara and the warrior in white stood against the Zekaran soldiers, dispatching them quickly before continuing on. Morgan finally pulled himself clear of the wheelhouse. Blood peppered his side from his wounds, but he was alive. Braden let the beam go, and the roof came crashing down. Morgan tried to stand up and cried out in pain.

"Come on, old man. Let me get you out of here," Braden said, and lifted the groaning admiral over his shoulders.

Braden leaped down from the ship and nearly lost his balance. Stumbling at first, he regained his footing and ran. A few seconds later, the focusing crystals on the *Raven* blew. The airship came apart as each of the crystal chambers blew, sending the splintering remains of the ship soaring through the air.

***

Members of the De'anjard raced to help Braden. Aaron and the others continued to help get sailors off the airships before they blew. Aaron glanced at the city walls and noticed that fewer gun turrets were actually firing. Could they be overheating? Fire from the Zekaran mobile command center relentlessly pelted the defenders.

They escorted the wounded to the gates, and the De'anjard began regrouping for another charge. The field beyond the walls was already littered with bodies. *So much death,* Aaron thought in disgust. He looked at the Zekaran mobile command center hovering over the ground with thousands of soldiers between them. The soldiers began pushing forward.

Tolvar raced through the crowd of soldiers, with none giving any indication that they knew he was there. The gates to Shandara were still open, and the line of wounded were going through. A volley of crystal-tipped arrows flew overhead and into the charging Zekara. The small amount of crystallized dust was not enough to stop a fully armored Zekaran soldier, but it did slow some down.

"Don't you sense it?" Tolvar asked, and gestured toward the tall statues lining the main thoroughfare in the city just beyond the gates. "You're the key. They will fight for you."

Aaron glanced back at the statues. They were tall and startlingly lifelike. Buried beneath the surface of the statues were crystals. Aaron pulled in the energy, and his perceptions sharpened. The crystals shimmered along each of the statues, and Aaron could sense the energy gathered inside. He focused the energy through the staff, and the runes blazed. Aaron raced to the middle of the street and planted the blazing staff into the ground. He unleashed the energy, and tendrils shot forth, racing along the statues that lined the streets. The crystals glowed beneath the surface. Aaron closed his eyes and pulled more energy in, feeding it through the staff. *The Safanarion Order calls upon you.* Aaron sent the message along the tendrils of energy. *Defend the city.*

The statues broke free of the pedestals and raced toward the gates. Aaron removed his hands from the staff, and the statues immediately stopped moving. Tolvar nodded toward the staff. There was no other way. Aaron clutched the staff and closed his eyes. He drew from his own lifebeat and fed the energy into the statues. His vision fractured and grew distant, stemming from each of the statues. He heard Sarah call his name.

"It's all right. He's still with us," Tolvar said.

"Form a circle around him. Nothing gets through," Sarah ordered.

Aaron saw through the eyes of a hundred statues stomping their way out of the city and heading directly for the Zekara.

***

Halcylon's mouth fell open at the latest sight to emerge from the city walls. It seemed the human still had a few tricks up his sleeve. The city was even better defended than he originally thought.

"Focus your fire upon the approaching force," Halcylon said.

The ground force weapons were able to deal a small amount of damage, but not enough to stop them. There were only a hundred statues, but what they lacked in numbers they more than made up for in size. They were easily thirty feet tall. Following close behind was the enemy army seeking to take the advantage.

The main guns were locked on the lead statue. The full charge signal flashed on the display, and they fired. The blast vaporized the target.

Halcylon smiled hungrily. "Fire at will."

The soldiers in the command center remained focused, but Halcylon could sense the growing excitement in all of them. Victory was near. Nothing the humans had could stand against what he'd brought with him. Their army was overextending itself in this foolhardy charge.

Suddenly the lights in the command center powered down, and emergency lighting engaged. The mobile command center lurched forward, and Halcylon braced himself as it hit the ground. Alarms blared, and a cascade of failure messages sprang up on the emergency displays.

"Status report," Halcylon said.

"Systems are failing all over," a tech said.

"Which ones?" Halcylon asked. As soon as he asked the question, the remaining holo displays went out, plunging them into darkness. Halcylon cursed. The power in his armor still worked, and small lights appeared from their helmets. Halcylon brought up his comms device and attempted to gain system access. He was denied. He frowned and tried to override it, but it didn't work.

"I want the systems back online now. We're easy targets in here," Halcylon ordered.

"Sir, it's not just us. We're receiving reports of systems failing all over— from flyers to mobile ground vehicles. It seems as if everything but personal armor units are offline," the tech said.

Halcylon heard the panic in his voice. So far, only networked systems were affected. "Remember your training. Our enemy must have a suppressor of some sort. It has to be close by. We find it, and our systems will reactivate."

"But sir—"

"Move out!" Halcylon ordered before anyone else could raise any questions. There very well could have been a suppressor out there, but that wouldn't lock him out of the command center systems. That was something else entirely.

***

Aaron focused on controlling the statues, and they fought as one. He plunged through the Zekaran soldiers and came upon the command center. The connection to some of the statues was lost along the way, and Aaron knew they had been destroyed. The Zekaran mobile command center suddenly plunged to the ground, and Aaron pounced. The statues heaved crushing blows, ruining the main turrets.

The skies over Shandara darkened as if a sudden storm blew in. A dark rift sliced through the sky, followed by a burst of light. The infected Eldarin landed upon the ground. Soldiers from both armies scrambled to get out of the way. Aaron felt himself clutch the rune-carved staff. He could sense the presence of other Eldarin. They watched from just beyond the dimensional curtain that separated the realms. He wouldn't call them into battle. The risk to their kind was too great.

The infected Dragon lord let out a mournful howl and spun around. Its great clawed feet shook the ground as it moved. It seemed to be looking for something. Its hide was almost completely black, and its eyes no longer shone with stunning brilliance. It cocked its head to the side, noticing the armies upon the field. The Eldarin's eyes narrowed menacingly. It lurched forward, snapping its massive jaws at man and Hythariam alike. It took several seconds for Aaron to realize that the victims weren't killed. Their bodies convulsed on the ground as if they had been infected with the Ryakul virus.

No, Aaron thought. *This is how it begins. How the infection spreads to the other species. It's through the Eldarin.*

Both armies moved back from the infected Eldarin. The statues of the Safanarion Order wheeled around and charged the Eldarin as it still sought to infect anything that moved. Aaron circled the Eldarin, keeping the statues between the Dragon lord and both armies. Knowing that the infection of any source could lead to them all succumbing forced Aaron to protect the Zekara as well.

The Eldarin attacked, smashing the statues with its armored tail. The statues rushed in, attempting to pin the Eldarin to the ground. For a few fleeting moments, it worked. The Dragon lord was pushed off balance. It quickly regained its footing and heaved upward, thrusting the statues away.

Bayen led a group of De'anjard forward and began dispatching the newly infected people. Free Nations Army soldiers joined them, using Hythariam rifles to incinerate the bodies before they could rise again. After a few moments, the Zekaran soldiers nearest them were quick to follow their example.

The Eldarin made quick work of the remaining statues, and Aaron watched helplessly from a statue head as Bayen blurred into view to square off against it. Aaron opened his eyes and released the rune-carved staff, gasping. Sounds from the battle rushed in with startling clarity.

"Are you all right?" Sarah asked.

"Bayen!" Aaron shouted, and turned toward the Eldarin and then back at Sarah. "He's—"

"There is no time. You must face the Eldarin. She's too far gone to save," Sarah said.

An ear-piercing roar sounded overhead, cutting off his reply. The fallen Eldarin was racing toward them. Aaron drew his swords and leaped into the air, putting as much distance as possible between himself and the others. The Eldarin swung around and was immediately on his tail. Aaron raced along, faster than he had ever been before. Streaks of white trailed him from the glowing crystals in his blades. Still, the Eldarin gained. He led the Eldarin through the Zekara, decimating their lines. Aaron landed upon the Zekara's mobile command center. The infected Eldarin pounced, leaving a massive gaping hole. Aaron sprinted to the ground and began to wield his swords into the bladesong. Bayen appeared at his side, brandishing his bladed staff. The Eldarin lashed out with its talons, and they both dodged out of the way.

"We have to kill it. It's the source of the plague," Bayen said.

"No," Aaron cried. Death couldn't be the only answer. If he killed the Eldarin, the sacred pact with the Ferasdiam marked would be broken forever. War with the Eldarin would doom Safanar just as surely as an unstoppable plague.

The Eldarin shook its head at some unseen force. Bayen cried out, clutching his chest, sinking to his knees. The Dragon lord lunged its head at Bayen, and Aaron stepped in front of him, slashing up with his swords. His glowing blades bit into the Eldarin's snout, and it reared back. Aaron swung his blades in a wide arc, using the energy to form a barrier. The Eldarin slammed down upon the barrier, its mouth and blackened teeth attempting to bite through it. The Dragon lord sucked in a huge breath, and a beam of energy spewed forth, slamming into the barrier. The ensuing glow blocked his view of the Eldarin, but the area around him erupted in flames. The crushing force drove the barrier to Aaron's outstretched hands. Aaron heaved and pushed out with all his might. The barrier expanded, knocking the Eldarin's massive head back, and dissipated.

The sky above them turned lime green. The presence of the other Eldarin felt closer than they had been before. A rift opened in the sky, and the Eldarin poured through. They circled overhead, too many to count. The infected Eldarin growled warily up at them. Aaron wielded his swords into the bladesong, keeping the infected Eldarin's attention on him. He reached out through the energy to the infected Eldarin. The Dragon lord's lifebeat was a shimmering mass of darkness with whispers of light peeking through. A low hum thundered through the air as the Eldarin in the sky merged their melody with Aaron's bladesong. The infected Eldarin shook its head and stood rooted in place. Aaron poured himself into the dance, moving at speeds faster than the eye could track. He circled the infected Eldarin, forming a barrier of light. He felt his physical body begin to slip away as he drew in closer to the Eldarin's lifebeat. The darkness was being pushed back. Aaron felt echoes of Bayen's presence being pulled farther away. The Eldarin howled mournfully from above, and a celestial glow surrounded Bayen. Aaron came to a stop. The barrier of light remained, fueled by his connection to the energy. Bayen lay upon the ground, his eyes oddly serene as he looked up at Aaron. His body was translucent, as if only part of him was still there. Bayen rose to his feet and stepped toward the barrier. Aaron went to stop him, but Bayen held up his hand. Aaron's feet became rooted in place. He felt tendrils of energy wrapped tightly around his legs.

"It's not your turn," Bayen said.

Aaron struggled to move his legs and inserted his own tendrils of energy to free them.

Bayen stepped closer to the barrier that was winding tighter against the infected Eldarin. "You can't. If you cross the threshold, everything will be lost."

"I can't let you do this," Aaron cried. A lump filled his throat, knowing that he was moments from losing his son forever. "Bayen!" Aaron called.

Bayen turned back, and the swirling vortex of darkness seemed to stretch against the Eldarin's lifebeat.

"My time is up," Bayen said, his body fading and his voice sounding as if he spoke from a tunnel. The Eldarin's light spread in a pool around him.

"Don't go, please, we've had no time," Aaron said.

Bayen glanced down at his fading body and back at Aaron. "They were wrong about you, Father, and so was I. None of this was your fault. I understand that now. You were defending us. You were always defending us."

A great thunderclap shook the ground beneath Aaron's feet as the time line tore itself away.

Bayen's body melted away, and his glowing lifebeat merged with that of the infected Eldarin. The darkness that dominated the Eldarin's lifebeat relented as the being was forged anew. The darkness didn't recede entirely but was brought into the fold. The Eldarin circling in the sky came to a stop and hovered, all their collective focus on the cocoon of light engulfing the infected Dragon lord. The cocoon of light collapsed, and a newly forged Dragon lord leaped into the air, joining its brethren. The sky over Shandara blazed overhead as more of the Eldarin came, dwarfing the city walls. They swam through the sky, washing the city in a warm glow.

The tendrils of energy that held Aaron melted away. He was free. "Bayen!" he cried out.

A lone Eldarin separated itself from the rest. Its hide was darkish gray and shone with a light of its own accord. It closed in and hovered in the air. Aaron felt a surge within him as he was drawn into its majestic gaze. The Dragon lord's eyes were at once both celestial and human mixed together, and Aaron saw something familiar in its gaze. A knowing.

Son.

The Eldarin's head lowered in acknowledgement.

We will meet again, the Eldarin said for him alone.

The sky split open in a streak of celestial light, and the Eldarin began going through, leaving the realm of Safanar. One Eldarin flew in a wide arc, circling the battlefield, and roared. The De'anjard and the FNA soldiers cheered back in response. At once, the sky that had been awash in color returned to normal as the Dragon lords left the realm of Safanar in a peak of glorious light.

Aaron sank to his knees and dropped his swords. Groups of Zekaran soldiers emerged from whatever cover they'd found. Thousands of their number lay dead upon the field. The FNA, along with the De'anjard, quickly moved in. The Zekaran mobile command center was a smoking wreck. A small contingent of Zekaran soldiers raced toward him, and Aaron recognized the armor of General Halcylon. Halcylon came before him, and his soldiers fanned out.

"You think you've won, human. Think again—"

Halcylon was cut off as his legs gave way underneath him. The vicious growl of a maul-cat was heard before anyone saw its shaggy form pin the Zekaran general to the ground with a metallic talon pressed against his throat. Thraw growled menacingly, ready to fulfill his imprint and take Halcylon's life.

Aaron regained his feet. The Zekara aimed their weapons at him though he was unarmed. They had seen what he could do and were wary.

"Would it be so terrible to throw down your weapons?" Aaron asked. "Look around you. There is no honor to be gained in death. I give you this one chance at life. If you're smart, you'll take it. Make any move other than surrendering your weapons, and I will kill you all where you stand."

The Zekaran soldiers divided their gaze between Halcylon and Aaron. Then one by one they dropped their weapons.

"Let him up, Thraw," Aaron said.

Thraw's talon sank deeper into Halcylon's neck. A trickle of blood came from the wound.

"He deserves death," Thraw said.

"You're right, he does. But if you fulfill your imprint and take his life, then *your* life is forfeit. You cannot return to Hytharia, and whoever did this to you is gone. The one thing that you can do is let him go. We will take him into custody," Aaron said.

FNA soldiers surrounded the group of them, and Sarah came to his side.

Aaron knelt down to be eye level with Thraw. The maul-cat gave him a warning growl.

"Please. Trust that justice will be served to him. You have my word. You saved my life when you brought me back to this world. Let me do the same for you."

Thraw's wild eyes looked uncertain for a moment, and then he backed off Halcylon.

"I am a patient hunter. I can wait to kill him," Thraw said.

Aaron thanked him. The maul-cat's gaze was fixed on Halcylon, who came to his feet. Hythariam soldiers removed his armor and took him away.

"You pleaded for his life?" Sarah asked.

Aaron looked into her eyes. "I kept a promise to someone else," he said.

Verona joined them. He carried Bayen's halberd and bracers. "There was nothing else left."

Aaron glanced toward the sky where the Eldarin had been. "Everything that counts is where it should be."

CHAPTER 29
CHANCE

The remains of the Zekaran army were disarmed and taken prisoner. Without their technology, they had no hope of defeating the FNA. Ring leaders were separated from the others, and Halcylon was kept isolated. There were pockets of resistance from the genetically enhanced soldiers that had been conditioned only for battle. They were hunted down. Iranus and the other Hythariam scientist analyzed the Nanites used in the Zekara and soon discovered the root of the unwavering loyalty to Halcylon. Protocols embedded into the Nanites exerted their influence when behaviors were exhibited that opposed his wishes. Roselyn surmised that the influence wasn't instantaneous, but over time those under the influence would be more agreeable. It was a form of mind control on a grand scale that rivaled any propaganda machine throughout history. Aaron ordered the Nanite protocols in the Zekara be overwritten with the only functionality being those that dealt with sickness. Most Zekara denied the mind control claims even when presented with irrefutable evidence. Stopping the Nanites from enforcing Halcylon's influence wasn't nearly enough to reverse what had been done to them. Their brains had been trained, and such conditioning could only be reversed over time, if ever. The few thousand Zekara left would be allowed to live out their lives peacefully if they chose. Aaron strongly urged them to seize this second chance at life and let the ghosts of their home world finally come to rest. Some would choose a peaceful life, and others would require a watchful eye.

The leaders of the Zekara were another story. Rulership over the Zekara had been consolidated into a powerful few. They were several hundred years old and believed themselves to be immortal. Aaron supposed with the Nanites they were pretty close. But if immortality came at the expense of one's soul, then that was something he could pass on. Life without end was a violation of the natural order of all things and was the road to stagnation and destruction. Beings were meant to live, grow old, and die. Hopefully, Aaron and his kind would leave something of themselves behind and the world in a better state than which they found it.

Thraw remained vigilant in his watch over Halcylon. They had found little information on the process used to imprint a target upon the maul-cat's consciousness. In the days that followed, Aaron urged Thraw to join him on hikes through the forest. Each day, Thraw would accompany him, Sarah, and sometimes Verona. They would venture farther from Shandara with each trip. Several times, Tanneth joined them, but there was an inherent distrust of all Hythariam from the maul-cat. Sarah was Thraw's favorite. They had met after the battle, and there was an instant understanding that passed between the two. Since then, Thraw had become quite protective of Sarah, and Aaron believed it was because she was pregnant. Not even an imprint could override paternal instinct.

Aaron stood outside Halcylon's cell. The Zekaran general smoldered as he sat upon the floor. The chair and bed looked unused as if the Hythariam couldn't stand the thought of touching them. The general had been given simple Hythariam clothing that covered his large frame.

"Have you come to gloat, human?"

Aaron shook his head.

"I'm eager to get to my execution. Have you come to escort me?"

"If I wanted you dead, then you wouldn't be here. I will keep you here for as long as I choose to," Aaron replied. He had to be sure there weren't any hidden traps or protocols that would be set in motion should the Zekaran general meet with his demise.

"What did you do to my Nanites? They're different," Halcylon said. He shifted as if he couldn't get comfortable and continued to fidget.

Aaron stepped closer, knowing that the cell's force field would keep Halcylon from doing anything. "We uploaded them with the same protocols that are used for the rest of the Zekara. Only the health protocols for sickness are engaged. This will help speed the acclimation of your species to the climate here. Then they will be turned off. You will age normally and grow old."

A look a fear flashed across Halcylon's face, and he narrowed his eyes. "Do you expect me to be appreciative of this mercy?"

"I don't care whether you appreciate it or not. The rest of your people, the ones not completely brainwashed, have been given a new lease on life. You'd be surprised at just how many people will leap at the opportunity for a second chance. A life without war. A life without you," Aaron said.

"You will never hold me here," Halcylon said.

"It won't be just me," Aaron said, and gestured to the side. Thraw's eyes flashed as he detached himself from the wall. "But I figured, besides Thraw, the remaining guards would be enough to contain one lowly Hythariam unarmed prisoner."

Aaron walked away, with Thraw staying next to him.

"I still say we should kill him," Thraw said.

"In time perhaps, but not yet."

Truth be told, he was sick of killing. It wasn't just the Zekara that were getting a second chance. They all were. Shortly after the battle, Roselyn had caught up with him with the results of her test of Bayen's blood. She confirmed what Aaron already knew. Bayen wasn't a clone. Initially, Aaron had avoided explaining who Bayen was to Sarah, but she had sensed something in him in the brief time they were together. How did one explain that their child who hadn't been born yet traveled back in time to prevent the end of the world?

"I didn't believe him. When he told us who he was, I had him taken prisoner," Aaron said.

"You were right to be suspicious. Given everything that Halcylon has done, this wasn't beyond the realm of possibility," Sarah said.

Bayen had only been among them for a few days, but Aaron felt his loss. There had been an understanding between them at the end. Sarah took his hand in hers, and they sat under the stars on the palace grounds at Shandara. Verona had a small campfire going and sat with Roselyn in the crook of his arm. They were soon joined by Gavril and Tanneth. Aaron sensed Thraw's presence behind them and smiled inwardly. He had left Halcylon of his own accord, which gave Aaron hope that Thraw would break free of his imprint. All of them here knew of Bayen and were sworn to secrecy.

"So Bayen is now with the Eldarin?" Verona asked.

"Part of him is," Aaron said. "His soul became one with the Eldarin.

The rebirth of the Eldarin cured it of the Ryakul virus."

"I'm not sure I understand," Verona said.

"It took me a while to get it straight in my head. The Eldarin are both physical beings and beings of energy. They can traverse among realms. I think of them as guardians," Aaron said.

"But they won't come here unless summoned by you or another Ferasdiam marked," Verona said.

Aaron nodded. "There is an ancient pact that binds the two together. I'm hoping there is more information in the palace archives on it. Bayen came here knowing that he would die whether he was successful or not."

Roselyn leaned forward. "This is what you asked me about. The possibility of time travel. We only have theories, but given that the keystone accelerators allow us to move through space, why not time as well? The strange thing is that it wasn't permanent. It's like part of him still existed in the world he came from, which means someone had to maintain the connection."

Verona frowned. "But Bayen said they were attacked right before he came—" Verona stopped and looked at Aaron.

"It was you, my love," Sarah said. "You were his link."

Aaron tried to imagine what it must have been like. The virus had spread to every living thing, including the Eldarin, and was attacking them. He must have maintained a barrier around a modified keystone accelerator that was Bayen's link to the future.

Aaron glanced at Tanneth. "Does the AI still work?"

Tanneth shook his head. "Not since the battle. We copied the data, but after going through it I noticed that the only information it contained was pertinent to the mission. It didn't contain a historical account of the alternate time line."

"You think that was intentional?" Aaron asked.

Tanneth nodded.

"It's smart actually," Gavril said. "The AI gave us the keys to unlock the Zekaran systems and allowed us in, but it was actually healing the Eldarin that saved us all. Do you think he knew, uh, the future you, that is?"

"I'm not sure. I don't think so because why would Bayen be given so little information then? We can go 'round and 'round about this," Aaron said.

"Why were the Forsaken and the infected Eldarin so keen on you?" Roselyn asked.

Aaron took a swallow from his tankard. The dark ale had been a gift from Tolvar's people. "It's because I'm Ferasdiam marked. The virus seeks to spread itself through the strongest host it can find. When it infected the Eldarin, it found a being that could allow it to spread to all living creatures. My connection to the energy is stronger than most."

Verona chuckled. "All, my friend," he said, and held up his hands. "I know, you're the possibility of what's possible."

"What I think happened in that alternate time line is that I killed the Eldarin, and the virus spread. Between that and the war with the Zekara, it all led to an ongoing war of attrition." Aaron stopped. They got the idea.

"So what will we do with Halcylon?" Verona asked.

"We'll keep him alive," Aaron said.

"You can put him on trial, and he will be found guilty. What then?" Gavril asked.

"We should put him on trial. But he can't be executed until we finish going through the Zekaran systems to be sure there isn't anything else in there that is a threat," Aaron said.

There was grim acknowledgement around the small group. The conversation turned to more mundane matters. They were later joined by many others, including Admiral Morgan, who delighted in torturing Verona by speaking with Roselyn about Verona's love of children. Apparently, Verona had taken it upon himself to make sure the orphanages in Rexel were run by good people.

Aaron slapped Verona on the shoulder. "You know, I think Morgan might be right. You *are* going to be next."

Roselyn turned to them as if she sensed their conversation and smiled.

"Well, at least we won't be having twins. After the wedding, that is. One baby at a time is quite enough," Verona said.

Twins? Aaron nearly spilled his drink. He turned toward Sarah and felt the strong lifebeat blaze within her... two lifebeats. His mouth fell open, and Sarah smiled at him. Verona took his leave and joined Roselyn.

"What is it?" Sarah asked.

Aaron slipped his arms around her. "Something Bayen said, but I couldn't see it at the time. He knew we would meet again."

Sarah smiled. "Oh, yes. We have a boy and a girl on the way."

Aaron kissed her and knew that wherever they were, from a hidden lake shore to the palace looming behind them, was home. The danger was past them. There would be challenges they would face in the future, but they had each other and their friends. Safanar was his home now, and there was still so much of the world he had yet to see. By the grace of the Goddess, or perhaps just luck, they would have time to explore it all.

ABOUT THE AUTHOR

I've been reading Epic Fantasy and Science fiction nonstop since the age of eleven. Before long, I started writing my own stories and kept adding to them throughout the years. As a father, I began telling my kids about the stories that became part of the Safanarion Order series. It was their enthusiasm and constant "Tell us more Dad," that lead me back to the keyboard. My main focus is to write books that I would like to read and I hope you enjoy them as well.

If you would like to get an email when I release a book please visit my website at KENLOZITO.COM

One Last Thing.

Word-of-mouth is crucial for any author to succeed. If you enjoyed the book, please consider leaving a review, even if it's only a line or two; it would make all the difference and would be greatly appreciated.

Discover other books by Ken Lozito
Safanarion Order Series:

Road to Shandara (Book 1)
Echoes of a Gloried Past (Book 2)
Amidst the Rising Shadows (Book 3)
Heir to Shandara (Book 4)
Warden's Oath (Short Fiction)

CPSIA information can be obtained
at www.ICGtesting.com
Printed in the USA
LVOW07s1729200617

538756LV00001B/163/P